THE GLASS

GW00599367

The Glass Sky

.

A Novel by

.

R. Barnett Beck

Elliott & Thompson
London

For my son, Clive

CHAPTER ONE

•

Louise decided to count her blessings instead of thinking about her husband, John Jacob, asking herself why he resented her sister so. She was content to have her two small children snugly asleep in the back of her car. She noticed the Johnsons had boarded up a broken window. She felt blessed that she no longer lived here where some of the isolated homes, needing repair, had nothing for protection from the sleet, wind or snow except plastic and wooden boards. The car windows were misted and she had to open hers.

Did not John Jacob remember how kin stuck together? It made her unhappy to disappoint him, but Hester was her sister and she had to visit her whatever he felt.

Icicle tears descended off rock shelves. Wasn't it her sacred duty to help others? A cyclops knot stared out of a beech, the tree clutching remnants of autumn. But why had he pointed angrily at her grocery cache and turned his head away? She gave thanks for the use of the Ford with its winter-wear tire chains. She saw a fern patterning itself greenly, and her face shone. She loved the beauty of the crescent moon-shaped fern. How pleased it would make Hester when she told her about it.

John Jacob knew that the bond between his wife and Hester was beyond his ken, it made him uneasy, and irritated him further. The car toiled up and up till it reached the last steep curve.

Louise stood in the doorway of the wooden shack, her large silhouette obliterating the view. She cradled her infant and carried a large sack of groceries. Clutching her skirt was Jake, her son, a small boy of six, a thumb stuck in his mouth. Hester greeted her sister, moving the soup pot closer to the heat of the wrought iron stove. All her children, except for Gladdie and the youngest boy, who was fast asleep, were out in the forest on their daily forage to feed the ever-hungry stove. Jake saw Gladdie, the only one he liked, and they both ran off to play. Neither woman glanced at Hester's husband Curt, who was sprawled on the floor.

'Good to see you. Thanks,' Hester gestured to the groceries and began unpacking them.

'Brought what I thought was needed.'

'Brung cough syrup for Ma?'

5

'It's there.'

'I'll take it to her.'

Louise lowered herself onto an old five-gallon lard drum. The sisters did not talk. They were as close as they were different: Louise, heavy and cumbersome in thought and action; Hester, lithe and quick. Their intense, unfaltering loathing of their father, old man Webb, bound them, yet even if their father had known how much he was hated, he wouldn't have cared. As a child Louise thought of her father as a huge black spider who jumped out at her from beneath any dark shadow. No one knew anything of Old Webb's history. They never even knew his first name.

High on a distant mountain slope, Webb's parents had farmed land which the bride's eldest brother had given to the needy young couple. Webb was never to know his mother who died giving birth to him. Her distraught husband put his newborn son to his favorite bitch that had recently whelped. One by one he mournfully drowned her puppies. The bitch suckled the infant for a few months; her milk and love nourished, but the babe absorbed none of her goodness.

The practice of buying brides had ceased years earlier but Webb never saw why he should lose out. After all, he'd had to buy their mother and felt determined to get his money back – and then some. A month after he made his purchase she ran the long, long way back home, her bare feet bleeding. Webb came astride a tired-looking horse to retrieve his goods. The moment they were sufficiently out of earshot, he dismounted and used the same whip he used on his horse. He mounted his wife. It was his land, his wife, his children, his horse, his dogs and chickens. All his to do his bidding and work as hard as he liked, and he liked to work them hard.

No one would want Louise, an ugly, worthless piece of his property. Webb couldn't believe his luck when Boardman from the hardware store said he wanted her. Quickly, he pocketed sixty dollars before Boardman would change his mind. Louise was fourteen. She had never prayed for her bestial father, she would never taint the Lord. Webb belonged to the Devil and was going to hell to be spit-roasted throughout all eternity.

Short and squat, Webb frequently beat his wife and children; he had no need of a reason and it was better if they never knew what was coming. Webb found Hester attractive. Most attractive. He broke her in at an early age. When she was twelve Curt Howard wanted her. He had to save up to buy a good second-hand Ford truck – the bridal price. He would not get her till then; it took Curt years, what with drink and family troubles. Maybe, sometimes when his son-in-law was drunk, Webb even planned to sneak in and have his daughter again.

Driving the bridal price truck a few years later, he had driven straight into a great oak and ricocheted into the side of the mountain. His leg had been badly broken and for the rest of his life he had to walk with a stick. They said he was lucky to be alive, but he cursed and blamed young, tall and muscular Curt.

The two women fell silent, Louise loosened the front of her dress and gave suck to her infant. Hester had six children, four boys and two girls and her work was back-crunching and ceaseless. But Hester achieved a rhythm, as though she heard music within, and the rhythm helped her do anything and everything. The flags she flew were her washing on the line. Sometimes young men from the university would come up to study her family. One even made red felt stockings for each child with their names written on them with Christmas gifts inside of coloured pencils, rubber balls and candy. Women students seldom came, for the authorities thought, privately, it was too unsafe. Once, a young redheaded 'Welfare' had brought her canned foods, baked beans, and sweet corn. Only when he found she had no can-opener was he stunned, racing back down to his jalopy roaring down the mountain road and returning with one, to demonstrate how it worked.

Gladdie was a beautiful five year old. She helped her mother look after the youngest and worked in the vegetable garden. She never left her mother's side. Gladdie had seen, under the tall jack pines where footsteps went unheard and where the brightness of day was shut out, here in the tree twilight, she had seen her grandfather hurting her friend. Billy-May Johnson was twelve and slow-witted. She sometimes came to play and was Gladdie's only friend. He had caught her in the curve of his walking stick. Hiding.

Gladdie could not hide from her friend's screams. Billy-May never came back again. Since then Gladdie had clung to her mother, even while her parents coupled on their bedding of corn shucks, and she heard her father grunt like her grandfather, and still she stayed close. She missed Billy-May. Every time she thought of her, Gladdie clapped her hands over her ears.

'It's the Lord's will. Even you can't guard her all the time. Of my six, only these two survive. Give Gladys to me. She will be my daughter. Yours too. The Lord despises selfishness. He despises the weak. Save her that she may be Saved. Give Gladys to me,' begged Louise. Then she paused. 'You know what could happen if you don't......' she trailed off.

'I don't know how I can do without her.' Hester was weary.

Scenting victory, Louise crossed her thick arms.

'Stop giving me the Lord stuff,' said Hester. Louise didn't reply.

'You know he's been seen. You know he's come back.'

'I don't think he would dare even try.'

'But she is so small! What if he's there just the one time when you're not?'

'In the spring. For two weeks.'

'Yes,' said Louise, slowly unfolding her arms.

'For a holiday.'

'Not today – in spring – late spring.'

Louise knew she would have to wait till then.

They were a team for their sisterhood had ensured their very survival. The powerful closeness developed during childhood and, as the only two surviving girls in the family, they seldom fought. In winter, they warmed one another on the floor of the one-roomed shack and shared what little they had. Although the younger, Hester was leader as she could fight and throw stones with lethal accuracy. Louise's screams slit straight through the undergrowth to their mother, their only ally.

Their father was mostly away. Mercifully, gone for months at a time – they all knew better than to ask him where he went or what he did. He always returned in a drunken fog, his behaviour never questioned. They were accustomed to it and knew no other way.

From the family's shack a path, worn by human feet, led down the mountain to a winding untarred road that snaked steeply, frightening the unwary traveler. Those who knew the road avoided it if they could. Poplars, oaks, beeches and hemlocks grew abundantly in the thin soil. The shack was made of wooden boards and the windows were covered by heavy shutters. A tubular black chimney stood out like a thin beckoning finger trailing a fine breath of smoke. The trees grew so close it was as if they themselves wanted to enter the dwelling.

Behind the shack was a small area where the mountain flattened. This was where the land was cultivated. The back had a porch overlooking the vegetable patch where a few chickens optimistically pecked and scratched.Not too far away was the outhouse, perched precariously beside a young hemlock. It seemed as though a strong wind could blow the structure, even the tree down. A cat and a dog slept together in an old coke box beside a disconnected refrigerator against the house, usefully employed for storage space. The snow had human tracks about the shack and all looked peaceful and clean.

Louise's car was being repaired, again. When fresh green unfurled, she took the bus to fetch her niece. There was nothing for Gladdie to take with her, except her uncertainty and she had not been to Aunt Louise's house before. Neither had she ever been off the mountain. They enjoyed the long scramble down the road. Squirrels hurried away, groundhogs scooted down their holes and Jake pretended he saw a bear. Gladdie teased that she had heard a dangerous mountain cat while Louise kept an anxious eye out for copperheads. The creek was running low and tree roots writhed down its banks and Gladdie had to force herself to resist the temptation to yell out 'Snakes! Snakes!' to her aunt. They jumped across a rivulet and walked through a snow of pale butterflies. Something lifted from Gladdie's belly. She hadn't known it had been there. Blue jays and red cardinals flashed, a redwing hawk hovered and Gladdie's insides whispered goodbyes. They heard a passing vehicle and knew they were near the road.
  'You kids play over here,' instructed Louise, indicating a flat grassy patch. 'I can see you, but remember more importantly, the Lord sees all.'
  Louise concealed herself behind a thick clump of myrtle while she nursed her infant. The children tried to see how long they could stand on their hands. Gladdie's thick plait lay on the ground, tempting Jake to pull it as he would a rope. If he did, he reckoned, she might fall and cry out and his mother would hear so it just wasn't worth it. They prayed three times before reaching the bus stop. Gladdie knew prayer wasn't serious because her mother had often laughed about her aunt; laughed as though at some humorous malady. Try as she might, Louise had only succeeded once in making Hester pray but it had ended badly. Hester couldn't stop laughing until Louise was furious with disappointment.
  'The Lord will punish you for mocking Him.'
  'If he exists, why would he bother with punishment?' asked Hester.

Hester and Louise first realised that their father's behaviour was strange when two of their mother's cousin's children visited them.

Louise ever-anxious, afraid and terrorized, asked the girl, Opal, if her father does it often to her. Opal didn't understand the question. Louise explained that her father says she is ugly because of her wart; she licked her upper lip gratefully from time to time. It saves me, she says. Louise considered Opal old and wise because she was fifteen, and felt disappointed when her cousin showed a lack of comprehension.

Louise resorted to mime, firstly, her own terror and struggle to escape and then she moved her body explicitly to demonstrate her father's activity. Opal was outraged that Louise could even ask such a question and then, seeing the shock on the younger girl's face, she understood. She was horrified. Her disgust consumed her but she was able, in a trembling voice, to explain that fathers don't behave like that. This part of life was for husbands and wives, it was how they made babies.

Opal was too embarrassed to confide in her mother about what Louise had told her. Until then, Louise and Hester thought all fathers behaved like that – they didn't think their mother knew about it – they hoped not, because of what Opal told them, and the way she told them.

Louise was always on the lookout, constantly afraid. She climbed trees, hid, even went without meals – anything to avoid him – he preferred Hester, although she was hard to catch. He caught Louise once. Barely five minutes later he slaughtered a young sow. The shrieking of the girl, and the squealing of the pig, ripped through the trees and the sound seemed to gash pieces of blue right out from the sky. Hester heard and vowed never to allow it to happen to Louise again. She promised her sister that she would distract him. She kept hog fat tied in a piece of cloth on her body at all times and felt little pain. Hester lied, it was easy for her, she said. She calmed Louise down as she helped wash her with fresh water from the creek. It was not yet the heart of winter and the ice was easy to break. They scooped up water in their cupped hands. The cold heart was still to come. And remain.

They were the only daughters, any other girl-child their mother bore died soon after birth. Their mother consoled the older two survivors, they died in their sleep; they knew no pain. Their mother thought it was better not to be born a girl.

Hester felt that she had two mothers; one who never laughed

and seldom smiled, the woman who gave birth to her and sustained her just as her other mother, the mountain, did. All the boys lived; Luke, Daniel, Jethro and Emmett. The little girls were buried in a row beneath a long skirted pin oak. Only Jewel, her first-born, and Gladdie, her last-born daughter, survived. Her mother was her midwife and she took Hester's girl babies to join her own little ones. There were five baby girls' graves around the pin oak. Vaguely Hester wondered if her mother had a hand in all those inexplicable deaths, those unlived lives, because at one burial her mother calls them the saved ones. Now they lay in the body of her mountain.

They lived in isolation, which consolidated their closeness, invisible steel vines fastened them together. Hester swore that when she got married her daughters would never go through this nightmare. She knew that she, although the younger, was the stronger. Louise tried to do Hester's chores for her, picked her the juiciest berries so that Hester could run off and play on the mountain. Dimly Hester understood that Louise needed to do this for her.

Hester glided and flew around the mountain every chance she got. It was during these glad times that she first began to feel as though the mountain was her second mother. She called it Ma Mountain. When she told her sister she was going to Ma Mountain, Louise tetchily replied that it was her mountain too.

Hester roamed like any other wild animal. She knew what she could eat and what to avoid, she had favorite viewpoints, special lairs where she could curl up and sleep if she wanted, she snuggled and rubbed herself against velvety moss and was hugged and caressed by the mountain. In winter, if there wasn't too much snow, she had her own black pine where she climbed up to the highest point and if the sun shone, she lay and stared through almost closed eyes back at the vaulting sky's eye.

Hester was scrupulously fair to Louise and tried not to abuse her generosity. Their mother was aware of their arrangement but made no comment. Hester and Louise looked so different, seemed so different, as they went about their days, no one could begin to appreciate their closeness. They loved one another with almost the purity of a mother loving her newborn and were as non-judgmental and indestructibly connected.

Gladdie sat on the bus, silent. She jammed her body against her aunt, her eyes downcast.

'I love you Aunt Louise,' she murmured to please, 'I love you.'

11

The bus bounced along, Gladdie was thirsty, she said nothing, she needed to pee, but said nothing.

'I love you Aunt Louise,' the repeating litany irritated Louise. 'I love you.'

'Enough,' said Louise, 'I've heard you enough. Once is enough. Rather tell the Lord that you Love Him, thank Him for this day, thank the Lord for the food you eat and stop looking at the floor. Look up, look up and see the beautiful world the Lord made that we may worship Him.'

Gladdie's eyes obediently darted up and saw a black and yellow butterfly, a swallowtail. She saw it splotch against the window and her large eyes filled with tears. Louise dismissed this – 'Gone to be with the Lord' – and patted the child's hand. But Gladdie knew it wasn't true.

Gladdie never knew her aunt was so rich, with real chairs and, amazingly, beds. That night, after first saying Grace at the table and eating with a spoon and then thanking the Lord for the food, she was put to bed. She had seen a photograph of a bed. Hester cut out all the pictures from magazines that a 'Welfare' had given her and papered the walls with them, using wet cornflour as glue. It never occurred to Gladdie that she would ever sleep in a bed. Her aunt tucked a comforter about her, determined, as an instrument of the Lord, to keep the child safe. Gladdie lay with her eyes wide open, afraid that by falling asleep she would miss the wonders of the day, or worse, wake up on the floor and know it had all been a dream. She lay and her eyes became diamonds holding her tears. She did not even blink them away. She couldn't wait to tell her mother about her day.

When the two weeks were up, Gladdie quite suddenly became terrified. She shrieked and screamed, like Billy-May did that day in the forest. The incessant howling and wild cries decided Louise that the child must never go back to her mother, because if she did the Devil would make her his ward.

'The strict worship of the Lord' ruled the house. Most things were forbidden. No music, no levity, no alcohol. Women could not wear makeup and the removal of any body hair was not permitted. It was forbidden to cut the hair on a woman's head. Fortunately attending school was encouraged so Gladdie was sent, with Jake, to the local elementary. This was a good school with high moral standards and the country people were proud of it, certain it was better than the citified ones. School was astonishing to Gladdie, she liked the teacher, who would throw back her head and laugh at the slightest provocation, just like her mother. She also wore perfume, which Gladdie knew was supposed to be a sin.

She was an eager pupil and when her school results were better than Jake's, something in the attitude of her aunt and uncle made her realize that this shouldn't happen again. She said nothing, but chose not to make the same mistake again and deliberately lowered her standards. Her teacher, Miss Macguire, chided her on her poor marks. She remained silent. After repeated questioning and responding by staring blankly ahead, unexpectedly she smiled. She smiled imagining what Aunt Louise would say about her teacher's perfume, short hair and infectious laughter. She couldn't keep the smile back; it had come to her face unbidden. She thought she would have to pay for it, but noticed that it had had a wonderful effect on Miss Macguire. Megan Macguire smiled back.

She pulled the little girl towards her and, hugging her, said, 'What a puzzle you are, Gladdie', and Gladdie knew she wouldn't be punished after all. She thought she could use this smile more often. Maybe.

CHAPTER TWO

•

When Curt Howard set eyes on Hester, young as she was, he wanted her for his wife. He found her wildness intoxicating and her vulnerability appealing. He wanted to take her away from her father and needed to protect her.

Webb drove a mean bargain. He made it clear that unless he received 'a bridal price', he would never consent to the marriage. Curt had no choice. It took him four years to buy the truck Webb demanded – at least Curt could keep his eye on her and see that she was kept safe.

He had no complaint about their life together and thought of himself as lucky, but guilty. Curt had not chosen alcoholism. Guilt was the unfailing partner to the disease and he was never able to rid himself of it. But he knew he was lucky. He had Hester. Hester, with her thick brown hair, smooth olive skin and quick smile. She had not left him for another man and was a good mother to their children.

The folks down at the fire station had taken Curt to AA; he owed them big time for he hadn't knowingly or deliberately harmed another person. Many were the times when he had woken in a strange bed, staring blearily, at the form lying beside him, unaware whether he or the woman sharing the bed was responsible for the foul-smelling vomit. His only urge was to get away. Get clean. Get back to his place on the mountain. Lie in the creek or the snow and then climb out and back. Back to his home, his sanctuary.

Hester didn't know what they did at the AA, but whatever it was, it worked. In the past, he binged and slept it off. She hadn't ever feared for herself because the only time he got out of hand she had hit him over the head with her heavy iron skillet. Knocked him clean out. Usually, by the time he crept and dragged himself home, the worst of it was over. She tended to his grazed, bruised and cut skin and she didn't grumble over so small a chore. She was fiercely determined that her children would be spared the terrors of her own childhood; she fought for this, but felt she could never entirely defend her young. He never struck them, but even so, they knew fear and uncertainty. Compared to her life as a child, she was happy that they had so much – it was rare for them to be hungry. Theirs was a life of relative plenty. The misery that she and her children had endured was, she reckoned, over. Their harsh lives were ameliorated by the kindness and care Curt showered on them; he dug a deep hole and constructed a new outhouse for them, he tore the old one down, burnt it and refilled the hole. He scattered seeds of wild flowers he'd collected on top of it. Then he built a railing to the new outhouse from the backdoor, so that if it became too windy, or the snow too high, his mother-in-law or the smaller ones had something to hold onto.

The most thoughtful thing of all was a rubber-covered flashlight that could be pulled along the rail at night; it took away the fear of going out in the dark and even Luke, his eldest son, was happy about that. He neatly stacked piles of wood he'd chopped and he worked in the vegetable garden. He got hold of two pairs of socks for every member of the family. He was paying off his debts. But what touched them most was one night, after the family had eaten, he told them that he was sorry that he hadn't been the father to them he would have liked to be. He told them that he wanted to do a better job as a father, and he told them how much he loved them. This was greeted by an embarrassed silence, and Luke walked out. Jewel told her father that she loved him too. Hester had nothing to say; she listened in wary surprise and carried on with her tasks. One of his sons, Jethro, stuck out his hand, that looked too big for his arm, and Curt grasped it and they shook hands. Curt's eyes filled with tears when his youngest son attached himself to his leg.

'You're not a bad dad,' Hester said, as she folded some clothes. He nodded his head mutely in thanks and poured out a coffee for her, which she waved away pointing to her mug that already had coffee in it. He drank it thinking that she had never loved him, would never forgive him and he didn't blame her. Perhaps it was possible, his optimistic and unrealistic heart promised him, that someday she would.

Curt did not know that her father had made it impossible for Hester to love any man. She saw that other women loved men but found this kind of love incomprehensible. She thought them fools looking for trouble. She tried to work out what it was that made women love men, and although she was happy because Jewel, her first-born, was happy, she felt a similar concern for her as when a flood or drought threatened. Her father had robbed her, as he had robbed her mother, of her capacity to love or trust. She knew about surviving and nurturing, her mother had used her own body as a shield to take much of the beating that was meant for her or her sister. When it was over, and because Webb grew tired or bored and left, their mother stroked their bodies to soothe their pain. She applied moonshine to sterilize any open cut or abrasion. It was essential not to cry. Webb never liked that. He even beat the tears out of them and didn't like the sound of whining, grinned when they couldn't hold back the gasp of pain. He did like the sound of his belt whipping into them – if they ran away – he beat their mother.

Hester was never able to rid herself of the engraved image of her father with one foot firmly pushing her mother's head down while he beat her body with frenzied wantonness. Neither Hester nor her mother Ellen-Agnes could call out. They had no money, no transport and nowhere to run to. It was around this time that Louise developed her breathing problem.

Curt seemed more at peace with himself, and when Hester mentioned this to him he smiled at her, thankful that she noticed. She had no notion of the gigantic battle he daily, hourly, waged against his disease. Sometimes, almost anything appeared to resemble a bottle and a killingly pernicious urge just about disemboweled him; it could be a cloud and he longed, longed to tear it from the sky and pour his pain away. The shine in a child's eye reminded him of the gleam of a glass. When he first learnt it wasn't a character weakness but an illness, it partially removed the enormous boulder he balanced on his shoulders, but even though he knew he should, he never succeeded in eradicating his sense of guilt. The love he felt for his fellow sufferers was returned tenfold by them. He had found God at AA. When his daughter Jewel met and fell in love with the man she wanted to marry, he was jubilant that, unlike her mother, she was free to choose. Nothing was forced on her.

It was just about impossible for people from the mountains to get a regular job, but Davis, Jewel's fiancé, had one. Many of the difficulties in obtaining work, besides under-education, were paradoxically caused by how closely-knit and interdependent families were. In winter the mountains were their jails and the weather their wardens. They hadn't enough money to move. Welfare kept them going. And they were going to their final destinations without the dignity of independence or the grace of self-respect.

Jewel's fiancé had managed to get a heavy-duty driver's license and was a long distance truck driver, a job to which Hester's son, Luke, aspired. It seemed attainable, gloriously possible. He worked as a seasonal tobacco picker and saved up enough money to take the test. Changed though Curt was, Luke wouldn't forgive his father and revenged himself by refusing to accept a single cent from him. Their second eldest son, Daniel, showed ability and was good with figures. Louise's husband self-importantly promised to use his influence to get him a job.

John Jacob worked in a hardware store, and whenever he saw his nephew he took time to teach him about the various items that were sold there. After all, as Louise reminded him, Daniel was kin. The others seemed disinclined to leave the mountain. There was work enough to be done anyhow; and besides, there was almost always enough to eat. They were ill-suited to towns where there was no support system, and it was common knowledge that town people didn't care about them. People from towns were judged as insincere, only interested in money. They felt pity for them because they didn't have a sense of community, or the implicit understanding of the value of kinship.

There was a certain amount of debate about where and when the wedding should take place. Davis was determined not to jeopardize his job, so the wedding could only take place when his leave was due and that wasn't for several months. Curt was finding out if the fire station could allow it there, or in the open lot beside it. Louise had offered her home, but it was scarcely a place for celebration. Hester wanted it on the mountain. Her daughter, in a daze of love and lust, took no part in the discussions. All she wanted was a pretty new dress since Curt's job was paying for the whole affair. Jewel noticed, for the first time in her life, how badly Hester dressed – that her hair, though clean, was unkempt and her feet were straight, strong but unshod. Hester's feet told a story, her soles were thick, her toes straight and their growth uninhibited by shoes. Ashamed of her disloyal thoughts, Jewel wanted her mother to show more appropriate interest in her appearance other than sticking a wild flower or leafy wreath in her hair.

'Mommy, if you tied your hair back you'd look really good,' Jewel quietly suggested. Hester cocked her head to one side and squinted at her daughter

'Davis said his mother does,' she added, and Hester immediately understood: 'You're embarrassed by your Ma. Don't worry. I'll make sure I look OK.'

Hester was in a quandary. She wanted to do everything just right, do Jewel proud. She had never, in her entire life, walked into a dress store and bought clothing. She had no qualms about accepting anything from other people – whenever she could share anything she unfailingly did. It was, for her, the natural way to live. She felt a surge of demoralizing unease not knowing whom to ask – Louise was out of the question. The people in the store would help, she suddenly remembered, relieved. She didn't think she wanted to spend money on a dress for herself and thought maybe she could fix up her own dress but was unsure. The lady from the store would tell her what to do – she wanted her daughter to have a good start and she wondered for a while why it was so important to her daughter that she looked nice. I'm me, she said to herself. Ain't that enough? It bothered Hester that it wasn't. I'll be darned, thought Hester, but I won't let her down.

She was unaccustomed to this sort of uncertainty. The vagaries of life and death were easy for her to understand; the moody unpredictability of the mountains was part of her. She skillfully killed rattlers or copperheads if they were dangerous to her children; if not, she let them be. She was fearless and philosophical about the ways of her world; and yet the idea of buying a dress filled her with a sense of bewildering inadequacy, a feeling previously unknown to her. She felt dread.

Hester had made sure she was within earshot of her mother for her confinement. But her second-last child caught her unawares. She had climbed up to a waterfall, knowing that soon she would be unable to do this, and lay down to breathe it into herself – its beauty, clarity and glister. Then, completely unexpectedly, her body whirled itself into a contraction. Birth would occur long before she could reach her mother. She found an arrow-shaped stone, seized it and sharpened it, rubbing it hard and fast across the rock face. Sparks flew. She chose well and worked well. She knew it would not be an easy delivery, they never were for her and she missed her mother's steady encouragements. The stone became knife-edged. She tested it with her fingers, a thin red line showed her that it would do the job. Between contractions she continued to sharpen it vigorously. She heard the voice of her great-grandmother speak, as the sweat of effort and pain poured slickly off her face and body. The voice told her not to lie down but to squat. She obeyed. The head appeared, and finally the bloodied, slippery infant was in her waiting hands. She cut the umbilical cord with the finely honed stone. The placenta spasmed out and she flung it away. She bathed herself and the newborn afterwards in the gentle softness of the waterfall's source. She licked this tiny girl baby's face clean, paying devout attention to her eyes, nose and perfect ears. Holding her newborn, cherishing each moment she slowly came home.

Hester found her mother waiting for her. She handed the baby to her to hold and then snatched her back. This was the child she felt solely responsible for, that had nothing to do with anything or anyone else. She breast-fed her for a full year. She carried her papoose-style, as she had all her children. They were part of her body, of her strength and vitality. They were only ever off her body to be bathed. She literally bound her babies to herself so that it was almost as if they had been in her womb until they needed to crawl.

CHAPTER THREE

·

Abigail Dunstable creamed her face carefully, swathed a scarf around her head and added a large sunhat. Complete with over-large designer sunglasses, she headed out to the small school in the country. She needed something unusual for her pre-Christmas party as she was combining her usual four dinner parties into one and her guests always expected something special. She was having cocktails and all two hundred and eighty-two 'intimate' friends would be surprised that the parties had been moved forward to the second of December. The truth was her surgeon, Dr Glazer, had said there was something minor he wanted to do about her left eye area and she would have to have it done on the twelfth. She gritted her teeth. Not too tightly – lines, she reminded herself.

Why didn't he do it when he last had me on the table – what does Christmas mean to him? Same as for most people nowadays, she supposed, to keep the retailers and hoteliers happy. He had to take his family skiing – or was it sailing? – and would be away for two months. Oh well, she thought, he is the best.

Abigail's friends and acquaintances, and those who pretended to know her, frequently speculated about her age, and what she had done prior to her first marriage. They went through her marriages trying to tally up the number of years spent, as well as fortunes acquired.

In fact, with all their adding and subtracting, there was much that they would never know about Abigail. During one of her more advantageous marriages what had started off as a hobby, an amusement, became a compulsive interest and stimulating lifestyle. Money. How to make it and become entirely independent of any man's whims. It started with a small share portfolio. Early on, she chose to try and deal with businesswomen to avoid any sexual innuendo or interference. She networked. It was slow but ultimately well worth the effort, and it was how she got to know many high-powered women lawyers, bankers and investment brokers. She had some ups and downs which she accepted with equanimity. She invariably paid top dollar for top advice, which she was not shy to take from as many people – women mainly – as possible. Then she applied plain old common sense. She had witnessed several of her highly effective business acquaintances passed over in favour of men and realized with a sense of outrage just how real the glass ceiling was. Those who attended Abigail's parties thought the only organizing she did concerned these occasions. For spring, she chose her thoroughbred horse farm in Kentucky; for summer, her home in Saratoga; for fall, it was back to Kentucky; and winter was at her castle in Scotland. Each place was chosen for its spectacular beauty and to celebrate yet another wondrously welcome season.

But now the rapidity with which each season flashed into the next frightened Abigail. The seconds seemed to tick away more quickly. Sometimes she felt she could even hear them. Tick. Tick. Spring. Summer. Autumn. Winter. Spring.

None of her usual party helpers had come up with anything truly memorable. Not Mandy, her secretary, nor Buffy, her hairdresser. Well, she'd show them, she'd find something herself, something different. Recently she had begun to feel bored with glitter and glossiness and had felt an urge to prove that she was a real down-home woman, one who knew the meaning of the word 'humility'; that was why she was visiting this little rural school. She had met the teacher, who had of course wanted a donation. Well, right in the capacious trunk of her limo was an old TV set, and she'd see what else she would contribute. When her gleaming car drew up, the pupils ran out excitedly, convinced she was a film star. There was a brief hush as she got out of the car and, as if by pre-arrangement, the teachers hurried out to greet her.

Megan Macguire had met Abigail Dunstable at a University Arts Function fundraiser for local arts and crafts. Kentucky folk art had been promoted by the beautiful Phyllis George during her tenure as the Governor's wife. She opened up her gardens once a year to hold a fair where their work could be sold. Their carved painted sculptures were excellent, often with a touch of whimsy. The painting of dried-out gourds with country scenes of bygone days, wooden artifacts painted to resemble watermelons, pumpkins and fruits were usually on offer; the work was invariably a sell-out. There were also things like coat-hangers in satins with bows and artificial flowers. Pot-pourris. Fun things. You could do all your Christmas shopping in one dash. It had been a brief meeting and Megan was astonished by this unexpected visit.

After the television set had been revealed, accepted with delighted gratitude, and Abigail had been given a tour of the school, Megan collected the children together to thank her for her kindness. Abigail found them touching.

'You need to showcase these poor little kids if you want the public to interest themselves.' She continued, 'Tell me, do they sing? I seem to recollect you mentioning a choir...'

'We do have a choir but sadly no piano. Would you like them to sing for you? We didn't know you were coming. If only I'd known.' Megan was flustered. 'We'd have prepared. Rehearsed.'

'That would be sweet. I didn't anticipate a concert,' she laughed.

The children were hurriedly gathered about in a semicircle and there in the schoolyard began to sing *Silent Night*, precisely the song she knew they would. They were a ragged bunch, but reasonably clean, and it suddenly occurred to her how charming they would look if properly presented. Little white surplices – she could get the yardman's mother to sew them out of white sheets. She was a nasty old critter, but a dab hand with a needle.

Megan conducted the singing with enthusiasm – secretly hoping for a piano. Abigail's attention was caught by a boy and girl who stood slightly apart and kept their mouths firmly shut. The boy would not return her gaze. She looked at the girl, a really pretty child with long braided hair. She smiled at the girl, who smiled back dazzlingly. Abigail recognized that smile; it mirrored her own. It was the same smile that had adorned her own face as a child when she craved approval: a ravishing smile, a winning smile, the smile Abigail still practiced. The children stopped singing and Abigail clapped her hands together, then quietly quizzed Megan about the two silent children.

'They belong to a fundamental religious sect, hard shell Baptists, and are not permitted music of any sort.'

'Not allowed music!' Abigail was incredulous, aware that this turned the two children into outsiders. She decided to alter that – everyone knew she deplored fanaticism. She divined that the girl, and the boy for that matter, would like to sing. She looked again at the little girl and saw that with her red hair unbraided and garlanded with flowers the child would be perfect. She reminded her so vividly of herself. She too had been beautiful as a child, perhaps without quite such enchanting colouring. Impulsively she turned to Megan and said she would like to have the choir come to her home on the second of December to sing for her many friends.

'Naturally you must come too. I'll supply a bus that can comfortably hold eighteen children.'

'What a wonderful idea,' a thrilled Megan responded.

'But, it won't work without the children who didn't sing. They have such an angelic look.' Sensing that she might be denied their presence, she became all the more eager for it and spoke with charming obstinacy, until Megan understood that somehow Mrs Boardman had to be persuaded. She undertook to make certain that all the children would arrive at the specified time.

'You're quite sure you can keep your promise?' said Abigail, managing to question and subtly threaten at the same time.

'Yes,' vowed Megan, 'you've my word.'

'You'll need to get in some practice, won't you? Rehearse a bit more perhaps.'

Abigail had often proved the value of great wealth to purchase power. She didn't like her power questioned, but enjoyed exercising it and she usually got her own way. Most people thought she had missed out because she hadn't had a child, not knowing that the thought of having her skin stretched was awful to her. But, she admitted to herself, if she had had children, she would have wanted them to look like the two little non-singers. Especially the girl.

Miss Macguire knocked on the front door, making Louise anxious, but her neutral expression concealed her misgivings. She invited Miss Macguire to sit and offered her something to drink. The young teacher thanked her gracefully, thinking as she sat down that the other woman's bulk had her at a disadvantage. She seemed so established, monumental.

'My boy has been behaving, hasn't he?' she enquired, her tone defensive.

'Certainly,' replied Megan, 'he works diligently.'

'My girl then?'

'She is well behaved, although her results are a bit disappointing.'

'She started well though,' Louise stated protectively. 'We don't mind if our kids aren't clever. We care only that they are good and pleasing to the Lord. We humble ourselves to Him and want only to praise His name.'

Quickly Megan seized the advantage.

'It's just that I want to talk to you about. Do you know of Mrs George Dunstable?' Megan waited, curious to see if the name had any effect. Louise's blank face answered her.

'She is a prominent member of our society, who helps the underprivileged. She wants your two beautiful children to join the rest of our school choir on an outing. She's sending a bus to fetch the eighteen children and, of course, myself as choir mistress.'

'Do you mean sing? My kids are forbidden to sing, we chant our prayers, the Lord despises frivolity.'

'Mrs Boardman, you are a Baptist, are you not?' She gestured out the window where a single boxwood shrub had been meticulously clipped into the shape of a cross.

'Mrs Boardman, as Christians we are required to do unto others as we would have them do unto us. The school choir is going to gladden the hearts of old people. The lady I am speaking of particularly wanted your two because they are so pretty. I feel that you will agree with me that it would be un-Christian to prevent this elderly woman from performing her duty. And denying your children their Baptist duty,' Megan hastily amended.

Louise shrunk back. Her kids would be unworthy if they sang. John Jacob would be furious if she let them go. Megan was desperate and knew she had to resort to a little embroidery – surely plastic surgery was painful, at least for a while. Megan knew that people like Abigail feared ageing even more than death, something they never allowed themselves to think about.

'This woman has suffered. She wears dark glasses and a hat at all times. Her hair is covered with a scarf.'

'Going blind, is she?' Louise evinced curiosity.

'No one can tell.'

'Going deaf?'

'I can't say.'

'Sounds like she's ready to meet her Maker.' Louise wanted to talk about the rich lady's maladies. Jake had told her about the big limo.

'Mrs Boardman, the children will be singing hymns.'

'Oh, I know that, Miss Macguire. Jacob watches Gladys and Gladys watches Jacob to make certain that neither slips up and offends the Lord.'

Whenever Brother Boardman was not there they all whistled, this was permitted, as did not birds in the trees whistle? Neither woman guessed that while on their own both children sang and loved it. Megan's shoulders drooped, try as she might to remain positive and erect. Unexpectedly, Louise acquiesced; she felt sorry for the sick rich lady, and the school teacher appeared desperate. Then she had a good idea.

'They can go. They may shape their lips to the words but not sing.'

Megan left as soon as she decently could. Once she was out of hearing distance she began to sing, her voice loudly victorious.

The choir rehearsed and rehearsed and enjoyed themselves. They couldn't wait to see what sort of presents they'd get. Expensive ones. Their parents wanted to hear all about Mrs Dunstable's house. They were pleased that citified folk would see how clean and well mannered their children were. They gleaned respect and basked in reflected glory. Finally the great day arrived; they all were scrubbed and their hair and eyes shone. The bus was equipped with a lavatory, which the children at first used as a novelty. Each child received a small basket with something to snack on before they arrived, and a meal beneath the snack for the return journey. Every possible need had been provided for by their hostess. Crunchy peanut butter sandwiches, a triangle of sweet milk cheese and fruit juices were on the top layer. There was deep fried chicken, potato chips and rich chocolate brownies for the return journey. A small refrigerator was filled with ice cream and sodas. They could eat the messy food on the way back. Wet wipes and paper toweling were included.

Megan made them rehearse, for the first fifteen minutes exhorting them to smile and show their happiness. After the last hymn they were urged to save their voices. The journey lasted only an hour and a half. She taught them the names of trees and made a game to spot evergreens, white pines, hemlocks and magnolia grandiflora. They learnt the word 'deciduous', a lovely-sounding word. Some of the children became sleepy so she made them comfortable and sang lullabies.

It was half-past five when the busload of children arrived on schedule. Passing through a town, they were surprised to find themselves back in the country. They drove down a narrow lane, then through an imposing entrance with large cement urns atop the gateposts. The urns were filled with fresh flowers. The beautiful blooms deflated Megan; her confidence leaked away. Large sycamores arched over the driveway, their trunks and branches gleaming as whitely as the light snowfall carpeting the paddocks. As they approached High Wings, a colonial mansion, after first being stopped by green and gold braided armed guards, Megan had to calm herself. She was determined not to be cowed by the blatant extravagance of exotic flowers at Christmastime, flown up from Florida, she reasoned. The children, seeing how quiet she was, thought she must be praying. The bus halted. Megan sprung up.

'Here we are, children! We're going to have fun and make .old people happy at the same time.'

The children filed through the kitchen, hushed and intimidated. The lady came and no one recognized her.

'Here is our hostess and benefactress,' chirped Megan. 'She gave us our piano.'

'Good evening Mrs Dunstable, and thank you for the piano,' they chanted, just as they had been taught to do.

Abigail had a coronet of fresh flowers in her hair. Around her neck hung priceless rubies with matching earrings encircled by diamonds. Gladdie didn't like the large drops of glass blood. They frightened her and a premonition nudged her spirit.

The children looked like angels. Abigail deftly unplaited the thick auburn braid and Gladdie's hair floated past her waistline. She wanted to tell Mrs Dunstable that she could do it herself but said nothing. She had to be polite. 'Perfect, you look just darling.' Abigail produced thick make-up brushes and with Mandy and Buffy she quickly rouged up a few cheeks that were a trifle pale. The children were surprised. Gladdie was certain her aunt would be furious – if she ever found out! She was excited – all the children were. The house was so big, the lights were so bright, and there were many strange people. But their teacher kept telling them how proud she was. She gave them confidence. Abigail dashed off after first instructing when and where the children should appear. 'Put her and her brother' – she pointed to Gladdie – 'in the center of the semi-circle.' Abigail and Gladdie smiled at one another.

The guests were happily drinking champagne, punch served from vast silver bowls, or mulled wine in antique pewter mugs. It was a tradition that these drinks were served at Abigail's pre-Christmas celebration, though bourbon and whisky had been decanted for a few guests whose preferences were known to her; she liked pampering. There were two ambassadors, the odd ex-basketball hero, a four-star general, a scattering of politicians and journalists, and one minor English royal. A few billionaires were de rigueur at such gatherings. A pianist at an ivory-coloured baby grand played unobtrusively, as did the others in the ensemble. The harpist was dressed, as requested, in a simple white dress with a gold cord around her waist. The men wore the matching gold bow ties Abigail had supplied. Male guests all received gardenia buttonholes, whilst the women, frangipani leis which they could twist around their necks, wrists or ankles. 'Get your beau to do it for you,' Abigail suggested to the more sedate or elderly.

The children were led to their position by Megan who had been obliged to wear a white toga. She exuded, she hoped, quiet confidence. As they entered, a beautiful reconditioned harpsichord was wheeled in. A gasp of pleasure arose from the crowd as the harpsichordist began to play. After a fugue by Bach, a sprightly minuet and a medley of rhythm and blues, he was applauded for his ingenuity. He stood up and bowed in a modest, almost sheepish way. Megan was sure that he resented wearing his gold bow tie.

Megan now came into her own. She stood before the children, holding them in perfect silence. Then their pure voices filled the air. All the old favourites – *O Come All Ye Faithful*, *All Things Bright and Beautiful*, *Silent Night*. Their listeners resonated, recalling happy moments, real or imagined, from their own childhoods. Gladdie and Jake mouthed the words just as they had vowed they would.

Abigail had been pleased to see her two beautiful children joining in with the rest but suddenly realised what they were doing and was furious. She was being cheated! The two were not singing, but she guessed they wanted to. Abigail's eyes scanned her friends' faces – she was looking for those she knew would be most critical. Faces glowed and the merest instant after the concert was over, spontaneous happy applause broke out. Fortissimo. But Abigail was not about to be foiled – after all, those children had been a major part of her plan: they were to break that ridiculous and unfair stricture, she had ordained it . . . . She stepped forward, clapping her hands, and asked Megan with mock humility if the 'two little soloists' could not end off the evening with just one more rendition of her favourite *All Things Bright and Beautiful*.

She moved amongst the children and firmly, playfully it seemed, thrust Gladdie and Jake forward. Megan was terrified, her eyes entreated Mrs Dunstable and she received a glittering smile in reply. Abigail propelled the two children into the exact position she wanted, bent down and kissed them, looking enchanted. Even the most begrudging knew that, once again, Abigail's parties were just the best. The two looked scared, and they were even more scared when they saw how frightened Miss Macguire looked.

Jake held Gladdie's hand tightly and, as they began to sing, with the lightest conspiratorial glance they promised one another never to tell. Their sweet sopranos lilted into the now receptive hearts of the audience. Megan felt life swirl back into her body.

The two had obviously sung together before this, because they sung each line separately only joining to sing the last refrain together. Megan signaled the entire choir to join in: 'The Lord God made us all'.

It had been an unequal battle of wills but Megan thought, considering how ruthless her opponent was, she had acquitted herself well. In the spirit of the moment Abigail embraced Megan and kissed her on both cheeks. Megan submitted. The crowd sighed at Abigail's modesty as she curtsied before the children, the ensemble players, and finally deeply to Megan. Megan would always be grateful and indebted to Jake and Gladdie.

The children were disappointed that they had to wait until Christmas to receive their big gifts. They gleefully admired them until they fell asleep or got home. Abigail deliberately chose not to give them their main present. She intended fixing a lasting impression on the children's minds and adopted this method on the assumption that anyone may someday prove useful. They trooped back to the bus feeling like the 'little heroes' their teacher told them they were. They ate the delicious food and some fell asleep, almost immediately. Jake, drumstick clasped in his fist, tried to stay awake but failed. Gladdie would not close her eyes and when she did the applause vibrated through her entire being. Megan fetched the overtired and overwrought child and put her on her lap. She gently rebraided her hair and wound it round the top of her head. Then she held the child and rocked her, hoping that she would fall asleep.

'I'm in trouble,' Gladdie whispered.

'We'll keep it a secret,' Megan hastily assured her.

'No,' said Gladdie, 'real trouble. I love music.' She sounded simultaneously despondent and delighted. 'I just love it,' she repeated to underline the gravity of her pronouncement.

'Oh, I see. We'll have to think of something,' said Megan, sounding less than confident.

'I won't stop loving it. It makes me feel happy. I love music,' she said, although her expressive face declared that this love was to be almost unattainable. 'It made my body whirr. Please will you help me? You can find a way, I know you can,' Gladdie said, worried by the expression on her teacher's face.

'I'll try,' Megan said, unable to sound positive.

'You always say we must try harder,' Gladdie said accusingly. Megan nodded her head and stroked the child's cheek. 'What will I do if you don't help me? Who will let me love music?' and Gladdie's eyes filled with tears. She didn't mean to cry.

'We'll find a way,' said Megan, brushing Gladdie's tears away.

'How? How?' demanded Gladdie, beginning to sob. 'How?'

'She's giving us a piano,' said Megan while she attempted to rock the distraught child.

'A piano,' sighed Gladdie and she quietened down.

'Perhaps we can make a plan,' said Megan. Gladdie clasped her thin arms around her teacher's neck and kissed her. 'My kisses are my thankyou's,' she whispered. Then, as though she had sealed a bargain, yawned and snuggled trustfully into her teacher's arms. All the way she lay still, as though asleep. But underneath her eyelids and against her eardrums was the pulse of her mantra. A piano. A piano.

Jake loved Gladdie. She helped him with his schoolwork and she was fun. Yet he was afraid that, being a girl, she might weaken and confess to his parents that they had sung. In front of people. Out loud. And enjoyed it. That's why he caught the lizard and slit its throat. It was the nearest thing to a serpent he could find. Then he nicked his thumb and her thumb and they gravely rubbed their blood together and made an oath. Never to tell. Never ... ever ... ever... betray one another. And it was done.

It was a given that not one choir singer, or their parents, would tell the Boardmans what they had done.

'Is a sin a sin if nobody knows about it?' Jake asked Gladdie, rubbing his thumb unnecessarily hard against the wall.

'But all the people heard us.'

'You know what I mean. Is it?'

'It wasn't a sin,' Gladdie said with composure. 'Not at all a sin. Nothing sinful about it.'

Jake stopped punishing his thumb.

CHAPTER FOUR

·

Meningitis raged through the school, through the little town, and Louise's baby became seriously ill. The prognosis was dire, survival unlikely. Jake and Gladdie were sent to Hester to prevent contagion and John Jacob Boardman took them back. They prayed all the way. He took them back up the mountain and they chanted Psalms till they had neither voice, nor breath. He surprised both children by making them promise to pray for Louise, to pray for her youngest to live, because if the baby died he feared for her state of mind. He was down on his arthritic knees, his bony hands on their shoulders, and they were astounded by how afraid he was. They had thought him above fear but his anguished doubts were painfully apparent. Jake felt an embarrassed, pitying love for his father – it proved to Gladdie how right her mother always was. He raised his hands above their heads and asked the Lord to bless and protect them; he stood up and led them into Hester's house, charging them to look after one another. They brought extra clean clothes, bibles and schoolbooks. Homer, the three-legged coon-dog, gave the children such a warm welcome it seemed he would wag himself off his feet.

Jake loathed going to his Aunt Hester's house. Even though Gladdie was with him he felt strangely apprehensive. He could not understand why, but he sensed that Gladdie too was scared. Gladdie clung, prehensile, to her mother. There was a battered sofa and a table that hadn't been there before.

'Got the couch from Uncle Clay, and Louise sent this fine table,' Hester explained, seeing Gladdie's pleasure.

'Got the trunk from the Welfare.' It had old clothes and other odds and ends piled on top of it, which was why Gladdie hadn't immediately noticed it. There was enough room for them to place their belongings in it.

'Quite the little stranger here, you are. It's good to have my pretty little one back. It's been nearly two years since you've stayed in your own home,' she whispered as she tenderly held her daughter in her strong arms. She'd gone down the mountain as frequently as she could to see Gladdie. Pushing her playfully yet reluctantly away, she added, 'There's chores to be done. Go get some greens.' They went looking for wild violets, lamb's tongue and wild onions.

'The polk is good, but only when it's young,' explained Gladdie, 'You can eat the stalk and the leaves, but if you eat it when it's too old, you'll die – it turns to poison,' she cautioned.

'Everything here is poison.' Jake couldn't help complaining as they searched together.

Gladdie didn't reply, then said, 'I hate rattlers.'

So he knew she agreed.

Hester, her children and mother had cleared about an acre. They planted every possible vegetable they could. They worked hard all summer so that in winter they would have enough to eat. A hole three feet deep and about four feet wide was dug for winter; they stored all the root vegetables, potatoes, turnips and carrots there. They stored apples and pears which they had sliced and dried on the roof during the summer. As needed, these provisions would be dug up and the dirt replaced. They had even raised tobacco, but gave it up when they discovered it was not viable. They carried buckets from their well, to water whatever they could when the rains failed them. It was heavy work.

The family had been through better times. Hester hoped that Curt's brother would be able to get her husband's job back for him. Curt had been a forest fire ranger, but drink had made him unreliable. He was foolishly brave; the other fire fighters requested him whenever there was a dangerous fire. They called on the wild forest ranger from different parts of the state as his reputation earned him almost legendary respect, yet these acts of daring were unknown to his wife and children. She knew the guys down at the fire station liked him and would pull for him to get his job back. They hadn't yet found anyone who'd lasted in that remote tower which he kept in immaculate order, the steep stairwell clean and clear of any object that might impede him if he had to move fast. All this too gave Hester grounds for optimism. They'd had a milk-cow, a Betsy, a few times but they usually ended up being forced to sell her. They all cried when she was sold and hated Curt for incurring debt through his alcoholic gambling and crazy investments.

Curt's family had no idea how desperate his drinking had made him. He had had two relapses. They admired his inherent masculine power but they were more than thankful that in the past his serious binges took place away from their home. Curt had invariably managed to crawl up the mountain to sleep it off, his face and body bruised and grazed. It was easy to tell when their father had been in a fight. When he returned to blurred consciousness there would be a look of ineffable sadness and defeat on his face. It wasn't because of the brawling, his fight was against an invisible enemy. He never struck his wife or his children nor did he ever knowingly hurt them and this was his only source of pride.

Somehow Hester always skillfully contrived to retrieve her Betsy. Curt's brother, Clay, lived not too far away and much to Minnie, his wife's more or less hidden indignation, constantly bailed the family out. Kinship meant all to mountain people. Curt managed to pay Clay back or any other man he owed money to, no matter how long it took.

Hester made her own soap. Her mother had taught her how to cut the fat off any slaughtered animal, clean it and then slice it into fine slivers. She collected enough cracklings to put into a huge four-legged iron pot and sprinkled lye crystals on top. Adding water, she then boiled and stirred, boiled and stirred. She would poke a clean stick into the mixture, and when she withdrew it covered in a creamy layer, she knew it was perfect. Whenever she had a big fresh supply of lye crystals she felt rich; it was used for the outhouse, or she used lime, her other necessity.

Once, Curt chose Gladdie to carry a burlap gunny sack and go into town to the Relief. He chose her because the older ones had work to do. She rode most of the way on his shoulders. It was cold -- they walked for six miles and when they saw the long lines, their hearts froze. Near the point where food was handed out there was a row of barrels where people in the line could keep warm; coal and wood burned so the sides of the barrels became hot. Curt warned her to be careful, not get too close otherwise she would get a bad burn. Her father had to produce his social security number; he held it ready in his sock-covered hand. The amount a man received depended upon how many children he had. It was usual at this point that whoever was running for judge or sheriff would be standing with fifty cents or maybe a dollar to buy their vote, if there was an upcoming election. Father and daughter wore earmuffs. That helped. The people in the lines exchanged no words, no banter, those who recognized one another gave no sign, few exchanged greetings. The feeling of charity unwillingly given was as ever-present as their loss of dignity. Gladdie had pulled her gunny sack back without complaint, watching the mist of her father's breath, unable to see her own. He led the way, his great bulk that evening confirmed his impregnability to her. She was later to remember that time with admiring affection. He was the strongest man in the world. His face ahead of her expressed humiliated desolation, but she felt so important; she was the one he had chosen to help him.

The children ran back to the two-roomed house, onto which a new small smoke house had recently been added. Hester showed her newly-returned daughter what to do, and it was as though she had never been away. Jewel, her elder sister, and one brother returned bearing wood to feed the voracious cast-iron stove. Hester would decide whether to boil the dinner in her huge kettle or fry it in her skillet. A younger brother brought in water that he had drawn from the well. Two of the boys had been catching crawdads in the creek; tiny lobster-like creatures, they had taken care to avoid a sharp nip. They welcomed Jake and Gladdie in a perfunctory way. Mostly they were awkwardly jealous that Gladdie had new clothes.

'Tomorrow morning is bath morning for the girls,' Hester announced. This news was received without enthusiasm.

Early next morning Hester unhooked the aluminum tub. There was enough wood left over and this time Jake learned how to lower the bucket into the well. It took him four trips before there was enough hot water to add to the tub. Jewel and Gladdie went first and the youngest boy, aged four, joined them as, to his annoyance, he was not yet deemed a boy. Hester soaped him herself and teased Jewel about how pretty her small breasts were. Gladdie was amazed to see that Jewel now had pubic hair.

'It'll happen to you too one day,' she told her little sister, and they all laughed.

Nothing ever went to waste. Watermelon rinds were pickled and put into jars. The previous summer gave an abundance of blackberries. Hester made one hundred and two gallons and bottled it all. They had a delicious winter eating it on the bread she made out of corn. People whom the Howard family thought wealthy sometimes gave them a hog's head. It was put in the aluminum wash pan to be boiled. They ate everything except the eyes. They added potatoes to the dish and found it scrumptious.

Hester's mother, Ellen-Agnes, ground the corn herself. On a large stone slab she rolled it with a heavy round stone. It was a matter of honour to her that, almost always, her grandchildren had bread. She grew Indian corn in her yard and tended to it herself. Her only luxury was the same one her mother had before her. She grew her own tobacco for her corn-cob pipe. Anything good enough for her mother was good enough for her. Ellen-

Agnes had a coon-dog that followed her everywhere. The dog, named Moon, was her constant companion.

Gladdie and Jake waited eagerly every day for news, hoping that they could get away from this place. Gladdie didn't feel even the slightest twinge of guilt or disloyalty – she wanted to leave, that was all she knew. Hester decided that they should attend school with the others, which meant walking two miles to the bus stop. The television had been repossessed, the telephone bill remained unpaid, and their radio was beyond repair, so they only knew that there would be no school if the bus did not come. Schools closed whenever there were heavy snowfalls. Then they all trudged back up the mountain. The school itself proved agreeable and, though they missed Megan Macguire, they didn't think they would fall behind.

The entire source of entertainment for the family was the mountain. The flying squirrels gliding by; huge vines to swing on; flashing waterfalls that would surprise and delight after rainfall; snow sculptures in winter; the creek to swim in; birdsong to listen to. The children would use the slate hill or a slick mossy slope and slide and slip gleefully along.

Summer nights were fun times, except for the skeeters and bug bites. They tied June bugs on a string and held the other end and watched them fly around in circles. They kept lightning bugs in glass jars as though they had glittery lamps, but let them go in the morning so they'd live. They had an old miner's hat, which Curt or Hester wore when they went to fish or frog gigging. The gigger was like a long broom handle with a three pronged head attached; they liked to wade and sneak up and gig their quarry. Frogs' legs were good eating. For bait they had earth-worms or, from the richly-laden wonky-tonk tree, caterpillars. They cut horse-weed in season to get at that fat juicy worm, or they used grasshoppers. Anything that moved. They had cane poles with twine, and sometimes they even had fishing lines to attach onto the hooks. The reward was, if you were little and real quiet, you got to wear the miner's hat. In winter they made ice-cream with sugar and a little vanilla mixed with snow.

One day huge machines came to cut through part of the mountain to make a new freeway. The children watched in wonderment, the boys enthralled by the equipment. They were all agile, they liked doing handstands and back flips and could run along the tops of dangerously narrow poles or planks with practiced balance. But now they sat quite still as they watched the huge caterpillar machines eating their way through lime and sandstone, large boulders they thought immovable were imperiously pushed aside.

After witnessing their monstrous power, Hester smiled mischievously. Happily old man Webb, her father, had not been seen for several months. She fetched her aged mother, who was awestruck and faintly terrorized. Hester's mother had never been off the mountains, she hadn't ever entered a store and had not handled money. She had a Betsy, who slept outside, but she took her chickens into her home in their small coop each evening so that the foxes or raccoons never got to them. She scrupulously cleaned off the small wooden board at the bottom of the coop each morning. This extra bounty was rich fertilizer that she hoarded and cooed over. She was fond of her hens; they were her pets: but when their time came, she killed them swiftly and, she hoped, painlessly. She petted them first then, holding them by their heads, she expertly swung them around and dispatched them with a quick flick of her wrist. She kept a rooster only until it did its job. As soon as enough chicks hatched, the strutting cock was soup. Her skeletal structure foretold her imminent death, but then it had been doing so for several years.

Hester was pleased to find an amusement for her mother. At first her mother predicted all manner of disasters for the men who worked on the machines; the mountain tipping, the creek damming up. But she was a shrewd woman, wise in Mother Nature's world. She knew the mountains were forever and reassured herself. After watching with Hester and her children she began to fidget; her hands fluttered about until they found a child to hug, but even that could not long hold her fussing hands. Braid the children's hair – the hands seemed independently to search for work. They could not remain idle, and after a while Hester was obliged to follow the commandingly erect body of her mother, who went directly to work in Hester's vegetable garden. Those gnarled fingers tugged relentlessly and tirelessly at weeds. Hester stood looking down at her mother, exasperated that the little entertainment had lasted so briefly. Abruptly and surprisingly, the old lady stood up and put her arms round Hester.

'You've always been one for a bit of fun, no matter what happened to you. Nothing ever trampled you underfoot.' The mother nodded her head as though in agreement with herself. 'Yes.'

She knew, thought Hester, she must have always known about

the assaults and been powerless. Hester was almost overcome, realizing that her poor mother was as unprotected as a skunk without odour. The savage tenderness she felt for her mother quelled her surge of rage. There wasn't anything she could do. Hester's mother hardly ever smiled. The two women looked at one another and Hester remembered that she had never heard her mother laugh.

'Why don't you ever laugh, Ma?' she asked, her anguish barely suppressed. Back to work went the work-addicted hands, going fast. Hester could not keep up.

'Curt leaves me alone now,' she said, attempting to offer solace to her mother.

'Good,' the old woman half smiled. No more kids, thought Ellen-Agnes. And no more girls. This last assuaged her anxious heart. Her incessant labouring was her way of placating the furies, of attempting to secure the safety of her children, of guarding against hunger. But she wasn't able to protect them from their brutal and malevolent father. Webb violated her thoughts and reverberated through her nightmares. Webb contaminated everything. She couldn't bear thinking about the man who had bought her. Work. If only he would never come back. If only he was dead. She pushed him resolutely from her mangled mind. Work. Work.

Hester was used to being held, being cuddled, throughout her life. There was always another body she could hold against her at night. She had no use for sex; there was little time and less privacy. Her father had raped away any thought of lovemaking.

The day after Hester's wedding, Webb took to the road after first giving Ellen-Agnes a severe beating. He broke her collarbone, but Hester thought the major problem was a wound on her right thumb that wouldn't heal. One of her brothers fetched her to help their mother. She had to trek to her mother's shack, look after her and tend to her vegetable patch.

Hester soon fell pregnant and had morning sickness. The coon-dog that they got for a wedding present died. She had loved the dog and was saddened. Her mother viewed it as a bad omen – her daughter would not have a happy marriage. What Ellen-Agnes meant by the word 'happy' was that Hester would not have to endure abuse.

Ellen-Agnes developed a high fever and Hester gave her cool elderberry juice to drink and rubbed her mother's body down with it. She cleaned the wound with moonshine. Ellen-Agnes wouldn't allow Hester to rub her right side. Hester made a poultice from the inner bark of an elm tree, something that the women had learnt from the old Indian settlers. At one point her mother was almost unconscious and when Hester rolled her over, she found a deep wound on her mother's buttock. Ellen-Agnes had been too ashamed for her daughter to see it. Hester cleaned it and went in search of burdock. As she searched, she remembered that Minnie, her sister-in-law, had told her that burdock, along with hoes, ploughs and nails, came to America with the settlers, and it was they who showed indigenous peoples how to use it. She chopped and crushed its root and made a salve out of it. She found her mother's stock of dried yellow root, which was what her folk called 'golden seal', she boiled it and steeped it. Her mother drank a cupful of this exceedingly bitter remedy. Even after she was well she continued to drink it for a few weeks. Ellen-Agnes' wounds healed; Hester never asked her mother why she tried to hide the one wound from her.

Curt had hardly seen his bride. He knew that Hester had to take care of her mother, yet he had been expecting regular sex on demand – once he had married. That was the custom. He had fallen so deeply in love that the depth of his feelings had come as an unsettling surprise. But still a woman, his woman, was supposed to open her legs whenever the need took him. After all, he married her, he loved her, but she went to take care of her mother all the time and was tired and listless by the time she got home. Frustrated and hurt, he went on a binge.

As the years went by, she found that after a binge he didn't seem to require her until his system was void of drink. This was the only thing, as far as she was concerned, in favour of his drinking. She made no attempt to understand why he drank any more than she tried to understand the vagaries of the weather. This was the way he was. She accepted that and had no inkling of his suffering.

CHAPTER FIVE

•

It was homework time. Gladdie and Jake kept gamely at it. They thought they did it for Miss Macguire's sake. Unknowingly, they bargained with God. The deal was if they worked hard enough, Louise and her baby would soon be well again. Then they could go back home and their inexplicable uneasiness, which shadowed them even in the noonday sun, would vanish. They were certain of a favourable outcome because hard work was rewarded. At night they heard the screech owls, they thought they heard a woman screaming, but it was a wild cat. They lay with their arms about one another and hoped there were no bats to tangle in their hair. They held on. They got through each night. Jake had got a lot stronger in a few short months. He'd had to, and he was pleased with his big muscles. He showed them to Gladdie several times. All the other children had disappeared into the forest and Hester left to visit her mother. Jake's chore today was to fetch water from the well because it was bath day tomorrow. On his third trip to the well an old man crept crookedly out of the trees, grabbed him roughly and dangled him down the well. Jake's loud cries brought Gladdie rushing out to find him – she saw a man who seemed to be rescuing her beloved Jake by holding onto his feet.

'Pull him, sir, pull him!' and the old man pulled Jake out but as he pulled the boy out he rapped the child's head against the rim of the well. He carried the unconscious Jake back to the house, the man leaning against Gladdie as she tried to help him. They laid him down and the man took off his bulky grey coat. She saw his walking stick. He took off his balaclava. He was her grandfather.

'It's your papaw – don't you remember me?' he smiled showing his crooked yellow teeth. Gladdie's flesh shrivelled; she tried to run, but he seized her long braid with his misshapen right hand, pulled hard, then he switched hands and now his right hand was free.

When Gladdie eventually regained consciousness, she saw Abigail Dunstable's red necklace. Now it was moving down her legs. She'd thought her friend, Billy-May, was screaming again, and then there was the sound of mewing so she looked around for the kitten. Then she knew it was herself because she felt that her belly had been torn out. She struggled to turn her head to look for Jake, saw that his eyes were closed, but she knew he was not asleep, knew he was badly hurt. She had to get help. When she tried to move it hurt so much that she broke into a sweat. She didn't want Jake to see the necklace. She had to get help but could not walk. She crawled and dragged herself to him. At that moment Hester arrived. Hester's mouth opened wide in an agonized, murderous, soundless scream. The sight of her mother's scream terrified Gladdie.

'I'm sorry Mom, I'm sorry Mom, I'm sorry Mom...' Tears streamed down their faces as Hester, with infinite gentleness, staunched the flow of Gladdie's blood and laid her down without a word. Turning her attention to Jake, she placed cold compresses on his head. He had a small jagged wound but the bleeding had ceased.

'Sorry Mommy. I thought Papaw was saving... sorry, sorry Mom... Jake, from the... the well. We brought Jake. I'm sorry Mommy. We brought him... something happened. He won't die, Mom, Jake won't be dead. He's not sleeping but, sorry, sorry.... He's not dead. His head. Doctor, Mommy, he must, the doctor, sorry, please the doctor. Sorry.' Hester's inner screams stopped as an immeasurable darkness of heart invaded her being. She started to prepare a sling to carry Jacob on her back, and in her arms she would carry Gladdie. As she lifted him into the sling of old sheeting, his eyelids fluttered.

'Jacob, Jake, can you hear me? Jacob my darlin' sister's son. My Jacob.' His eyes opened – unfocused, but opened. He started to smile and then, as the pain continued, he cried a little. Because it hurt more, he soon stopped. He must live. He would live. Hester was as grateful as she was grim.

Down the mountain she carried them. She found a pace and moved as surely as a mountain cat. She never paused, she never stopped, through raging pain and thirsting fury. She followed no trail, taking the shortest route. She sped down Rattlesnake Ravine through a perilous area that she had forbidden to her children. She did not feel the sharp rocks beneath her feet. Gladdie slipped in and out of consciousness and Jake whimpered occasionally. Good, Hester thought with each whimper that she heard through her own rasping panting. Good. He is still alive. She couldn't stop to see. Eventually she reached the road and kept going. The first vehicle appeared. She simply stood in front of it. The startled driver, afraid of the mountain woman stopped. She croaked 'A doctor', and he took them to the town and the emergency centre. When he left, she nodded her head in thanks.

'What happened here?' a horrified Dr Jergens asked when he saw Gladdie.

'Fix them,' was all Hester said.

'I'll notify the police first.'

'Doctor – fix them right now else I'll cut your balls off and make you eat them.' Her tone was steady as stone. He hesitated briefly. Looking into her eyes he understood that she was capable of carrying out her threat.

'I'm no gynaecologist,' he muttered apologetically.

But he did do what he could for Gladdie. He gave her a local anaesthetic, stitched her up and put her on a saline IV containing antibiotics. He gave her sedatives. Jake had sustained a concussion; how serious it would be, he could not yet assess. They were to stay overnight in the hospital. Dr Jergens, frightened by Hester's wild eyes, resisted asking her if she required tranquillisers. Once she had seen the children attended to she seemed calm, unthreatening, thankful even. Though there was threat in her reiterated 'No cops!' She went to the bathroom at the nurse's suggestion. When she saw herself in the mirror, she stretched out her arm and rigidly pointed at her reflection.

'You,' she accused, 'you.'

The nurse brought her hot coffee, thickly sweetened and drew a bath for her. She brought her a clean shirt and some britches. 'They are nobody's,' the nurse said. 'Somebody left them behind. You take them.' She brought her shampoo. 'Lie in the bath for a while.' Then she put bath salts in the water.

'You,' Hester accused roughly, her arm and finger still stiffly unyielding. 'You.'

'Fresh green pine,' the nurse said soothingly. As the fragrance filled the air and the nurse's compassion enfolded Hester, she began to weep. The nurse put her arms around her and asked no questions. She rocked Hester and patted her on the back. Gently she turned her to face the bath. Hester lay in the first full-length tub she had ever been in. Her wet hair floated around her shoulders and her tears slowly ceased as the warm water cooled. She washed her body, her hair, her clothes. She cleaned the bath and put on the fresh clothes she'd been given. The children lay sleeping and safe. She could no longer put off going to her sister.

In this instance, John Jacob had judged rightly. The death of her baby had driven Louise almost insane. Her house was in a mess, dishes were piled high, cobwebs claimed the corners, unwashed clothing formed a vaguely menacing grey mass. Her husband had tried to help but was exhausted by the time he got home from the hardware store. He would find his wife where he left her, in bed, her hair uncombed, her body unwashed. Hester had visited after the baby died and instructed him to see that Louise ate and drank a lot of water. Before leaving, she had made a big pot of soup. It was filled with vegetables and John Jacob had been annoyed when she added a whole chicken to it. But his wife had no appetite, and every night for two weeks he had the soup for dinner. He had to admit to himself that it was good.

It was past ten when Hester arrived at her sister's door. If only Louise had been a sturdier sort of woman, then Hester could have brought the children back sooner. Dark night animals loped back and forth inside her skull. She had chosen to shield the children from her sister's crazed anguish and she bore full responsibility for that choice. Because of that choice, this thing had happened. But to feel guilt was pointless. She understood that all living things were at the mercy of chance. All you could do was cope with what came as best you could. Hester thought Louise was not meant to be a mother. She had no luck with her children. Now all that Louise had left was Jake, and who knew how he'd end up. Hester would have to give Gladdie to her to keep full time. It would help Louise and would be better for Gladdie. That was that. A bleakness took possession of Hester's soul as she knocked at the Boardman's front door.

When John Jacob Boardman opened it and saw her leaning against the wall, she who was so strong, he was afraid. He knew that further sorrow was about to enshroud him. His eyes beseeched Hester. He couldn't utter a word.

'Jake is safe,' she said, dully noting that he wore long johns in summer.

His entire body sighed his gratitude. 'Gladys?'

'She's alive,' said Hester. 'Alive. It will take time. I don't know how long.'

Louise barely seemed to notice Hester snapping on the bed-side lamp. Her eyes had watered and the wart on her upper lip seemed to pull her face into the grimace of some gargoyle. The room was steeped in sorrow, awash with incomprehension and grief. Anger and despair lent Hester inspiration. She wiped Louise's face with all the tender meticulousness of a cat licking her kitten. She hauled her into a sitting position.

'Go get fresh strong coffee and plenty of sugar,' she ordered

John Jacob. When he had closed the door, the tabby became a lioness. Snarling, Hester systematically began to slap her sister's face back to life. Hard, but not too hard. Seeing intelligence flickering back into Louise's eyes, Hester felt a relief so profound that for an instant she was bereft of purpose. Her acute need to ensure a home for the two children flooded back into her and when John Jacob returned to the room he found Hester carefully mopping her sister's tears. She fetched the coffee from him and he shrank away. She intimidated him, and yet at the same time he knew that something beyond his understanding was happening between the sisters. Something that he suspected would return his Louise to him. He could not obey and follow his Lord without his wife. She was the altar that inspired and ennobled his prayers. Deep within he was aware that Louise's purity of spirit and absolute love for the Lord was infinitely greater than his could ever be. Her being lent him grace and he left the sisters alone.

Hester spooned brown sugar into the steaming mug. She stirred it. Filled the spoon, blew on it, and fed her sister. Obedient as a child, the large woman swallowed.

'Too sweet,' she gurgled, but when her hands stopped shaking she took the mug and gulped down its contents. Then Louise began to quake with anger. It was quite a daunting sight. The flesh on her arms hung loose and wrinkled like crepe. Observing this, Hester saw her sister had not eaten for days. Waving her arms and heaving her ample but empty breasts, Louise finally was able to voice her anger.

'Britches,' she gasped, 'a woman wearing the garb of a man offends the sight of the Lord, and in my own home! Get down. Get down on your knees to pray for Our Saviour's forgiveness.'

Thank God, thought Hester, thumping down on her knees. Maybe He does exist afterall. For now she knew she could go back to the mountains, back to her brood, as soon as she knew the children were alright.

While the children slept at the emergency centre, Hester swiftly cleaned Louise's house. She didn't want Gladdie to see it in that chaotic state. Louise took a shower and washed her hair. The next day, Hester took Gladdie back to her aunt's house, she slipped into her daughter's bed and lay beside her, holding her firmly. The child stared at her mother as though newly examining her, and eventually fell into a deep sleep. The hospital kept Jake one more day until they saw he was on the way to recovery, and John Jacob fetched him. By then Hester had left.

Five days later Hester reappeared at her sister's house. She went to Gladdie's room.

'Honey', she said gently, 'I need to look at you.' Gladdie seemed to be dreaming. Dazed, she allowed her mother to examine her. Quietly she watched as Hester lit matches to disinfect thin nail scissors by scorching them. Then her mother rolled up a piece of cloth.

'Bite on this,' she told her daughter, and after she again scorched the scissors she cut two ugly black stitches and carefully removed them. The internal stitches, that neither knew were there, would dissolve.

'You can stop biting now,' Hester directed, but it was difficult for Gladdie to unclench her teeth.

'I thought,' Hester said, 'I'd have to take you to that kind nurse.'

She removed the cloth from her daughter's teeth and then she stroked her child's cheeks. She stroked her head, her soft young neck, smoothing her shoulders, her arms and little hands. Each finger, one at a time. Then down the sides of her thin torso, her legs, feet and each tender little toe. The rigidity drained away and Gladdie lay peaceful as Hester quietly left.

The sisters did not speak. They could not look one another in the eye.

CHAPTER SIX

•

The moment Megan saw Tom Burns, a tall, lanky man with a gentleness she found irresistible, she knew she wanted to meet him. She was at a book fair when a small child started to cry. Tom scooped the child up, his eyes scanning the crowds looking for a parent, when Megan came up to help.

'Yours?' he asked.

'No, but I look after children. I'm a teacher.' He smiled at her.

'You've arrived just in time to find the mother.'

'Or father,' she replied. Together they calmed the well-dressed child and found the parents at the Information Desk. Reunited and relieved, the parents asked the two, whom they assumed were a couple, to join them for coffee. And that was how Megan and Tom met.

Thomas was called Tom by his friends, but Megan always used his given name. They often discussed the miracle of their coming together – their happiness, shared interests, values and even ideals. They flung themselves with lovers' recklessness to their fate, convinced the gods would be kind to them. They talked about what they had together and knew it was too precious to lose. For what is life without love? Nothing, they agreed. Nothing.

Tom had found his years as a student social worker crushingly depressing. They had led to disappointment in himself. Enthusiastic, impatient and young, he had found it impossible to accept how meagre his effectiveness would ever be. He resorted unwillingly to anti-depressants and feared his parents might have to endure the misery of his possible nervous breakdown. The extra miracle of their meeting was that Megan understood his dilemma. She thought he empathized too deeply, which she assured him was not a bad fault. In fact it made her love him all the more. That book fair, held in Cincinnati, had changed their lives forever.

They duly introduced their parents. Megan's father was a professor of philosophy, her mother a semi-retired landscape designer. Tom's parents owned a small chain of restaurants called Fat Fred's, named after their favourite labrador. They were married in the spring in the Macguires' garden. Megan, an only child, had promised herself six children.

She carried a sheaf of white dogwood and they chose the Painted Desert for their honeymoon. They wanted to make love in the desert dawns and sunsets, and by moonlight beneath the stars. Their love made them feel part of the light. They became their own light.

Tom's parents gave them a new branch of Fat Fred's. They wanted to guarantee the active participation of the newlyweds because, whilst ideals were good, there was no profit in them. Megan was a fiery idealist, and they were worried she might re-ignite their son to the point where he lost interest in their commercial creation. Fat Fred's could be the source of a considerable fortune. They congratulated themselves that one day it could become a dynasty and now, with Tom settled and the prospect of grandchildren, they could scarcely contain their pleasure. The young couple were excited at the prospect of working together, though Megan would continue with her teaching for a while.

When Megan, already pregnant, returned from her honeymoon, entered her classroom and breathed in its unique aroma of chalk, fruit, dust, children's perspiration, remnants of school meals, she knew how pleased she was to be back. She noted the Boardman children had not returned and decided to find out where they were. These religious ones were the worst. She found out that Mrs. Boardman's baby had died and had been the only fatality; a major achievement for the school district.

The children had brought many flowers on her return. She carefully disentangled all the white ones from the various pots and jars and made a passable little bouquet to express her condolences. Armed with both sympathy and prudently hidden indignation, she was determined to get the two children back to school. She hadn't even knocked when the door was opened and Louise ushered her in.

'You've come about Jake and Gladys,' she said, taking the flowers from Megan. She gestured to a chair and left the room, returning with the flowers in a jug.

'Thank you for remembering my baby,' she said. She was silent for a while. Before Louise spoke it was clear that she had put a great deal of thought into what she had to say. 'Jake was in an accident. They told us he got concussed, had a convulsion and it's epilepsy. We pray for the Lord to guide us. I hope it's not the Devil who shakes his little body, but Brother Boardman says the Devil inhabits our son. We pray for guidance about medication. God created man and man made medicines. That's how come the Lord made medicine. But Brother Boardman says the Devil will shake himself out of Jake. He says it is a spiritual matter, that we are not allowed to interfere. He says, like Abraham, he is being put to the test. The Lord will not find him wanting. All he permits us to do for our boy is place a rolled up rag in his mouth to stop him from swallowing his tongue. I don't know what I've done for the Lord to visit his wrath upon us. I suppose I shouldn't tell you all my troubles, please excuse me.' Louise spoke quickly and coherently. Her arms were tightly clasped around her large frame.

'How is Gladdie?' Megan asked.

'She's OK. She only lost her voice. The last time I think I heard her she was whispering to my husband to please give Jake medicine. She's totally dumb. Voiceless. And,' she said, hugging herself more closely, 'I can't send my child, an epileptic, to school, or one that can't speak.'

Megan found she couldn't speak either. In the ensuing silence Louise thought maybe her husband was right. Maybe the Devil was in her home. Why had all her babies died except Jake? Maybe He took Gladys' voice away. What had she done wrong?

'Look, look at everything. It's as clean as can be. Always we say our prayers; even Gladys mouths the words.' Louise called through the doorway, 'Gladys, Gladys.' They came in holding hands. They had heard every word.

'Look at Gladys' hair; not one strand of it have I cut.'

Gladdie's long chestnut braid seemed to have lost its light, as had the child's eyes. She seemed dulled. Jake came up to Megan, painfully confused.

'If the Devil lives in me,' he asked Megan, 'am I the Devil?'

'Oh Jake, of course you're not the Devil. I don't believe in the Devil.'

At this Louise seemed shocked, clasping herself tightly, as if afraid that if she let go, all her vital parts would escape and go winging across the room. Especially her heart. Her hurt heart. Turning to Gladdie, Megan said, 'You know that Jake's not the Devil, don't you?' Gladdie bobbed her head up and down in agreement.

'Jake,' Megan said, shaking her head and stroking his. 'Jake, epilepsy can happen to anyone who has bumped his head. How did you do it?'

'An accident,' answered Louise.

'At a well,' said Jake. 'That's all I remember.'

'That's all he remembers,' Louise echoed.

'Mrs Boardman, will you allow me to speak to your husband? I can assure him that epilepsy is easily treatable. I know a man who is a doctor. He has the same problem, yet people trust him. He is a devout Baptist,' continued Megan, seeing Louise wanted to be convinced. 'I can bring him here to meet your husband. He is living proof that epilepsy is something that can be controlled.'

'How did he get his?' asked Jake.

'He was going down a hill,' improvised Megan, 'when the front wheel of his bicycle hit a bump in the road and he fell off. He was on his way to church!' She ended with a flourish. 'This is such a fine Baptist home – I would be honoured to come and give the children lessons right here in your shining clean house –,' her voice demure and reasonable, 'and get them back to school. Soon.'

She looked into Louise's eyes.

'Tomorrow,' said Louise. 'After we have all prayed. But I think I heard the Lord say tomorrow.'

The Lord's voice sounded suspiciously like Gladys', but Louise quickly banished the remembered tone.

'As for Gladdie, if she can't speak at least she can hear – isn't that so, Gladdie?' Again she bobbed her head.

When John Jacob found out that his Louise had heard the voice of the Lord, the exhausting strain of his grief began to diminish. How could the Devil dwell in the fruit of her womb, in his Jacob, his only surviving child? Hadn't his wife herself heard the voice of the Lord?

That night Megan and Tom discussed what could be done to help Gladdie. He shivered slightly when he thought of the little girl's plight. Megan determined to find the cause, get hold of the facts and reach understanding. Surely with understanding, healing would come.

As he renewed himself in and of her, Tom recreated her sturdy sense of self-belief. Their lovemaking made them feel indestructible, yet vulnerable. They were not naive about the ways in which even the best of relationships could wither; they wanted to be different. They did not believe in happy endings; rather, they believed in constant new beginnings.

Their own branch of Fat Fred's soon began to improve. The area had been well researched before being selected. It was so good that the larger restaurants chose to be there… Tom had a battle royal to bring in the customers.

'If only my customers would be like dear old Fat Fred,' said Tom wistfully. 'He was loyal, obedient,' he smiled.

The dog ate everything, like a vacuum cleaner.

The emblem of Fat Fred's was a large, seated labrador, with his front paw extended and head tucked beguilingly down; more or less how Fat Fred had looked.

'What would happen if,' suggested Megan, 'you had a labrador family or a puppy for children to play with?'

So it was that they acquired a labrador puppy, given the name Pudding. Children and adults alike loved he r and she was given her own comfortable enclosure. There was a sink and antiseptic liquid soap with fresh paper towels with their logo on them for customers to use after they had patted her. Pudding was the start of many things, including puddles, but she did the trick, and more and more customers came back.

Next morning, Megan was pleased to see the Boardman children were back at school. No one thought it peculiar that they shared the same last name, and assumed their fathers were brothers. The other children were pleased to see them too and were thrilled by the livid scar on Jake's temple. They wanted to know how he got it and Megan told them how he had fallen against the side of a well and how brave he had been when he had the stitches. They were all impressed by his adventure and were a bit envious when Megan left them with the spare teacher to take the two children to see the doctor.

When her dumbness first began, Gladdie could not stop thinking about her lost voice. It seemed one moment it was there and the next, gone. But where did it go to? Where? She imagined that one day (when she was singing when she wasn't supposed to be) a bird flew out of a silvery tree and picked up the threads of her song and flew away with it. A white bird circled around trailing her song, like a long dewdrop-covered ribbon, with the sun shining through each note. Then the bird flew past her as though to say goodbye, and a tear fell from its eyes. It was sorry it had to take her voice, but it was a mother bird who needed it for her children. But what she didn't know and couldn't work out was why? Why? Her head felt cold; she tried to rub it warm. She put her cushion over it but then she couldn't breathe. She wondered if people could kill themselves like this. If she could kill herself this way.

If something bad happens, her mother told her, look for the good.

In a secret chamber of her innermost heart, Louise feared the

Love of God might not be enough to help her little boy. She had never told John Jacob that she had implicitly given Megan the right to look after her children. It was a relieved Dr Jergens who finally could give the boy the correct dosage of medicine and explain to this sensible teacher how to monitor his epilepsy.

'It may take a few months for it to be reliably effective. I don't want the boy to be unduly stressed,' he told her. Megan felt more confident and secure. She had been right to bring along the carefully folded cloth, the perfect size to fit into Jake's mouth in case he had a seizure.

'I can't find anything wrong with Gladys,' Dr Jergens added, hardly glancing at the child. He had been shocked when the girl entered the room – he would never forget those wildly haunted eyes.

'Maybe it's psychological. Perhaps she had a shock,' Dr Jergens hastily suggested. Megan could scarcely contain her annoyance.

'Seeing her darling Jake bleeding and unconscious naturally shocked her,' she said with asperity and left.

The young doctor sat with his head in his hands, his eyes tightly shut, trying to forget that dreadful night. Nothing could have made him tell the conscientious teacher the truth. He had not contacted the police, and if that came out he couldn't bear to think about the ruinous consequences. He had to protect himself. As for the little girl, she looked well and alert, her darting eyes and briefly clasped hands had seemed to implore his silence. Only seven and small for her age, skinny and weighed down by her thick chestnut hair, she looked like a six-year-old. He saw his knuckles gleaming whitely and he pounded his desk. He remembered that he had allowed himself to be afraid of the wild woman and that she had shown him to be a coward.

For a while, Megan artfully arranged her classes around the Boardman children's needs and they were given extra books to read at home. Louise sedulously co-operated with her children's teacher.

One day Louise told her Gladys had been stung by a wasp and hadn't uttered a sound and Megan's anxieties doubled. Who could fail to cry out with pain? Was it possible that the child would never speak again?

CHAPTER SEVEN

•

After Hester removed Gladdie's stitches she returned home to the mountains. She could have hitched a ride at least part of the way but instead chose the long hike back. She revelled in it. Her bare feet seemed of their own accord to enjoy the feel of the road, the pathway and above all the strength-giving earth. Yes, her feet told her. Yes. You and I are one.

Luckily Curt was away. Happy to see her, her children rushed to hug her, fetch her wild flowers and show her the garden. Her mother too was waiting for her. Not one of her children asked her what had happened; they smelt sorrow and wanted no part of it. Only to be with their rugged, cheerful mother and celebrate her return with walking on their hands and skipping about. Excitedly they chanted snatches of what they'd learned at school, they wanted to hide their resentment of what had been her preoccupied air and seeming abandonment. Their mother had never before left for more than a day and, when she did, they knew where she had gone to and why. Hester sang songs to them; she felt her heart opening like a huge, many-petalled flower, forever opening one more petal. For once her mother smiled, her strong teeth gleaming.

A week after her return Hester told her mother to watch over the children for a while. There was work, she told her mother, that could wait no longer. Foreboding twisted her mother's heart. An owl must have flown over Webb's house, Ellen-Agnes thought, as she held her hand to her eyes, as if shielding them from a drenching blackness. She noticed that her daughter had tied a long thick rope around her waist.

Hester rejoiced as she climbed towards the road-builder's earthmoving equipment. She liked the sun glistening on the rocks. She marveled at the sheen on the leaves. Closing her eyes she embraced a large tulip poplar and placed her cheek against its bark. Listening, she pressed her ear against the trunk. A small waterfall glittered and pebbles shone as she sniffed the different fragrances. She plucked a yellow May apple and ate it. For sheer reckless joy she swung herself on an old climber that hung seductively in her path and as she swung the medley of all that was good in her childhood seemed to swing with her. She was in her early thirties, but she looked older. She didn't think much of men, yet there were times when they gave her pleasure, a pleasure derived solely from her power over them. She well knew how to use them and she was too hardworking to let them waste her time.

She could see the lights flashing to warn motorists and could smell the pungent molten tar. When she got to the machines and the men she was particularly fascinated by the heavy treads and felt an electric frisson when she saw them. The men indulged her curiosity over the large scooper, the grader and the machine that spread tar on the road. They laughed at her pretended fear over the dangers of the tar spreader – an outdated old model, they informed her. Then they broke for cigarettes and coffee. When they returned to work, one remained behind with Hester. Their snickering and envious glances back at the temporary road builders shack told them they had lost out. But the one Hester had chosen, Hugo, she quickly used up. She pulled down her skirt and pulled up his trousers and shared a cigarette with him. She puffed and coughed, unused to smoking. Hearing his shouts of laughter, the men sighed sheepishly. She must be some woman.

Hester talked to him, minutely interested in his words about the huge machines. Wanting to know everything about how they worked. The men watched from afar as he showed her the levers and pulley on his earth digger. Then they came down and each showed her how he operated his specific equipment. They wished she'd give them all a go with their very own machine. She teased them and then left them, disappointed and curious.

She left and made her way to find the place where her father lived with a young runaway. This wasn't the first under-aged girl he'd got for himself.

'Ma wants you,' she spat.

'What the hell for?' he shouted hoarsely. 'She don't need me for nothin'.'

'You betta come,' she said menacingly.

'What's that used-up ole cow want with me?' This said for the benefit of the young girl. He grabbed his walking stick as if to strike her but then he scrambled and limped after her.

'Move it!' her grating voice flat and hard, commanded. Her eyes expressionless as flint stones. He didn't know what to expect, but somehow he could not disobey her. He was angry because he felt tense and uneasy.

It was inexplicable that Hester had come to fetch him – why

would Ellen-Agnes want to see him? He found it mysterious. They walked along a little too fast for him, but he wouldn't admit to it.

'Is she dyin'?' he panted.

'She don't want you.' They stopped walking for a moment.

'You lyin' to your papaw,' he said, spluttering copious amounts of spit as he began to raise his walking stick again. She snatched it away with panther-like ease.

'She ain't dyin'.'

'Give me back my stick!' he shouted hoarsely, suddenly remembering the severe beating she had once given him – and the reason why. For the first time, he felt fear.

'I was lyin'. I've got something special for you.' She simply unwound the rope and tied a knot in it and before he knew it had dexterously slipped a noose around his unwashed neck. Then she gave him back his stick. He thought it a good sign she gave it back to him. Now the rope, that was another matter. 'Keep goin',' she said. He did as he was told but exaggerated his limp.

'I didn't never have no mother, my uncle's brung me up. Taught me to read the street signs. That's how come I could drive,' he said, making conversation with her, which he had rarely done in the past. She made no reply. Instead she smiled and her smile frightened him. He couldn't work out what the hell was on her mind.

'Nobody looked after me when I was a kid,' he said, and tried to recollect when someone had come looking for him. It was only when one of the uncles needed him for chores. They told him he was a lazy runt.

'I wasn't as strong as the other boys,' he panted. Of course girls were different – they were easy. Now this girl, his blood, was leading him along like a cow to be slaughtered. He tried to pull away but the rope tightened on his neck.

'Nearly fell down there,' he quickly said. She made no reply. She fiddled with two black pieces of cotton in her pocket: Gladdie's stitches. They were walking along, father and daughter, among the trees and were almost opposite the road builders. He felt a surge of optimism, certain that she would do nothing if they were within sight and earshot. He was about to call out when she seemed to guess and the noose tightened. She swerved towards a tall black pine, and made a sudden leap to catch one of its branches to haul herself up. Before he knew it she began to pull him up after herself. He struggled, choked, tried to yell but could not breathe, so he began to climb up after her to lessen the pressure on his neck. Fear lent him strength and he desperately grasped her ankle, but she jumped down, the rope still looped over a branch. He held on as long as he could but slowly, jamming her feet against the tree trunk, she hauled him up. Then she kept him up, her body straining, then holding still.

The branch she had looped the rope over was a good choice. He made a desperate effort to carry his own weight by clutching onto other branches but they gave way. He tried for a foothold, but lack of oxygen became too much for him. After a while he ceased thrashing about, but still she didn't move. She didn't trust him. Her arms and legs began to ache, but the only movement she made was the steady rise and fall of her breath. She became a clamp. She hated herself because she hadn't done this sooner. Sweat ran off her face and body. A wasp alighted on her cheek; she didn't even flinch. It flew away after investigating her face.

Finally, she let go of the rope and the body came tumbling down. She put her arms around the trunk, put her lips to it, and kissed it. Trees, her dependable allies and friends, never disappointed her. It would be a simple matter to drag the body, in the dark, across to the road building machines. Put him away for all time. Never to harm another child – never ever. She looked briefly at his face, his popping eyes and purple tongue, and felt satisfied. She waited for the dusk to deepen. It would not be long.

The next day the road builders returned to go over the work they had done the previous day. It seemed the road had added on a yard or so during the night. Hugo, the man who'd had all the luck yesterday, went back over his work in the steam roller to make sure the patch was as smooth and even as the rest.

'Fucked your brains away,' they mocked. 'Can't remember what you did.' They could laugh all they liked – smugly, Hugo knew what they really felt. But what a woman. He shook his head again. He'd been saying that all night. What had she done – it was all over so fast. She had manipulated his body in a fury of dexterity. Her powerful ability frightened him. He knew he'd never experience the like again and, in truth, he didn't want to.

There were nights, and days too, when Curt did not come home. The shack seemed more isolated, more prone to some extravagantly violent act that nature might hurl at them. It seemed as though their father's absence provoked a subterranean fear, one that the children would not acknowledge but deeply sensed. If they felt hungry, the smaller children wondered what a hungry bear would do – or a wild cat. Branches scratching against the window could well be claws. A flash flood, the creek becoming a rising river, their home floating away … a tornado sucking up a heavy tree trunk, dumping it on the shack and flattening them. The heat, the humidity or a forest fire devouring the air. Oh yes, there was plenty to fear – especially in the summer. Winter somehow evoked less terrors.

Hester was fearless. She didn't bother with what may or may not happen. It was not arrogance, just acceptance that she could and would handle whatever came her way. She tried to make provisions for the suffering that was part of living. She had an axe that she kept sharpened and a shotgun that was old but well oiled. More importantly, she had food and fuel reserves for the winter. Those were her concerns and she felt she had the weapons to deal with them.

She knew of her children's fears. So she taught them everything she thought they needed to know. Above all how to grow food and how to store it. She taught them all the medicinal remedies that she knew of. She taught them how to survive.

'People want things that they've no need for. That's foolishness,' she said. 'People want things that are never going to happen, like to never be afraid. That's foolishness too. It is sensible to be afraid of copperheads and rattlers, even though most snakes are harmless; a little fear spices up eyesight. Keep your eyes open, otherwise you might miss the beauty in nature,' she warned, 'that's what you've got eyes for. And look out for each other. One may see what the other may miss. That's how we share. If we don't share, one may go hungry or get cold. That's why we share.'

Their mother made a game of it.

Why is it good to sometimes be sleepy, she would ask, and the sleepy one, or the one pretending to be sleepy, would answer with a smile – so that we can share laughter. Laughter, they had been taught, was the richest of all things to share.

And so Hester gentled their fears away. She was adamant they believe in themselves as individuals and as a family. She made jokes about Brother John Jacob and his fire-and-brimstone talk. The only hell on this earth is when one of you runs a fever – I hate that, she admitted to them. I hate that.

There wasn't much time for long talks with their mother unless they were working alongside her. Hester was not a dreamer; she had no worldly desires. She expected nothing from life. All she wanted was the strength to work for her own survival and that of her family. She wanted them to have fun, enjoy the bountiful beauty that surrounded them. She had heard of the Garden of Eden and imagined that they lived there. She told her children that too. Her mother had explained to her that no religion has dominion over another. Hester supposed that God may exist, but not if the God was male; not if the God was a man. The sky was neither male nor female, nor were the mountains; in fact she reasoned many things were not of one sex or another.

It was simply not possible for her to respect any man.

She taught her children that all beings were equal; if a boy was stronger than a girl in one way, then she was stronger than he in another. She held most objects in deep respect, if not awe. She respected the iron in her skillet, the strength of her stove, the sturdiness of a chair. She swept away their fears with the same gentleness that she stroked their hurt bodies or feverish foreheads.

When Gladdie thought about her, she remembered the way her mother stroked moss growing on rocks and how she bade her do the same, to feel the textures of leaves, bark and petals, the wind on her hair, the feel of the water in the creek. Her mother taught them her favorite fragrances that abounded in the forest, the smells of wild violets, the faint perfume of a wild iris, and the earth after a good rain.

CHAPTER EIGHT

•

Abigail Dunstable stood looking at herself in her full length mirror. Then she sat at her dressing table and flicked on her state-of-the-art lighting. The best make-up artist and most expert lighting consultant from Hollywood had constructed her equipment. She scrutinized her face in an enlarging mirror with the fervour of a scientist examining a promising microbe. She was pleased the face that gazed back at her was almost flawless. If the skeletal structure was slightly too prominent, the lustrous dark eyes and perfectly arched brows framing the face more than compensated. The full lips hinted sensuality. Her hair was silken, thick and jet black – and was her trademark.

Gratified, she smiled at herself. She still could get away with it. Dr Glazer was worth his weight in gold. Dimming the lights, she looked even better. She put in the contact lenses that had been carefully chosen to enhance her dark eyes, with a slight purplish tinge which made her eyes fascinatingly hypnotic. Then, unintentionally, she glimpsed her reflection in a sideways mirror. It was not her 'mirror face' she saw, it was as others saw her. She saw age.

A brief shriek of terror tore through her. She felt a frantic need for some form of comfort, so she rushed to her safe and rummaged through one of her jewel boxes. Priceless jewels were her consolation and pride – the friends who never betrayed and faithfully gave her their allegiance. She picked up a large opal egg pendant. She popped it in her mouth and then she smiled as she withdrew it. It was so big it felt slightly uncomfortable. So she put it in again, drooling a chain of diamonds and opals.

She was still a sexual being, anxious not be cheated of a worthy mate. She was sufficiently pragmatic to know that she lacked youth but she also knew that she still had much to offer in addition to her money: a renowned hostess, she knew all the people worth knowing in many fields, both political and cultural. She was a status symbol, people dropped her name. She never name-dropped.

From her short list of possible husbands she chose Roberto Albuquerque, an American with impeccable Spanish lineage, who was a cultured, desirable young banker. He was slim, narrow-hipped and his walk had an elegance in keeping with his well-groomed style. His eyes were dark brown and the length of his eyelashes caused many a woman to complain how unfair it was – no need for mascara. He had long been a generous Democrat supporter and was in line for an ambassadorship. His wife was known to be gravely ill. She had never heard what the illness was but the general view was that she would not last long. Abigail knew the future ambassador – her future ambassador – loved the sea, so her next party was to have the sea as its theme. What would be entirely novel, imaginative, unforgettable? Of course the Seamen's Rescue Mission would benefit. Her party-planners all had the same boring ideas, including a yacht in her swimming pool! No one but she understood the importance of this occasion and how much depended on its being unusual and beautiful. She became impatient and cross with her assistants, and with herself too, because time was passing and still she had no inspiration.

Then it flashed upon her – Mermaids! A pageant of mermaids and mermen could be ravishingly beautiful – the girls would have to be chosen for the perfection of their breasts, of course, which might slant it towards the vulgar, which would be unbearable – discretion and good taste were vital. But it could be handled in such a way that the danger was avoided. Abigail remembered the great success she had achieved with the innocent simplicity of the school choir. If she used those two exquisite children she had rescued from their silence, they would provide the innocence she needed, the balance. This would have to be her spring party. The next one, her winter party in Scotland, she now saw, would not suit Roberto, as he was a creature of the south. She overcame impatience by appreciating the time gained for planning perfection.

On her instructions, Mandy asked Roberto's secretary to lunch. They were to gossip and Mandy's brief was to find out as much as she could about Mr Albuquerque. In fact the secretaries rather liked one another. Mandy was the older of the two, and both were devoted to their employers. They admitted this to one another and this similarity allowed them to speak freely. They developed a friendship and saw to it that they lunched together or went to a movie at least once a fortnight. On certain subjects Lillian, Roberto's secretary, would not be drawn. On Mrs Albuquerque's illness, all she would say was that it was extremely serious, and confessed she had never met her. Mandy suspected that she was in love with Roberto, which Lillian blushingly denied. Mandy reached across the table and touched her hand, smiling compassionately, drawing them even closer. They commiserated and complained together. They called their employers by their first names, although they never did so in person. Mandy passed on to Abigail the morsel that Mr Albuquerque hated grouse-shooting and fox-hunting, so Abigail rejoiced that her instincts had served her well. Mandy wanted to discuss the winter party but Abigail, uncharacteristically, told her to use the old lists and her imagination.

'Alter the colour scheme,' she exclaimed imperiously. 'Use more pipers to pipe them in. I'm working on the spring. The spring.' Abigail sent Mandy on a quick business trip to check up on several of her ventures and went herself to England to see what progress was being made on an entertainment and shopping mall she was financing in Leeds. She didn't neglect her 'hobby', no matter what.

Abigail worked out at the barre, used weights and all her ballet training. She worked in grim silence, hardly ever using the excellent sound systems she had installed in all her houses. The problem with music was that it could bring about fits of weeping and swollen eyes. She would lie with slices of cucumber on her eyelids to cool them and reduce the swelling. Loneliness and self-pity were her constant companions. She wanted to marry Roberto, but in the meantime, there wasn't a single man she wanted to have an affair with. It was exasperating. She didn't want to break her rule and use a former lover.

Roberto Albuquerque was a courtly man with exquisite manners. He spoke several languages and the idea of his someday representing his country in an ambassadorial role was pleasing to his family. He was, he knew, supremely well qualified. He'd studied Political Science and International Relations, combining them with Maritime Law and Economics. He had dated many women, he hadn't merely played the field – rather, he had played the continents. While studying for his Masters at Yale he had met Evelyn Carter.

Eve was unlike anyone else. They'd worked at the same table in the library. A shaft of light from one of the high windows had softly lit her face. Dust motes like moonbeams shone about her. The large round spectacles she wore as she worked were incongruously granny-like. Her head drooped like a graceful flower. She felt his intent gaze and glanced at him, flipped her fine-boned hand and then shrugged her shoulders, gesturing that studying was not all that easy, but returned to it with a wryly determined smile. And he to his. When later she pulled her chair back, he was enchanted to see that this small, delicately built girl had breasts that belied her boyish slimness. That was how his Eve turned out to be: she was one thing; she was another thing; she was all things. She was like her contradictory appearance. She was deeply serious; sometimes capricious; childlike yet wise. The more he got to know her, the more she confused him. She was confused herself, something she cheerfully confessed to him. Ambiguity was essential to her, yet she disliked change. He could not categorize her or place her in any one of the fields in which he had previously strayed. With resignation, and faint regret, he recognized that she was the only woman who would ever mean anything to him. The anything became his everything. He courted her for two long years, during which time her stubborn indecisiveness nearly drove him mad. His ambition to serve his country she politely respected, but felt there were more valuable ways to be of service. She did not want commitment, but when finally, impulsively, she agreed to marry him, he experienced heights of gratitude that he had not known existed. At last he felt his great love, if a little vulnerable, was safe. There was no doubting his happiness any more than there was his acceptance of her waif-like waywardness. Oh, she led him in a dreamy, mercurial tango. When at last she gave in to him and ceased practicing contraception, he knew a delirious delight. And when she fell pregnant he felt his entire life validated.

Six of the most exhilarating and love-filled years died when she did. Roberto felt crushing guilt and grief when Evie of the moonbeams, of the sunbeams, died in childbirth. The babe, along with her hopes, was stillborn.

The only way in which Roberto was able to continue living was bizarre and tragic. He kept up a fiction that he had an ailing wife. This distressed and distanced his family and intimate friends who knew the truth of the secret double funeral; two white coffins, one scarcely longer than a shoebox. However, for the sake of his fragile sanity they colluded, hoping that with time Roberto would achieve a measure of peace and acceptance. Years passed and yet there seemed no change. Friends realized with formidable fortitude that this might be the way Roberto would live his life forever. He attended to his work and at official functions it was made known in subtle fashion that his wife's illness was serious and not to be spoken of. He was courteously dismissive if anyone questioned him. His close friends and family were blackmailed by his desperate state into being accomplices. There was nothing that he and his stalwart friends would not stoop to, to keep his dreadful truth secret.

Roberto loved to sail and that was the one source of happiness in his life that Eve had not shared. She had a delicate system and he grieved that he had not understood this till it was too late.

That day when she posed on the prow of his boat was numinously etched into his being and whenever he went sailing she accompanied him. On the tenth anniversary of her death he had to be honest with himself. Yet the power of her remembered presence made him glance around eagerly as he lifted anchor. And yes, as the wind billowed out the sails he saw her form, her face, everywhere. Each anniversary he had had to lose her, all over again. The pain was intolerable. He thought the wicked luxurious thought he used to comfort himself in his darkest moments; he thought of suicide.

This virile man of forty-three, with his deeply sun-tanned face, his gifts and skills, fantasized frequently about different ways of ending his life. It was his hidden, treasured extravagance. A mountain-climbing fall. A crash against a wall, careful to be the only victim. A fatal drowning accident was his favourite method. His body would never be found and would feed the creatures of the sea and return itself to the vast deepness, that oneness. At this point tears would trickle down his cheeks – it was something he could never do to his aged father.

At their last meeting his father had wept, pounding his chest with surprising vigour for a man of eighty-six. 'She is dead, dead. Your behaviour is unseemly for a man and it's destroying the last years of your father. Accept, my son,' he said. 'Accept. Accept what has happened and live your life.' Roberto recollected that his father had always thought him too sensitive, much more so than his brothers.

It was at the bullfight when he let his father down for the first time. He'd been nine years old and his father had taken him alone, without his brothers. He never forgot the music, the lights, the sensation of going into another world, and his father's arm slung across his shoulder, giving off his unique smell. In came a bull with curly black hair between his horns; he didn't want to fight and kept circling back to the gate. The crowd booed him, and so did Roberto's father. The picadors did their best to inflame the bull. It kept returning to the gate from which it had entered. The toreador, with an insolent contempt, put paid to the bull. Roberto closed his eyes. The crowd cheered.

In came another bull which had the courage to meet and defeat his death – had been taught it was possible; his rage-filled eyes knew it was not. The crowd loved him and so did Roberto. He gored one of the picadors, a famous woman, and Roberto cheered. The toreador returned and now the crowd was hushed as the bull made dangerous, malevolent moves against his tormentor. The moment the bull went down on his knees, Roberto could taste blood in his mouth. He kept his eyes shut. He thought he would open them when it was all over, but he opened them too soon.

He saw the bull on its knees with blood pouring out a pattern of black redness into the sand, soaking it. He quickly shut his eyes, but it was too late: the image was imprinted forever on his mind. He began to cry loudly and didn't mind who saw him or what they thought of him. His ashamed father had to take him home. He had spoiled everyone's fun. The magic had gone, yet he had always remembered the time before the bull was killed.

CHAPTER NINE

•

Megan began to teach Gladdie to play the piano, with Louise's approval but without John Jacob Boardman's knowledge. It was soon apparent how abundantly gifted she was. She had only to hear a melody to play it. In no time at all she learnt to read musical notes, and was soon stretching her hands to play chords. She practiced her scales without fail. The other children stopped mocking her muteness for in other ways she was so normal. Agile and swift, she loved playing games, jump rope, hopscotch and catch. Questions she answered in rapid handwriting unless she could answer with her expressive face and articulate body-language.

Gladdie was a busy and seemingly happy child with limitless energy. Her musical vocabulary expanded as her need to speak diminished. She practiced on any surface, on the school piano, but she practiced chiefly in her head. Jake's work was average, but Gladdie's was excellent and Louise was proud of her. After all, she couldn't speak so there was no way she could outshine Jake. Louise would have felt shame and remorse had she understood herself.

Hester came down the mountain whenever she could. She made no attempt to get Gladdie talking. She petted her face, stroked her limbs and held her as she had when her daughter was an infant. They needed time. They had time. Weren't there things that she, Hester, never talked about? Things as dark as ancient congealed blood. Hester foresaw conclusively that one day Gladdie would speak.

Megan asked her mother-in-law, Francesca, to come and listen to Gladdie playing. Pleased that her daughter-in-law valued her musical opinion, she hastened to accommodate her, and after hearing the child, volunteered to give her lessons twice a week. Gladdie had thrilling promise, and in some way she reminded Francesca of her son when he was little. She soon realized that Gladdie was infinitely more gifted than she herself had been. Honest with her husband, Randall, she conceded that although competent, she lacked the blue flame of passion, nor did she have the equally important quality of perseverance. You saved your passionate Italian blood for me, he teasingly told her.

She began to cast about for a more experienced teacher. She

made enquiries about the various schools of music. It was a serious responsibility, she told her husband. What is genius, Randall had asked her, then answered himself: no one can say. With the nurturing teaching that you are giving her, he'd added, it has more chance of expressing itself. But they both knew it was something more. Something inexplicable.

The idea of sending Gladdie to music school was tactfully put to Louise, who was shocked and disappointed that this 'heresy' was even suggested to her. She could not, would not budge. There was absolutely no possibility that John Jacob would ever let her go. He had caught her in the act of practicing her finger movements on the kitchen table, her face glowing, her body swaying. Gladdie had had to stick her fingers in her ears and run to her room in the ensuing row, sobbing in her soundless way. Louise had wailed loudly as she confessed to her 'sin'. Have pity on her, she had entreated. This is the only way she can speak! Have mercy, she had begged. He had castigated his wife pitilessly and smote her with verses from the Good Book about bearing false witness. His bitter disapproval of her, and her own sense of worthlessness, whipped her. She always tried to win praise from him, unaware that his nature was against her. Vulnerable, Louise felt she should try harder to please, but he never allowed himself the dangerous luxury of pleasure. A profoundly superstitious man, he feared that showing pleasure invited punishment. The youngest son of a large, unruly brood, he had been sent to his grandmother for a time. After her death he had stayed at home and ended up nursing his mother. His rambunctious siblings were relieved of the burden which was all that was left of a once energetic and hardworking mother. It took her a decade to finally fade away.

He wore his suit, vest and tie without exception, whatever the weather. A man is judged, he believed, by his outward apparel. Louise saw to it that his shoes shone and his shirts were freshly washed and ironed. Sex was for procreation. His libido was low and this suited Louise. But she liked to snuggle up to him at night.

'You're not starting,' he would warn.

'No, no,' she reassured, 'I can't sleep 'less I hold you.' Relieved, he allowed her. It was comfort enough. Louise wept until finally, after what he judged to be sufficient time, he ceased chastising her. After all, they had to set a good example. Her menstruation ceased along with her tears.

• •

Jake and Gladdie were happy children. There was much to give thanks for. Louise and her body decided not to have any more children. She felt there was something about her that caused her to lose them. Perhaps the Lord had something in mind. It was not for Louise to question this, but she did ponder.

Jake was a fine boy and gave no trouble. As long as he took his medicine on a regular basis, there was no reason why he would not take after his father. If her son became a preacher-man, the Lord would be mightily pleased and the family's goodness would be beyond dispute. It would prove Jake had not been spared in vain, but for a grand purpose. John Jacob congratulated himself, remembering that his Louise, whom he magnanimously forgave, heard the voice of the Lord saying, 'Tomorrow'. She heard it when the teacher first came; yea, his wife was innocent and pure. In truth, John Jacob could not function without her, he humbly and a trifle rancorously admitted to himself.

Gladdie was a great help with household chores. Louise taught her how to bake bread and its fragrance caused a satisfied smile. Louise herself did not lack for work, for did not the Lord despise idle hands? Her home positively gleamed. Louise thought strangers would be sure to know that this was a dwelling of God-fearing people, though actually no strangers ever came. People who prayed there belonged there.

In her spare time she went about doing the Lord's work, for she loved Him wholeheartedly. She visited the sick and old. She was ceaselessly helpful. Her husband's small congregation believed that they were members of a chosen elite who would enter the Kingdom at their appointed time; for had they not prayed and praised their Lord's glory every minute of their days? And when they erred, had not they repented from the depths of their fear-filled hearts? Hallelujah! Brother Boardman had baptized and sermonized. This was the one ballpark where their golden tickets were reserved. This was the one blessed certainty that no one could take away from them. Hallelujah!

Jake and Gladdie developed their own sign language; when necessary she wrote details down for him. Sometimes they fought and that worried Gladdie who, ever mindful of what the doctor had said, thrust her anger aside. No undue stress. For Jake's part, his frustration was snarled up by his compassion; she couldn't speak. Their relationship was more complicated than most children's. More like brother and sister than most siblings yet their squabbles were quickly settled.

Then too, they were not permitted to argue in the Lord's House. The Boardmans' home was not a church; it was too small and the ground on which it stood was not officially consecrated. But the congregation gathered there regularly to pray. Brother John Jacob would lead the prayers and afterwards, on Sundays, offer up a sermon instructing his parish on the Unknowable Ways of the Lord. He bellowed, his harsh voice grating, his delivery rapid, punctuated by rasping gasps of air. The Good Book was focused on in a literal fashion. The Lord had called him to be a lay preacher and at the age of forty-eight, soon after he married Louise, he became one.

Gladdie was giving Jake a hard time. He didn't want to learn, he resisted her excited advances and cunning ploys and he used whatever devices he could think of. None of the other boys did it and they would laugh at him if they found out. Laugh, mock and make fun of – surely Gladdie didn't want that to happen to him! Skipping was for girls. But Gladdie persisted and eventually succeeded. She showed him pictures of the great Mohammed Ali, skipping! Jake couldn't argue about the muscles. They were there and they were big.

There was something called God, but Gladdie contended you didn't need a religion to reach God. Jake didn't like what she was trying to say. Then it got complicated because Gladdie thought God was nature. If this was true then it meant God could be cruel. There wasn't anyone she could talk to about this. It meant a lot of writing to her mother, and if Aunt Louise found out, there'd be hell to pay.

John Jacob knew he didn't play with his son as other fathers did, but then, he consoled himself, other fathers didn't provide what he did. They didn't teach about the Good Book, about the Right Way to Live and Worship. They taught nothing. What was playing ball? Nothing! Even so, he felt he was letting his son down.

The prime reason that he welcomed Gladys was that Jake could play with her and exercise his body. Jake could not risk being seen by other children. They thudded and pounded the floor of the house and John Jacob contained his irritation over the punishing noise.

In a fit of religious passion, he ungrudgingly forgave Gladys for being Hester's child. The thudding was driving him insane, but he put up with it for it assisted in the development of patience.

On the day that Hester's eldest son, Luke, appeared unexpectedly, darkness enfolded Louise. Luke looked down at he. He was wearing his shoes, and that in itself was a bad sign, for he only wore shoes in winter and here it was in the heart of summer. Meekly Louise gazed up at him, not wanting to hear. He told her that Ma was dead. She was seized by a spasm of grief so violent that it flung her onto the wooden floor: she lay where she had fallen, writhing in anguish. She quieted, her body forming a swollen shape like a silkworm before it spun its cocoon. Then she stretched out her hands and Luke awkwardly pulled her up. 'We'll get ready to go to her funeral.' The two children stared.

'Ma has gone to her Reward. She is safe in the arms of Jesus!' Louise told them, pretending, they knew, that she was very thankful and pleased. They looked at her, their eyes owl-like. Didn't she know, they signed one another, that they had seen her, had heard her, heard Luke? They were sad about their grandmother. But their sadness was muted by unnamable scuttling shadows.

The children didn't want to go to the mountain at all. Gladdie was unhelpful as she lay foetal-like in her bed. Jake thought that she was ill, so he did the chores and the packing. She clasped something wrapped in newspaper. Luke carried her to the car last. All the food that Louise had prepared was loaded in and two extra white sheets were carefully folded. They would stay the night. Luke was excited to be going in the car, it was the best one he'd ever been in. He held Gladdie, who seemed scarce able to move, on his lap. Someday, Luke vowed, someday I'll get me a Camry.

'This is what happened,' Hester explained to Louise. 'Ma came to me and said she wanted to sleep here because she was tired. She got onto the couch and said to me it was her time to go. "Go where"? I asked her. "Tell Louise that she has been a good daughter to me."'

Hester forbore to add that Ma had also said, '...but you were my best and bravest.'

'I told her to have a good rest and a sleep and that she would be well in the morning. I covered her in the fine quilt you gave me. She looked well, nothing wrong with her. I thought I'd give her a little milk so I went out to milk Betsy. When I came back Ma was facing the wall and her eyes was closed. I knowed she was not asleep. I went up to her and see'd she was gone. She'd made up her mind that this was the time she wanted. Just closed her eyes and went to sleep and from sleep to death. Easy.'

John Jacob said how happy the two sisters must be that their mother had not suffered. They glanced at one another. Louise was grateful that John Jacob knew so little of her mother's life, or of her own childhood. Somehow it made him more noble and pure to her, more fitting in the eyes of the Sweet Lord Jesus to whom she was certain her mother had gone.

Ma had not been a member of their own hard-shell group, and, as John Jacob always said, hard-shell was the one True Baptist way. For a fleeting instant Louise worried whether her mother would be accepted in Heaven. Old Mrs Webb had been against any denominational church house but was far too courteous to express her feelings. In common with many Appalachians, she never wanted others to lose face, so she kept most of her opinions to herself.

Outwardly she appeared to agree, but inwardly she laughed at their foolishness. Louise didn't know of her mother's strongly-held view that no church should reign over any other or consider itself superior; this was vainglory, something abhorrent, to be avoided at all cost. The only thing that Mrs Webb had approved of in John Jacob was that he received no pay for his ministry because he had been gifted to be called by Spirit. But Ma was a good woman, Louise quickly consoled herself, a hard working mother. I, her daughter, have prayed enough for both of us. I, her daughter, have made it possible for the Sweet Lord to accept her into the Life Hereafter. Louise felt a wave of relief. Now her mother was safe in His Kingdom. She would never again know hunger, terror or grief. Her mother would know the love of Sweet Jesus our Saviour.

All that Hester knew was that her mother was dead. She was sorry that she had experienced so much hardship, and she would miss her.

When Jake got there he thought that it wouldn't be so bad. He felt safe. He signaled to Gladdie that it would be alright. Luke started to carry Gladdie in, but when she saw her mother she ran to her. She clung to her mother as she had in days of old, all the while holding her parcel. Gladdie didn't know why she was so afraid; she remembered that this was where Jake hurt his head, that this was a bad place. She furtively hid her parcel in the branches of a hemlock and went to play with her brothers and sisters, but they seemed like strangers to her. She was by now more familiar with her school friends. Her brothers found her changed and different. Stuck up. They were all dark-haired and olive-skinned, and she was the only one with chestnut hair and tawny greenish eyes. Secretly, for the moment anyway, some were not sorry that she was dumb.

The burial took place where their mother had wanted her grave to be; as this was about the only thing she had ever firmly requested, Louise acquiesced without argument.

'Fix me the same as they fixed my mother, nothing new fangled, then just bury me beside the wonky-tonky.' The wonky-tonky was a mature Catalpa tree near the creek in a small family graveyard. She wanted no headstone. Hester wondered why she chose to be there rather than with the little graves of the dead baby girls, with their small unnamed stones.

Louise expected that they would argue about the headstone, but that was for later. Curt dug the grave himself in one of the last plots left. No one else wanted it. It hadn't been hard work as the earth was soft and damp. It wasn't the place he would have chosen.

Curt had got his job back and was painfully, exhaustingly sober. People revered the brotherhood and camaraderie that firefighters shared. But he preferred being a forest fire-ranger high on top of the hill – there was no temptation there. He used his CB two-way radio to report any fires sighted and regularly checked in to the manager station. He had the use of a dark green truck with an attached camper to keep all his fire-fighting equipment at the ready. He used powerful binoculars, watching out for smoke.

The weight of his responsibility added to his loneliness. He wanted to take care of every tree, of the forests, the mountains and the valleys. His protective spirit soared with the eagles. Here at last his work gave him some liking for himself. He felt particularly empowered when he rejoined the Forestry Service because that gave him the opportunity to plant out saplings using a dibble bar. His great strength was a bonus because after fires the ground mostly hardened. They were reforesting where a fire had ravaged and raged and all wore Kevlar chaps over their legs, which were as strong as bulletproof vests, in order to prevent snakebites. Occasionally, horrifyingly, like a glorious butterfly suddenly metamorphosing into a deadly spider, the outline of a mountain, a stone or a tree took on the shape of a bottle. The sheen on a rock or leaf became the shine on a bottle.

Then his despairing, ongoing battle filled him with bottomless fear. As he dug, he reflected that his life, and that of his family, had gotten better.

The calf his brother Clay had sold him very cheaply had grown into a good milker and he had two hogs, one of which he had slaughtered for the funeral feast. In the past they seldom ate meat. Sometimes they ate squirrels or groundhogs, but the latter were particularly fatty. He didn't regret slaughtering the hog, even though he knew that had it lived another four months or so it would have been much bigger. He guessed he hadn't been much of a son-in-law, any more than he'd been a good husband or father. He saw his chance to pay the old lady back and perhaps Hester would see him in a better light. When he made love to his wife, all that interested her was to get it over as quickly as possible. He asked himself again if she had ever loved him. He doubted it.

The funeral was simple and dignified. John Jacob cut the service short. Curt had unceremoniously instructed him to be quick, and it was plain that Hester was behind this fresh outrage. Once again, he bitterly resented her power. Bile rose in his throat. She diminished him, because she had no respect for him or all he stood for. The gravity of the funeral was eased by Emmett's strange little posy. He had gathered feathers from different birds and had added his treasured collection of chicken legs and wishbones. His grandmother would have understood and appreciated – wings to fly and wishes to make.

Soon the grave was piled high with leaves and flowers, the only store-bought wreath, of red and white carnations and gladioli, came from the fire station, and Curt was proud of it. Nobody questioned the absence of the dead woman's husband. Curt had dispatched one of his sons to inform him that he was now a widower. He had long since left his wife and, had he known just how much this pleased her, he might well have moved back in with her. Webb was nowhere to be found.

The next morning, when dawn was just beginning to sing, Hester leaned up against her tree trunk. This was how she began her day. The tree poured strength into her through her shoulders and back, from its heart to her heart. Sometimes she embraced the tree so hard that marks of the bark were etched into her cheek. Half-smiling, she traced the ridged patterns with her fingers. The air was dense with katydids' song.

Gladdie glided out of the morning mist holding a tin bowl and a pair of dressmaking scissors and motioned her mother to follow. Hester knew that Louise and John Jacob would be incensed and unforgiving. Seeing her mother's hesitation, Gladdie snatched up a handful of her hair and hacked away at it. Hack, hack, hack. Hester didn't try to stop her, and strands of hair fell to join the pine needles on the forest floor. Hester sat her daughter on a convenient log, meanwhile Gladdie hacked away at her hair. Hester knelt down behind her and put the bowl on her daughter's head. She had allowed Gladdie's hair to grow because she was proud of it. As she snipped away she remembered Gladdie's father, the young student who'd brought her the can opener. Remembered how she'd lured him into the forest, how on a bed of pine needles, not unlike the one she now knelt upon, she'd slipped off her dress and taken him. She'd teach him how it felt to be always receiving, receiving. Oh yes, he received a great deal that day and lost his virginity in the process. She reckoned he wouldn't return. But, to her surprise, he came several more times, blushing to the roots of his red hair, mooning helplessly about. Sometimes she forced him to receive and receive and receive. But never again did she allow him to enter her.

Hester turned the bowl around so that Gladdie could try to glimpse her reflection. Gladdie felt herself growing lighter as a shadowless burden lifted off her and she smiled her thanks even as her eyes shone wetly.

'You're welcome,' her mother smiled back at her with overly bright eyes. 'You're welcome. You look so pretty.'

Louise instinctively understood that Hester needed to deal with the burial her way, so didn't buy the beautiful satin-lined coffin that she'd set her heart on. Reviewing her mother's funeral, she conceded all had gone very well. With, of course, a few exceptions. The two white sheets that she'd taken to carefully wrap her mother's body in and line the coffin could have been whiter. That night the family had stayed awake, although some of the younger ones had strayed, horsed around or fallen asleep. Hester had borrowed four extra kerosene lamps to light the darkness away. Louise approved of the decent pine coffin that Curt, with the help of a carpenter friend, had made and of the carefully dug grave. Curt went up in her estimation. Her mother's mouth had been stuffed with clean sheep's wool and her lips neatly sewn together with cotton. Coins had been tenderly placed on her eyelids.

Ellen-Agnes was the only one who knew that the custom of putting coins on dead people's eyes was to pay the ferryman to carry the soul to the other side. It had been one of her chief reasons to request that she be buried as her mother before her.

The food had been plentiful. Thinking of it caused Louise to salivate. It was their everyday diet, but more varied and much more of it: cornbread, pinto beans, cow's foot and sweet potatoes fried in delicious hog's lard. The pork stew had been perfect and Louise had eaten more than her share. Some of Hester's older children had picked blackberries, a task she had forbidden Jake to do as the briars were filled with thorns. Everyone seemed to get chiggers when they went blackberry picking, pinpoint red dots showed where the miniscule insect got in just under the skin. They itched like nature had no conscience. They used rubbing alcohol – a waste of good paint-peeling moonshine – and Hester tried caking the bites with soap. A new and common remedy was nail polish. Bright patches of red or pearlized purple were to be seen in the unlikeliest places. Worse still, copperheads and rattlers lived in the thicket, as did fearsome wasps.

Gladdie, of course, knew the ways of the mountains and so it was not necessary to warn her about anything. Hester had prepared a great feast and they hadn't needed to use any of the provisions Louise had brought. She left them there anyway. John Jacob had developed more sophisticated taste buds and greens all fried in lard were now outlawed. All the bouquets and flowers were lovely, except for the one with the chicken bones. Honestly, Hester had a lot to answer for, those children of hers were allowed to run riot. How could she have cut Gladys's hair! That was just about unforgivable. She felt a bit ashamed of her sister, an unusual feeling because she had always been proud of her, but she knew that with time she would forgive her. Was not forgiveness one of the major teachings? That was how she had presented her case to a wrathful, livid John Jacob. She was careful not to provoke his quick temper – it often appeared as though he would have a fit.

CHAPTER TEN

•

Fat Fred's was doing well. Tom was targeting new areas, and he worked long hours. Money was needed for the new welfare project he and Megan wanted to build and call 'The Friendly Family Planning Centre'; but a private poll revealed that the anti-abortionists were against the name. They could ill afford adverse publicity, so they called it 'Peace Place'. It was to be a home for battered wives and shattered families. It was to be kept small; they wanted to create a homely, welcoming atmosphere, a sanctuary where rape victims could receive counseling. In his disappointed heart of hearts he knew that the most useful thing for him to do was fund the project. A strong, imaginative man, his failure as a social worker still occasionally haunted him.

Tom and Megan delighted in one another, in their shared, active lives. Every weekend they rose early to go for long runs. They were proud of how well Megan carried their child throughout her pregnancy and especially during their runs the promise of her belly was displayed with pride. On occasion Tom felt a fist of fear clenching his heart – he savaged himself for his shrinkage of faith. He cheered himself thinking that, though small, his wife was strong. Tom was the sort both men and women found attractive. People liked being in their love-filled ambience; they were warmed, as though sitting beside a glowing fireplace, and hoped this warmth would burnish their own lives.

The gynaecologist performed a sonogram and found out that there were twins. It all looked normal and fine. Both future grandmothers redoubled their effort to ensure that the babies would lack for nothing. T hey conferred with one another and complete layettes were readied. The young couple smiled conspiratorially at one another and gave their mothers full rein. Megan's parents concealed their concern about their petite, narrow-hipped daughter. They hadn't wanted to know the sex of the infants, but the doctor told them to expect a boy and a girl. At one thirty in the morning, Megan felt her first real contraction and was about to awaken Tom when he, so at one with her, asked if it had started. Her floral valise was already packed. They believed in natural childbirth and had attended classes regularly and appeared quietly calm; the maternity nurse was surprised to note, when Tom filled in the forms, that this was

Megan's first confinement. They went through the breathing – the relaxing and the reassuring – and all was going as it should. Tom was breathing too deeply and Megan had to slow him down. Excited and nervous, Megan quickly called their mothers, as they'd promised. The two sets of grandparents raced for the maternity waiting room.

Suddenly, horribly, complications set in. The umbilical cord was twisted around one of the twins' necks. The surgeon refused to perform an urgently-needed caesarean section until the required forms granting him permission had been filled in. Megan was lapsing into unconsciousness and, by one of those impossible quirks of fate, the forms were briefly mislaid. Tom quickly wrote a statement swearing that, whatever the outcome, neither the doctor, hospital or nursing staff, would be sued in any unforeseen eventuality. Desperately he rushed into the corridor to find witnesses to co-sign but the correct form was found just in time which he rapidly signed. Megan was rushed into surgery. Distraught, Tom could only watch his mother saying her rosary. He stared mesmerized at her hands which were as familiar to him as his own, yet they seemed like mechanized calamari.

A nurse came to call them and told them that they were very lucky, given the circumstances. The baby girl was lost, but the little boy was perfectly fine if a little underweight. The patient was doing very well but she'd had a further complication. They had been quite unable to stop serious haemorrhaging. There was no choice: a hysterectomy was performed. They were not to be alarmed when they saw Megan having a blood transfusion as the blood had been tested and there was no possibility of it carrying any disease. She was young and healthy and would soon be well again.

Megan seemed to be sleeping but, opening her eyes, gave Tom a quick smile before she went into a deep, drugged sleep, her system entirely unused to analgesics. Tom was the first to hold his son in his arms – his entire being overflowed with a sense of profound tenderness and marveling wonderment. That night Francesca whimpered in Randall's arms. 'I know I should be grateful and I am. But I'd so hoped Tommy would have a large family.'

'We couldn't afford one – and we're happy, aren't we? Megan will be well, and we've a fine grandson,' Randall said, stroking his wife's cheeks. 'It could've been worse, and it nearly was,' he said, attempting to console her.

'But Randall, I wanted a granddaughter,' she cried. He, of course, knew.

'At least you've got your little piano prodigy. I know it's not the same, but you've put your heart and soul into her.'

'And I will continue to do so.' Francesca decided that what she had would have to suffice. She lay wide awake, pretending to be asleep. He chose to accept her pretence and after a while fell asleep with one arm around his wife. Francesca prayed much of the night sitting in her armchair in the bedroom and reverently handled her rosary as she prayed.

The children at the school heard the news and they were excited about their teacher's new baby boy, named Benjamin. Six weeks later Megan was back at school. She insisted on breast-feeding and used a breast pump so that, when she was teaching, one of the grandmothers could feed him. If the two doting mothers had any differences, these were put aside, and they formed a flexible rota. Each spent three or four days a week in the home of their beloved children and agreed with a smile and a wink that they wouldn't interfere but would obey instructions. They liked and respected one another.

Lying in wait for Megan, like a shadowy bat caught in a web, was the time she would mourn the daughter she had lost.

The Boardman children had their own surprise for Megan as they had composed a little ditty. At play-time when the other children charged out of class, Gladdie came and gave her a gentle hug then handed Megan a note which read, 'Please, Mrs Burns, sit down. We've made a present for you.' Gladdie accompanied Jake's sweet soprano voice:

All the birds were singing
All the bells were ringing
To welcome in your baby boy
He will bring you lots of joy
We think he will be kinda neat
We love his little baby feet.

Megan glowed and accepted their tribute whooping and clapping. She asked them if they would sing it for her husband if she brought him because, she told them, 'He will love it as much as I do.' In truth, she wanted him to love them as much as she did.

Tom was busier than he had ever been. He couldn't wait to

get home to bathe his baby and he tightened his schedule so as not to miss that particular time of bliss. Three new branches of Fat Fred's were in the process of being built. He was committed to the concept of not expecting more from his staff than he himself gave, so it was imperative to set an excellent example. He kept rigorously to his principles, sometimes to the annoyance of Megan who thought he went too far, but he was adamant that he had to earn respect and loyalty from his people. Any notion of nepotism had to be extirpated.

He oversaw in minute detail the building of the home for abused, embattled women. The architect Jonas Beardly, an old friend of his father's, was asked to round off corridor corners and, even though it would be costly, he asked for arched windows and an arched front door. He wanted Jonas to create a feeling of gracious security, a place that was welcoming yet quietly elegant. Since Tom was now a father himself, the establishment of the centre became even more important to him and he made certain the builders executed the plans with precision. The front door and window frames were to be painted a specific shade of yellow. He interviewed several possible candidates to fill the position of manager. But in the midst of all of this he agreed that two weeks hence, the first opportunity he had, he would take an afternoon off to meet the Boardman children.

Louise had told Hester about the baby's arrival and about a proposed school concert. Gladdie was first to play something by someone called Moses, something like that. It sounded great to Hester but she was undecided as to whether she would make the trip down the mountain to go to it.

'You simply must see Gladdie,' Megan excitedly reported to Tom, 'she looks so cute, her hair has been cut, she reminds me of you.' In the Burns' spare time – and there was little enough of that between taking care of baby Benjy and their work – they took to planting out a garden on Sundays. They made it into a very private shrine to the overwhelming love they felt for one another and for their little son. They took Pudding home and replaced her with a former seeing-eye labrador who generously allowed himself to be petted by all and sundry. True to his breed, he ate every morsel offered him. Fat Fred's prospered.

On a Sunday summer's evening Megan and Tom hosted a barbecue. The air was filled with delicious smells of steaks, and smoke mingled with the rosemary that Tom had added to the grill. The delicate residue of a day drunk to the full, scumbled pinks, reds and pale greys towards the darkening horizon. The last of the barbecue's embers reflecting in their eyes and hearts lit their awareness that, yes, life was good. Holding a glass of wine or beer they were momentarily hushed by the beauty of their day and the warmth of friendship. Tom strove to keep Megan occupied because she had confided early in their relationship her dream of a large family.

If only her baby girl had lived. She told herself to count her blessings, especially when she thought of the dreadful difficulties couples went through. Guiltily she remained devastated and had no idea how to handle her desolation; she, who had once been so open with her husband, kept it from him and in doing so largely succeeded in hiding her feeling from her conscious self. Tom expected that, with time, she would get over what he mistakenly saw as moodiness.

No one mentioned the daughter she had lost. It was as though she hadn't been born. Megan had to work out a sensible answer when people asked when she would have another child, a little girl to make a pigeon pair. She didn't want to say she'd had a hysterectomy, not just yet, she decided to say she wasn't sure. It was true because for a time she wasn't sure about anything.

As soon as Megan received the news that Abigail wanted to meet with her again, she couldn't wait to tell Tom. What did that woman want from her? She alerted the school and told the children that Mrs Dunstable, the lady who gave them the piano, would be visiting with them in a few days time. Every child had heard about the big house, from the choir. They looked forward to seeing the lady and tried to guess what she might give them this time.

'I'm ashamed of myself,' Megan admitted to Tom. 'The cream and white arrangements of exquisite blooms all up the drive to her house,' she paused searching for how to express herself, 'They completely cowed me.'

'Why, you're much too spunky and intelligent for that!' he protested.

'No, no, I haven't described it well enough. They were strategically placed on columns about every twenty yards along the entire length of her very long driveway.'

'Sounds grotesquely ostentatious.'

'And they were well lit; I think the lights had a dual purpose. They kept the flowers from freezing,' she reflected.

Tom sighed, exasperated. 'They must have been imported or

maybe they came from her greenhouse. Or both.' He grunted with distaste.

'The anthuriums were almost the size of your hands and the hydrangeas were larger than your head!' Megan exclaimed, at which point she'd raised his hands and put them were she wanted them and then held his head in her hands, her eyes pleading for understanding.

The next day, Megan tidied her classroom, made certain that the piano shone and on her desk was a bowl filled with shiny russet apples. Tom had cautioned her to be prepared for a surprise visit and he had proved prescient. As the limousine pulled up she asked her class to continue with their lessons and went out to greet Abigail with easy aplomb. Gladdie knew she was expected to play the moment she heard the car.

'Hi, I've come to see, and hear, what use you've put my piano to. I suppose it's a help for choir practice.' Abigail breezed in like a welcome old friend, much to Megan's annoyance. Her familiarity irked Megan.

'We sure have, Mrs Dunstable, and we will be most gratified to show you.' What a phony, thought Megan, irritated that she too was obliged to pretend false feelings. Abigail scanned the group, looking for the little girl and her brother, as Megan motioned a young boy at the piano to begin playing. Abigail was so transported by the boy's talent that she stopped looking for the two she required for her spring gala. When the short piano recital was over, she applauded more ardently than anyone else. This boy was a find, he was superb. With better teaching and improved technique, who knew where he would end up? She had found him! The thin child stood up and bowed deeply, then turned and smiled at Abigail. Instantly Abigail recognized that smile. It was her smile. The marvelous fall of chestnut hair must have been cropped, but there was no mistaking that radiance. A wig, thought Abigail, a wig would do the trick; her party plans were not about to be spoilt.

With her tight helmet of deep, glowing red, Gladdie looked quite different. She seemed like a boy rather than the idealized picture many had of beauty in a girl child. There was no doubting her happiness; her feet barely seemed to touch the ground and her fingers skimmed and rippled across the keyboard. Everything she did had a lightness about it, an airy quality of a child completely at ease. Untroubled.

Abigail complimented Megan upon the child's playing and then asked the choir to sing for her. This they did, with Gladdie playing the accompaniment and Megan conducting. It was obvious that there had been an improvement but, with the addition of the piano, something had been lost. The children's voices, soaring like birdsong, had become too organized, too disciplined, too cohesive. The little impromptu concert was over. One of the children, chosen by Megan, made a cute speech to thank Abigail and, in an unrehearsed gesture of friendship, took an apple, rubbed it on her butt for an extra shine, and presented it to her. The class laughed at her boldness. Megan, wondering why she had come, escorted Abigail out of the classroom to her limousine. As they were leaving, Abigail reached out for Gladdie and with one hand on her thin shoulders, gently steered her out of the room with them, enthusing over her playing.

'When did you begin to play and who taught you?' she asked gaily of the child. Gladdie smiled back at her, her body and shining eyes speaking of her happiness. Abigail didn't see how she could include the piano playing into her plan for the party.

'Well, what do you have to say?'

Gladdie didn't reply. Instead she put her arms around Abigail. Megan smiled; Gladdie was always demonstrative.

'Aren't you going to answer me?' asked Abigail kindly, pleasantly surprised by the unexpected though pleasing embrace. Then the child looked downcast.

'Sh–she can't speak,' stammered Megan. 'She's lost her voice.' But Abigail wasn't listening to Megan, so intent was she on the child and her plans for her spring party. Megan was irritated because Abigail didn't respond.

'She has lost the power of speech. Therapists haven't been able to help,' Megan said distinctly, omitting to add that this had been done without the permission of Gladdie's parents.

'I think there is some reason why she can't, at present, speak. A psychological cause inflicting speechlessness on her. We haven't discovered exactly what it is yet.'

'But that's not possible,' snapped Abigail, 'she has perfect pitch and a beautiful voice.'

'We've done our best.'

'It's not possible today that a child can lose her voice and that nothing can be done,' Abigail said trying not to sound impatient. Her hands became fists and Gladdie's eyes filled with tears. Both women felt like crying too, though for different reasons.

'She is very close to Jake. She plays well with the other children, is a bright and attentive pupil and, of course, thanks to your generosity, can express her feelings musically.' But Abigail was not to be comforted. She kissed the child on the tip of her head.

'I will help you,' she promised, and with a gentle pat on the shoulder set Gladdie free to run back to the schoolroom.

'What happened to her?' she rasped. 'What happened? Why hasn't she been helped?' she demanded.

'We've not given up hope,' answered Megan, thinking perhaps this socialite had connections that could be useful.

'I will find the best therapists in the country, or in the world, if need be,' Abigail declared.

'She saw her cousin, who is more like her brother, receive a head injury when they were out playing one day. Jake was unconscious and bleeding. She hasn't spoken since. Her aunt told me that even when Gladdie was stung by a wasp she didn't utter a sound. Deep inside of me, though, I believe that Gladdie will speak again,' Megan explained.

'And what do her parents say?'

'I've never met them,' replied Megan, mortified, thinking perhaps she should have done. 'They are hillbillies and, I'm told, live in an inaccessible area. During winter they get snowed in and the dirt road is hardly ever used and then you have to climb up a trail. She lives with her aunt and uncle. I do want, however, to meet her parents as soon as I can.'

'I too,' Abigail said, 'I too will meet them. I've a Range Rover that can tackle the most difficult roads, and I think some of my help came from the mountains. They must know the area and other hillbillies.'

'I'll go to Louise Boardman – that's Gladdie's aunt – and see if I can extract Gladdie's parents' address. They don't like giving any information, but I'll try. Maybe, if it is to help Gladdie...' Megan left the sentence hanging.

Back in her car on the road, Abigail mused on what had drawn her to this child. From the first moment she saw her smile which mirrored her own, she had felt something... possibly a sort of love, a real affection. Could it have been caused by that ubiquitous banal question – would her life have been richer, more fulfilled, if she'd had a child? She knew she wouldn't find the answer and didn't care about the little shot of schadenfreude that her being childless gave her friends, because she didn't particularly like babies. It had been more than enough looking after her various husbands and their progeny. There was much that she and the child had in common: their talent, good looks, and, obviously, that the other children would not easily accept her as she was. She was too different from the rest. And because of my secret, so am I, thought Abigail. There was something magical about this little girl, she possessed a mysterious ability to draw people to her. Look, thought Abigail, how she has affected me.

CHAPTER ELEVEN

•

Tom wanted to discuss his business news, but when he got home that night he never had the chance. Instead he was assailed by a whirlwind of questions about the most effective way to handle Louise. They resolved to take along a speech therapist and a psychologist and then diplomatically coerce Louise to join forces with them. Megan succeeded in making the vital appointment. They were to meet her at four-thirty the following Friday afternoon. It was only after sharing events with one another that they developed reality, meaning and colour.

Louise, her home gleaming with polish and cleanliness, was ready to do battle with these people who had come to interfere with the Lord's will. She and John Jacob were ready for them. Their oppressive self-righteous presence took possession of the disinfected air. Feigning patience, they listened to the arguments put forward on why it was necessary for these people to meet Gladys's biological parents. They listened to these experts, who knew better than God, who knew more than the Good Book, what should be done to help their little girl. They sat, stubborn and immovable, waiting for the group to talk themselves out contributing nothing to the conversation except blank faces. Louise's deep courtesy prevented her from contradicting her ignorant guests, and at the start she had offered refreshment. Having been forewarned about the coffee, everyone knew to ask only for water. In the midst of their discussions Louise leveraged herself out of her chair and lumbered off to make coffee, which they dutifully drank. Megan exclaimed a trifle too enthusiastically about how good the coffee tasted. She's trying to get round me, Louise realized, keeping a smile off her face. She felt strangely powerful. Before the delegation arrived the Boardmans sent the two children on errands and instructed them not to return until after their visitors left. The group had put their persuasive points forward, but one by one they ran out of steam, defeated by the obdurate silence that met every salient detail or tactfully put question.

After a few minutes of exhausted silence, Brother John Jacob began to give his unwilling captives a sermon about the Ways of the Lord. They had no idea they would be preached at; his voice was loud, grating and harsh, and they had to resist the temptation to clap their hands over their ears. There was some involuntary nose twitching and eye rolling. As the dejected group left, having been thoroughly routed, Tom, the last to leave, asked almost as an aside for Gladdie's last name. John Jacob glared and spat out her name, Howard. It was of no importance because, after all, the Will of the Lord had prevailed.

Tom was quieter than the rest of them. He had recognized the name Howard – could it be the same family? If they lived in the same place, he knew he could locate it – his mind raced on, threatening to overtake him. The party got into the car feeling hot, tired and dispirited, and did not have much to say to one another; too much inbreeding, was the general incorrect consensus. Soon Tom and Megan were home, and the first thing to do was put their son to bed. Benjy and the babysitter were fast asleep on the sofa, the teenager's homework littering the floor. Tom picked up his son and whispered good night to the future mathematician. The moment Benjy was safe in his bed, they threw off their shoes, took off their clothes and stepped into the shower together. They brushed their teeth more vigorously than usual, so eager were they to cleanse themselves of the Boardmans and their stifling, thrusting version of Christianity. They embraced one another for the sheer joy of confirming the warmth of life and the strength of their love.

'They remind me of Blake's poem,' said Megan, and she went to get her copy. Tom looked at her adoringly as she read:

> *I went to the Garden of Love.*
> *And saw what I had never seen:*
> *A Chapel was built in the midst,*
> *Where I used to play on the green.*
>
> *And the gates of Chapel were shut,*
> *And 'Thou shalt not' writ over the door,*
> *So I turn'd to the Garden of Love,*
> *That so many sweet flowers bore,*
>
> *And I saw it was filled with graves,*
> *And tombstones where flowers should be:*
> *And Priests in black gowns were walking their rounds,*
> *And binding with briars my joys and desires.*

'They would try the patience of Christ himself if he existed,'

Megan goaded Tom, a more or less lapsed Catholic, but he didn't rise to the bait. They lay in their cool bedroom and the fragrance of a small cottage-style bouquet of lemon-mint, rosemary, geraniums and lavender slowly eased into them. Hesitantly and cautiously, Tom told her his thoughts.

'There is a possibility that I know Gladdie's family. It's a name I recognize from when I worked as a student. I didn't mention it to the others, I don't want to raise any false hopes.' Her reply was nothing that he could have anticipated, and it stunned him.

'Gladdie's muteness screams at me. I don't sleep, it disturbs me so loudly. I keep trying to imagine what she saw that was terrible enough to rob her of speech. Images too horrible and awful encroach on me. Perhaps if I saw the place where the accident happened...' Her voice trailed off, followed by a sob. Then she recovered herself.

'Would you recognize the house?' she asked anxiously 'Can we go and look for it?'

'Soon,' he soothed, stroking her hair. 'Soon.'

Megan and Tom underestimated Louise's canny intelligence. The visitors' sudden interest in Gladys's parents rather than herself and John Jacob had alarmed her, offended her even. It was no strangers' business! The very next day she set off to warn Hester that her husband had made a serious blunder in giving Gladys's last name.

'They will come on a weekend – maybe next weekend,' she warned. 'They want to take my Gladdie. John Jacob told my girl's last name.' So intense and dogged were Louise's pleadings that Hester quietly agreed to make it appear as if her family no longer lived there. She would leave Luke and Jewel to look after the place whilst she and the younger ones joined Curt at his forest lookout.

Hester made haste to reap what she needed from her vegetable garden, collected eggs, collected enough to take with them until the strangers gave up. It was to be a camping-out jaunt. The children relished joining their father in the tower lookout; each shared with him the chance of being master of all they surveyed. They felt special because he was warm and loving, and it was a nervous novelty to feel proud of their powerful father. He was sober.

They never could have guessed why he was such a swift runner. He had run up the mountain many times; he ran until he exhausted himself, to the point that when he dropped he could not get up. He ran to outrun his craving: to flee his corrosive despair; his dread fear of failure. Defeat by the bottle, vanquished, finished. Bartenders he had known materialized from behind boulders, out of dark shadows under trees, crooking their fingers. He ran on, fell, picked himself up; his chest bursting, his calf muscles seizing up, he ran on. All those friendly bartenders metamorphosed into reptilian sirens beckoning him on. Have a drink, the trees whispered tantalizingly in the wind, have another. Branches whipped him; he welcomed the pain of thorns slashing him and rocks slicing him. He ran on. It was a race to beat the drink, a race to regain his position in life, to be a husband, a father. His breath desiccated his lungs, his heart leapt about in his throat like a frog trying to jump out, trying to leap into a pool. A pool of alcohol – any alcohol would do. Finally, his body was felled into unconsciousness. This was a kind of oblivion – not the way he wanted it, but oblivion. Respite from his screaming brain; a beneficent unknowingness, a time free from craving, a period of peace.

His family knew nothing of his constant state of war.

Once, he left his look out tower and ran to drink from the creek. He lay on his stomach and drank until he was like a hot water bottle about to explode. He tried to slake this other thirst. Would he ever win? Was it possible? He drank to cleanse his system of his raving, insatiable longing for a shot of alcohol. He drank till his belly complained painfully and he vomited. He lay on his side, irrationally convinced that he could dilute his cravings, wash them away. He drank more, vomited more. He tried to vomit it out of himself. Then he lay on his back, semi-comatose.

Ellen-Agnes had heard the peculiar sounds of a wild animal roaring and howling its agony. She approached cautiously and found her son-in-law lying there. She rinsed him clean and went to fetch Hester. Together they hauled, pushed and pulled him back up the trail. His colour was waxy, pallid and his eyes were deeply embedded in his head. Hester made him as comfortable as she could in her chicken coop, then covered him with a quilt. She regarded him more as a problem than a husband. But she took care of him and made him a weak broth; it was crucial to get him well as soon as possible. He had to go back to his job. He was pathetically grateful for the smallest thing she did for him, he kissed her on the hands, he wanted to kiss her feet. He left even before his powerful constitution allowed him to recover.

He loved her. She was the world he wanted to live in. On the very few occasions when they went for a walk alone, she allowed him to make love to her. There, on a thick rift of fallen leaves, he felt she became the mountain, its ridges and streams, its softness and harshness, its sheeted waterfalls. He fell upwards. He swooped, spiraled and then glided down. He lay with his head on her stomach, she stroked his hair and he cried. She meant to help him out more often, but didn't get much chance. It was so important to him, she felt a vague unease that it was of so little value to her. She felt so sorry for him the day her mother found him, an injured and sick animal. Doing this made him happy. She disliked lovemaking, but she liked to be held by him at night. She treated it as a tiresome activity in which she was obliged to participate. It gave her pleasure to stroke his hair as she would any injured child.

In his solitude from his lookout, Curt had long hours to think and remember. His sister-in-law Minnie at all family gatherings would lecture how, when the settlers first arrived, 'there was as much land for the taking as the eye could see.' Whenever she uttered this, some would mouth her familiar phrases and roll their eyes. He would smile recollecting this. She spoke of how they had escaped poverty, organized hierarchical churches and as a result had no freedom. She instructed them to be grateful. Minnie had so loved her great-grandmother who had brought her up – 'Keep your sense of family – they're the ones who'll help you' – that she felt constrained to keep her words and ways alive. But, thought Curt, we're still poor. Yes, we love our own folk; but instead of being poor over yonder, we're poor here. He felt the feeling he was supposed to avoid – he felt guilt. His eyes swept the mountains – he should have done better for his family.

Curt admired and respected his fellow hillbillies. They didn't simply belong to, but were owned by, the mountains. They accepted that seasons had wayward changes. Death was an expected welcomed or unwelcomed guest, never giving its arrival date. Nature lived as a being, brutal or bountiful. Nature was as full of frailty as they themselves. This knowledge was as engraved as a thumbprint on their shared psyche.

Hester trekked back to see how Jewel and Luke were doing. She re-schooled her children in how they should fool the strangers. Tall Luke was to act like he was married to his sister Jewel. They were to give false names and say their dead father's great-uncle had given Luke this land long ago. Only answer questions, never volunteer information. If asked where their father's great-uncle was, they were to say they didn't know. Nor did they know when the land had been given. They were to act helpful and offer coffee. Act stupid but give nothing away. They were looking forward to pulling the wool over the eyes of the city slickers, those fancy folks who thought they were better than the Howards. Hester was pleased to see her young had worked hard. Everything was as it should be. They had even made some fresh cheese for her. They had known that she would, of course, come back to see how they were doing. They gave her five hard-boiled eggs to take back for the rest of their family.

Louise had been right about when they would come. That Saturday, Hester secreted herself away, even from her children's eyes, in order to observe, or help in some way, if the need arose. She first heard, then saw the Jeep, long before it reached her home. She watched a tall man wearing a baseball cap help his wife out of the vehicle. It had been a bumpy journey. She watched his solicitude with astonishment. She had never known a man to be this helpful to his woman. He must, she supposed, be what was known as a gentleman. The two climbed up to her dwelling, the man supporting his wife on one arm and carrying a large sack in the other. Perhaps she was ill, thought Hester.

Her children did not disappoint, and she chuckled to herself as she watched the downcast and defeated couple leave without the parcel. When the man took his cap off and kissed his wife, Hester recognized him instantly. Well, well...he was the Welfare who'd brought her the can-opener all those years ago. No wonder the Jeep had moved up the mountain road with such sureness and had stopped in the right place. So. The past had come to visit her. Well, she would meet it head on. She would go to the school concert to meet this teacher and her husband after all. Louise had sensed that they wanted Gladdie, not why. There were times, smiled Hester admiringly, when Louise just knew.

CHAPTER TWELVE

·

Abigail broke with certain social conventions. When people invited her to attend their functions, large or small, it was up to them to find her an escort. She invariably arrived and left on her own. In the most discreet fashion, it was made known to a few hosts how entertaining she thought Roberto. This was how he found himself seated beside her at dinners, balls and at the opening of an art exhibition. His conversation with her was as charmingly polite as it was charmingly distant. The more she saw of him, the more convinced she became that, when his wife conveniently expired, he would become hers. She could wait, although time was not on her side.

At one rather small dinner, shortly after she had seen Gladdie, she surprised herself by telling him about her. He was interested by her plainly authentic but uncharacteristic concern. Brittle women were familiar to him; all had had several marriages, large amounts of money and appeared to have gone to the same cosmetic surgeon. He understood them and knew their monetary value which, as a banker, he held in respect and esteem. He treated them as clients or potential clients. It was in his interests and that of his family's bank that he pay them court. His father relied and depended upon him. In a business sense at least he did not let his father down. His family's need for grandchildren had been met by his brothers, so at least on that account he wasn't pressured.

His attention to Abigail strayed when she reverted to being amusing and he hoped she'd not noticed. Of course she had. She had also particularly noted that when she had mentioned the mute girl he had shown interest. Cleverly, she reopened the subject.

'I sent Eugene – he works for me on my stud farm – to see what he could find out about Gladdie's family, but he came back with nothing. He's a hillbilly so I thought they'd open up to one of their own. Her family seems to have disappeared. Megan Burns, her teacher, failed too. The aunt and uncle Gladdie lives with belong to a sect known as hard-shell Baptists. They regard themselves as being the height of religiosity, they refuse to cooperate.'

'Why do you suppose they won't?' Roberto asked.

'Megan says they're obdurate, stubborn and obstructive. Holier-than-thou types. They say it's God's will!'

'God's will?'

'According to their religious beliefs, which they put above the child's needs. Megan took therapists there and they refused to answer one question. Not one. I don't know what to do. I'm at my wits' end...' Abigail trailed off, pulling her mouth down despondently. For a moment her involvement with Gladdie overrode her desire to impress.

'There is one thing I am proud of,' Abigail said, her eyes gleaming. 'I'm proud I gave the school a piano, it's an upright and I really didn't need it. This child is a prodigy. Given the opportunity, she could become superb, yet we can't even trace her biological parents!'

She flung her arms up in disgust. Her disappointed hurt momentarily reminded him of Eve, and unexpectedly, he suffered a pang.

'I have a suggestion for you,' he offered. 'Try to find out what they want and offer it to them. The Almighty Dollar...'

'No,' she interrupted him, 'no, you haven't understood. They don't care for material things. I thought of it immediately, but they can't be bought.'

'Try – you may achieve your objective.'

'They're not bribable.' She was depressed now, pulling her lips down with her fingers and looking like a dispirited clown.

'Look here, I'll come with you. I'm not a fairly successful banker for nothing. I'll do the negotiations for you.'

At this, Abigail's cheeks flooded with colour and her eyes glittered with exhilarated gratitude. On all counts.

'Well... since you're not a fairly good banker but the best, I'll give you a chance,' she teased. 'You handle one of my portfolios and it's excellently balanced!' she congratulated.

He hadn't been aware of this and wondered what name she used for her portfolio. The others invariably utilized time with him for free advice. Tonight, her company was pleasant.

'We will discuss a strategy in the New Year. We go to Spain for Christmas.'

'I'm going away myself, to Scotland, for a few weeks in winter,' she replied. Of course, he remembered, that's where she has her winter party.

'How is your wife?' asked Abigail in a soft voice.

Abruptly, he turned his head away, visibly distressed. She knew it was a taboo subject, but when he'd said 'We go to Spain' she'd thought it only polite to enquire. Why did I do it? she reprimanded herself. Why? His whole body had stiffened as they stood waiting for coffee to be served. Their hosts had brewed the herbal tea her chauffeur had delivered earlier along with a polite note instructing how long to steep it. She only permitted herself one coffee in the morning because she'd heard that it was ageing. She had asked him about his wife and spoilt her chances. She nodded her head dismissively to the waiter and offered her cup instead.

'This is my herbal brew of lavender and rosemary. Please try it.'

He tried it, his hand trembling.

'Thank you,' he'd said, aware that for some unfathomable reason he couldn't lie to this woman, who was quite old enough to be his mother. But what shocked him was that he had been so tempted to tell Abigail the truth. This was the first time it had happened to him, and he felt stirrings of resentment both towards himself and Abigail; but chiefly against himself.

Abigail thanked her hosts, fetched her wrap and left. She was shattered. His rigid body language, pallor and shaking hand eloquently expressed a tragedy of ghastly proportion. Now, unreservedly, she accepted it was not to be, no more loitering hopes. Roberto had stirred longings. Relinquish all such thoughts, she directed herself.

In Scotland, her sense of isolation returned uninvited and unwanted. The lakes, the majesty of the mountains, the beauty of her castle with its tapestry wall hangings, sculptures and paintings didn't touch her heart. Dutifully she held her party; the bagpipes played, the dancers danced. The guests were happily drinking champagne and quantities of whisky and the evening was as usual, a success. Yet all the while she felt numb, as though indifference had wrapped itself about her. She smiled; she laughed; she did all that was expected of her.

When the last guest had left and she retired to her room, she lay in the vast four-poster bed. She remembered being told that the canopy had originally been made to keep insects and mouse droppings from falling onto those who slept beneath. That the enclosing curtains had been made for privacy and to keep out the draught. Suddenly she imagined a spider crawling across her face and shivered. She felt alone. She was not made for celibacy, she thought as she convulsively brushed the non-existent spider off her face. She thought spiders were like rat droppings, rat droppings with legs. She imagined all the other people who had used the bed through the centuries, but not only for sleeping. She didn't sleep that night.

On the evening of the concert, Abigail drove fast along the mountain roads and parked beneath her old friend, the American ash. Megan came out to greet her. Louise followed, panting and puffing her way in, steering her two children. Gladdie was wearing an old hat that partially concealed her face. She had only consented to grow her hair provided she could wear this soft old fedora. Where she had found it no one knew, but everyone accepted it as being part of her uniqueness, part of her strangeness, of being so different from everyone else in class.

The concert was held in the largest classroom in the school. The adults sat cramped at small desks; some stood at the back wall. Louise, her cheeks flushed with pride, leant against the side wall. Megan laughed at Tom's long legs crunched between two of the larger school desks. She fitted neatly behind an average sized desk, while Abigail nimbly folded herself onto a child's chair. The children sat cross-legged on the floor.

Almost tangible anticipation vibrated like an invisible bell. The children briefly surrendered their excited chatter, silenced by the palpable expectation which was echoed on their parents' faces. Nervousness replaced by pride in each child's role now shone on the softened expressions of mothers and fathers. The concert culminated with Gladdie playing Mozart's 'On the air, Ah! Vous dirais-je Maman', her body swaying to the music.

Those among the listeners who understood Gladdie's gift were spellbound. Everyone, even the children, applauded rapturously. Abigail and Megan found this evening's proof of her astounding talent so overwhelming that it moved them almost to tears.

It was during the applause that Hester, wild flowers in her hair and an enigmatic smile on her face, arrived in the doorway. While the adults looked in astonishment at this powerful mountain woman in her shabby old jeans and greenish T-shirt, she strode down the makeshift aisle to where Benjamin was playing on the floor at his father's feet, scooped him up, gave him a kiss and slung him onto her shoulder.

'I heard the music,' she said, 'it called me in. I'm on my way up through this town. These children make sweet music. Who taught them?' she asked Megan, who didn't reply. She was afraid of offending this wild-looking woman who was making so free with her little son. But Hester handed him back to her with tenderness, then turned and said to Gladdie, 'I like your hat and your music, child.'

As she turned to go, she glanced piercingly at Tom. On seeing her face directly, he went grey with the shock of recognition. Then she mischievously looked back at Gladdie.

'You should all be proud,' she murmured faintly, smiling slightly. She saw with satisfaction that he was utterly undone. She hesitated an instant before leaving and looked at Abigail.

'Hope you enjoy your visit, stranger. I see you're not from these parts.' For a while their eyes latched with hostility, and then she was gone.

'Who was that?' Abigail's voice rang out. 'Who?'

'She's a mountain woman, is all I can tell,' replied Megan.

'Never seen her here before,' claimed Louise, looking away from her children.

Jake chimed in, saying they'd never seen her here before and he started to sing one of their songs again. The adults felt uncomfortable but the sweetness of song dispelled and diluted the uneasiness and the evening ended calmly.

Louise, however, was still feeling upset by Hester, then she started for home with her children. Abigail fell in step beside her.

'You're a Baptist aren't you? I'd be interested in learning about it.'

So the Lord was smiling down on Louise after all. Hoping that John Jacob would never find out that Jake had been singing, she took the chance that the sweet Lord Jesus was giving her. She gave the children a pat, they ran off ahead, and she led the strange lady to her home. Abigail walked all the way with her to develop a feeling of togetherness. As Louise trudged along, slippery freckles of perspiration dotting her face, she preached. Elevated by the prospect of saving another soul she preached continuously. Unendingly. Abigail's patience was put severely to the test, but it held.

Abigail had never been in such an ordinary little house. How did people exist with so little space or privacy? It was tidy and clean, however, and she suffered herself to be seated and undergo further teachings. Several times she thought Louise had played herself out but now it was hard to see how she would ever find out what a woman like this wanted. But she did discover that Louise's home, in which she evidently exulted, was used as a gathering place for prayer.

'Brother Boardman left the mines when he was only twenty. His father died of black lung, his two uncles and one brother had it. They never paid them no disability. Took forever fightin' lawyers and all. Died before the case was heard. That's what they do. His ma saved some money and sent him to his grandma. She raised him till she died and then he went back home, that's how he was saved from black lung. He says the Lord chose him!'

Louise confided to Abigail, who struggled to keep her pretence of interest up and her boredom at bay. She was well aware of greed-struck coalmine operators who despoiled the land, desecrated rivers and creeks and legally evaded those and their families who sought compensation. Kentucky, she had heard from the governor himself, was making an attempt to legislate in the victim's favour, but was hesitant to ask substantial owners for too much because they could jeopardize big contributions come election time. In some areas the Forestry Department had exercised its authority with success, Abigail reminded herself. This was the first time she had met anyone who knew people who died of pneumoconiosis. Louise was gratified that Abigail was interested in everything she taught her and almost clapped her hands.

'The Good Lord blessed my husband John Jacob with strong lungs. In good weather he holds prayer meetings in the yard, but when it's too cold everybody comes in, and even if we're in different rooms, we hear him through the walls,' she said, sounding well pleased. Can it be, speculated Abigail, that they could be tempted by the offer of a church?

'Do you not long for a proper church?' she asked tentatively.

'The Lord in his mercy hears us wherever, and whenever, we pray,' Louise admonished piously.

'But in the heart of winter, wouldn't it be nice to be warm? Wouldn't it be easier for the people to concentrate on the preaching if they were in a church?'

'Well – yes, it would be. But the Lord hasn't given us a church and we must not question His wisdom.'

'I see. But it just happens that I am looking for something worthwhile to donate funds to. The money would come from trust funds and as such would not come directly from me, but I would be required to ascertain exactly how the money was spent. I can't think of a better way to spend such money.' Louise's mouth hung open.

'I would so love to meet Gladdie's birth mother.' Louise closed her mouth and walked Abigail all the way back to her car suspicious and afraid – why had this woman made this enticing, tempting offer?

'Yes, I really must meet Gladdie's birth mother,' repeated Abigail, her voice gentle, but her tone final. 'I would give a great deal for that.' She drove off and Louise fluttered her sweat-drenched handkerchief in farewell. Her stomach clenched itself in. Her baffling dilemma would take quite some time to sort out, but with the Lord's help, and Hester's permission, peace would replace mind-boggling uncertainties. This was something to deliberate over at great length with John Jacob, or perhaps she shouldn't discuss it with him... just yet. Her thoughts churned back to Hester. What, oh what, had possessed her to come in?

Abigail was disgusted by the size, the bulk, the fatness of the woman. She supposed herself to be sensitive, but it never occurred to her that as a child Louise had often gone without enough to eat. Abigail had never known hunger. Never knew that hunger is as absolute a master as acute pain. That it is all-consuming and that while it is master, nothing else is of the remotest consequence. Louise could never have enough to eat. Her remembrance of her own hunger and that of her family enforced a perpetual hunger upon her; she ate as though to stave off hunger for all those who felt it. She thought there must be something wrong with Mrs Dunstable, so rich yet whose skeleton was there for all to see.

CHAPTER THIRTEEN

.

On her way home from the Boardman's house, Abigail noticed a disused tobacco barn that housed farm tractors and other implements. These barns were comparatively easy to move; it had been done before. I'll paint it brick red, she thought. It will work like a charm.

She saw black-eyed jersey cows in the fields and silos standing in sharp relief. The highway cut through hills of shale. Annoyingly a van was tail-gaiting her; she let it pass. She paused to push the button to open her gates before the security guard did and observed that he wasn't concentrating on his job. She deliberately didn't greet him. Slowly she drove in, savouring the beauty of her farm, her land, her horses in her paddocks.

That evening her thought kept returning, she couldn't understand why – to the mountain woman who had invaded the concert.

That woman had eagle's eyes, thought Abigail. They had made her remember seeing a Martial eagle sitting in a dead tree. They had driven towards it and as they passed its impossibly bright eyes stared straight into hers, filling her with awe. There was something fearsome about that woman's strength. Who was she? Her piercing glances round the room had suggested a purpose, but what was it? Who was she, where did she come from and above all why had she come?

There was a change in the morning mist, in the birdsong spangling the air and the frogs' continuous croaking. Leaning against her tree Hester could feel spring stirring in her bones as it was stirring in the tree's sap. Today she would begin to hoe the land, turn the dirt so that it could ready itself to accept and nourish the seeds she had assiduously collected the previous autumn. Mulch from dead leaves would contribute their thick bounty. She had stacked all of Betsy's cowpats and her chickens' manure into a heap which she would add to the receptive earth. Betsy would be milked today by Jethro, her third child, who was doing it under pressure. He was inclined to laziness and Hester would not tolerate it.

'Look at the squirrels,' she explained, 'see how they prepare for winter; they wouldn't live otherwise. Look at the bluejays,

94

see how they hunt all day to feed themselves; and when they have chicks they work even harder. Life is work. Work is life.'

Still, her son was unsure if life was only that. He wished it wasn't true. But watching his mother, always busy, especially with the washing, he dolefully thought that maybe she was right. Again.

Every summer's evening Hester caressed and massaged her children's heads and taught the older ones how to do it for the youngsters when time was too short for her to do it herself. The little ones protested when their mother couldn't do it, couldn't search for ticks. Once found, she crushed them. While waiting their turn, if small hands found one by themselves they would pipe up helpfully, 'Got one for you, Mommy! Got it.' Her method turned this summertime necessity into a form of pleasurable bonding, much like the grooming of primates.

Hester heard the familiar sound of Louise's vehicle. She hadn't seen her sister for some time, dropping her hoe to run down and greet her. Louise struggled out of the car. She intended to confront Hester. She had at last decided to get the church, knowing that unless she persuaded her sister to meet the people who wanted to help Gladys, nothing would come of it. Perhaps those people really could help the child to join the rest of the world. The speaking world. But before she quite managed to dislodge her bulk, she found herself being firmly pushed back into her seat by Hester, who, her eyes sparkling, cried 'Take me for a ride, Lou.'

'I've come up to talk to you. You tell me why you came into school like that! Do you want them to know you are the blood mother? Well maybe they should.'

Hester was nonplussed; what had happened to change her sister's mind? Louise had been obviously furious when she appeared at the concert, yet now she was suggesting she should own up to being the blood mother.

'You talked to John Jacob?' she asked.

'Not so far,' replied Louise truculently.

'Maybe better not,' said Hester, dismissing the matter and returning to her own private excitement.

'Let's go for a ride along the new highway,' she urged.

'But, what for?'

'Let's go and I'll show you why and I'll show you where to stop.'

Louise switched on the ignition and the car stuttered into action, but she stuck to her guns.

'Well, maybe we should find out if other people could help Gladdie, and if they want to talk to you and Curt, just let them.' Hester wondered if maybe the thin dark woman with the big limo had something to do with this turnabout of Louise's. She remembered her eyes and reckoned that she probably did. But she was too full of her own plan to give it much thought.

'Go slowly now; real slow.' Louise obeyed.

'Do you ever think of Pa?'

'No. Haven't seen him since way back when... before Ma died.'

'Well go real, real slow now. OK. Pull up. Reverse, go back over this spot. That's it.' Hester's tone had an edge of intensity sharpened by hoarse pleasure. Louise agitatedly waved a car past and acceded to her sister's weird request. Slowly, looking nervously and repeatedly into her rearview mirror, with Hester's murmured encouragement, she reversed, stopped and went forward again.

'Don't you ever wonder where he is at?'

'No,' answered Louise.

'Well, Lou, you just drove over him. Isn't that just the sweetest thing.'

Honest to God, thought Louise, there's times when Hester frightens me. Then suddenly, with a gasp, she realized exactly what her sister meant.

'Turn off at the next ramp, Lou.' Looking at her sister's face, Hester let her laughter come bursting out, and after a moment Louise joined in. They laughed and giggled all the way back, Louise driving even more erratically than before. They were children again, their laughter releasing and uniting them. When they got back to the shack, both were gasping for breath. Hester unloaded the provisions Louise had brought for her.

'About Gladdie: she can speak. She cain't just yet. When she is ready she will. We don't need no experts,' Hester stated.

When Louise drove away she was mournful, thinking that she didn't know what to do. Hester said Gladdie would talk, which meant it was true, so now how were they going to get that church? She prayed that the Lord would tell her what to do.

In spite of her worry, every now and then a hysterical wheeze of laughter escaped her. How had Hester done it? Why didn't they do it before? Why didn't their poor dead mother do it? Now he was roasting in Hell. If Gladys knew where he was, would that help her? And when she spoke, what would she say? Certainly if people found out what Hester had done, there'd be no church.

By the time she returned home, her predicament dizzied and confused her. She wanted the child to have her voice back; yet how would John Jacob react if she told him that Gladdie could speak, but wouldn't? Or rather couldn't just yet, but someday she would. They, the entire congregation, had all prayed loudly and vigorously for the dumbness to leave her, all had bowed their heads in acceptance of the Lord's Ways. It wasn't conceivable that Gladdie had willfully deceived and defied them. Louise hoped that Hester was for once wrong, mistaken – for had not the child remained silent when stung by the red wasp?

Louise recollected how painful a wasp sting was. Her father had once begrudgingly removed some chewing tobacco from his mouth and placed it on her forearm to draw out the sting and keep the swelling down. She hated wasps. She remembered the sharp pain and associated it with the only time in her life that her father had ever shown her kindness. Then she whimpered, remembering how her mother, holding a heavy stone, promised to brain him if he didn't give her the saliva-soaked plug. Her respect and admiration had grown for her mother. She was awed by her bravery. After this had happened, she remembered how her father had yelled at her. 'No man will have you, Louise, you're so ugly. Ugly.' He laughed raucously, taunting her, sneering angrily at her.

'You're 'bout as invitin' as a sow's tit with a tick on it. I'll never get a buyer. You've cheated me out of some good money, you ugly bitch!'

His laugh hurt her eardrums and tore at her heart.

Well, it's my turn to laugh now Pa, now the worms have eaten you and you and the worms are roasting in Hell. 'Oh dear God in Heaven!' she shrieked out loud. What if once they found Hester, then they found out what she had done? She didn't know she knew the word 'patricide', but suddenly it started to throb in her temples. It was one of the words John Jacob had taught her early on in their marriage when he had worked on improving her vocabulary. A preacher's wife needed to be able to know more words, he had kept on telling her. She learned because she had to speak better: it was incumbent on her in her lofty new position.

CHAPTER FOURTEEN

•

Francesca, Megan's mother-in-law, supervised Gladdie's music lessons and showed her videos of as many different piano players as she could find. She understood the world of music was Gladdie's natural habitat.

The child soaked up music like the parched earth after a long drought. Gladdie was given a key to the piano room – as it had become known – and three hours before school began could be heard practicing. As much as she longed to play pieces, she was diligent about her scales. She saw herself rising from beside a Steinway grand – and bowing – or curtseying, she could never make up her mind which one to do. She practiced a few curtsies, but thought that to bow was more dignified. The place in her dreams was always the Carnegie Hall as she had seen it on one of Francesca's videos. She smiled over her scales, happy as she imagined listening to applause sounding like a heavy downpour on the tin roof of her mother's house. Her concentration was like the deepest meditation; nothing entered her mind, her entire being was the music.

At times when Gladdie longed for her mother, there was a game she played. In her mind's eye and her memory's ear, she would go home and listen to her father playing the harmonica. The sequence of her game was that after he played his harmonica he would knock out a joyful tune using two spoons, tapping on his thighs, chest or table with wildly happy-sounding clicks. Jethro played on the washboard and Luke on a Jew's harp. She imagined them all laughing. She wished her father had a guitar. One day she was going to buy him one that was even better than Uncle Clay's. There were nights when sleep evaded her and stole away her dream time and it was then that she played her trick on sleeplessness. She would relive especially happy times. Her favourite one was the song Uncle Clay made up; she could just about hear her family rolling around and screaming with laughter. She went over the words in her mind:

O America
Land of the free-ee
Richest in all history-ee
Here is no electricity-ee

98

A heck of a lotta poverty-ee
The water lines don't run
It ain't a whole lotta fun
Without the warmth of the sun
In winter you freeze up your bum
Oooooh America
Land of the free-ee
You have to go outside to pee-ee
To pee-ee-ee.

Then happiness blew around her room like a friendly whirl-wind. Contented, she placed her hands beside her cheek and fell asleep.

Spring would soon be here, and the children watched excit-edly for signs. They were tired of wearing layers of clothes and irritable when cold weather and swift-falling nights prevented them from playing outdoors. Although Gladdie and, increas-ingly, Jake did not believe in fire and brimstone or eternal Hell, they nevertheless were far more obedient than most.

Tom had to resolve his stupefying dilemma and kept his sanity by being constantly occupied. He blocked out, for as long as he could, the awful unwanted reality. He could not face thinking about Gladdie – after all, he only had sex with Hester once! She must have had many, many different sexual partners. Wasn't it possible, probable even, that the child was not his? He remem-bered the exact date – how proud he had been – he had seen him-self as no longer a boy but a man! He feverishly did his arith-metic – he wanted his doubts resolved into certainties. Perhaps she was not his daughter. The mountain woman was out to blackmail him! But it was the child's colouring, her flaming, accusatory auburn hair. She had his complexion and Megan, his beloved, simply adored the child.

A black shaft was digging its way into his being. The con-structive life he led was being eaten up by armies of ants destroy-ing his foundations. Their sharp pincers were his guilts and regrets. How could a moment of lust be returning to revenge itself on his precious wife and son? How would Megan react if she found out? He felt himself crumbling, disintegrating. His act of youthful irresponsibility had brought an innocent and beautiful child into a world of darkness, ignorance and super-stition. He had to cease his incessant inner dialogue. He could think of no way to help his gifted little daughter, whom he found that he couldn't help but love, and somehow simultaneously protect Megan. Megan, who had lost her own baby girl.

Tom distanced himself from a hurt Megan, who had no idea of what was happening. She realized that he had completely immersed himself in Fat Fred's, as if he wanted to escape his family. Tom flung himself into his work with overzealous industriousness and with the same degree of concentration – away from her. She became distraught and afraid, it was obvious that he was hiding something from her. When she'd asked him what it was, he rounded angrily on her, loudly commanding her not to question him. She was aghast. She couldn't believe this was her Thomas.

Two days after his outburst she started crying and couldn't stop. Like a violent storm from which there was no shelter, she sobbed until there was no breath left in her. Only when Benjy was with her did she quieten. When Tom came home late that night and saw her swollen red eyes and heard her exhausted sobs, his legs gave way and he dropped onto their bed.

'We have to talk,' he gasped, then could not go on. She froze. 'I don't know how to tell you,' he blurted out. He took a few deep breaths.

'I don't know how to say this. But I must tell you. I have another child.'

She didn't comprehend what he said. She began slowly to quieten down and looked at him dazedly.

'She's a girl.' he said. 'A beautiful little girl.'

'What? What did you say?' she asked, rubbing her eyes as though that would clear her confusion away. He started to cry.

'What's wrong – what's happened – why are you crying?' These bewildered words were not even questions. Her nurturing nature came to their rescue; all she wanted to do was comfort him, she had no need to understand.

That long night, the story came out and they held one another and tried to soothe away their pain. Reality was blurred for Megan.

That, Tom expected, would come later.

Peace Place was being run compassionately and effectively by Elsie McNab who shortened its name to 'Peace', and that was how everyone now referred to it. It was soon known by other centres which, once they investigated it, sent victims there. Elsie wasn't an earth-mother. Her physique was anything but ample. She was tall, thin, her movements gawky, her nose bent and squashed, her light caramel-coloured skull showing through thinning hair.

'When you meet Elsie, you are made too aware of her skeleton,' Tom said. 'That can't be good.'

Sometimes, when she heard the stories of the women's lives, Megan was amazed that they had the courage to continue living. In her daily life, as she did her chores, taught the children, looked after Benjamin, she was embarrassed by her own riches. Yet, as she was about to fall asleep, a heavy hooded cloak enfolded her as she remembered the baby girl she lost and the other children she should have borne. Sadness stole into her happiness. At night she would creep closer to Thomas and try to breathe in rhythm with his breath. Beneath each breath lurked, unacknowledged, her festering sorrow, her grief. And now there was a new fear. A joy, a fear, Megan could not decide which it was the most... Gladdie. Maybe she was Tom's child... Maybe she wasn't....

That awful night when Tom came home drained and pale, his blue eyes ringed as though by dark bruising, and blurted out, 'We have to talk,' she had felt indescribable relief. As long as he would at least talk to her – whatever it was he had to say.

'You can say anything to me,' she managed, her voice strained and quiet. 'Anything.' How old, she thought, then her mind screamed. How old? How old is this child?

'Well, when I was studying social work, when I was seventeen... I met... she didn't have a can opener...'

'"No can opener",' she repeated, covering her eyes to mask her relieved expression. He was seventeen! Only seventeen!

'No. I bought her one. I was just seventeen. Well. She seduced me. Only once. Not that I didn't come back for more... I began to feel like a used can. No use to anyone... anymore.'

'You're everything to me,' she lifted her head, her heart thundering in her ears.

'I was a virgin... till then. And to think I have a daughter.'

'We. We have a daughter,' Megan imperiously interrupted as her confidence bounced back.

'It's Gladdie.' His admission shocked his wife into silence.

'She lives with those people,' he choked out. 'Religious bigots. Bigots,' he sobbed. 'She can't even speak – she's been traumatized. Her mother lives in a shack! My daughter was born in a shack – a miserable little shack.'

'We'll adopt her.' Megan broke her silence, suddenly joyful. Gladdie, Gladdie, Glad, gladness, her being pealed like a bell.

'They'll never let her go,' he whispered, and she realized he had already thought of it. Megan felt a healing salve gently massaging, caressing her heart, restoring her strength.

'We've got so much love to give her. So much,' she said.

'I couldn't tell you. I was ashamed of Hester. Ashamed of myself. Disgusted and disappointed in myself. I realized I've always felt superior to the people I wanted to help. They must have sensed it. No wonder I was a failure. I kept going back again and again. Not because I wanted to help... Oh no, I wanted Hester.'

'You were only seventeen,' she excused and absolved.

'I thought that it was because of what I secretly termed "the Hester episode" that I finally gave up welfare work. She taught me how futile my efforts were. How puny I am.'

It was then that Megan smiled softly at her husband. 'I take issue with that word. Perhaps in saving the world, the word applies to everyone, to all idealists; but we need them. As far as I personally am concerned, the word is entirely inappropriate.'

He understood her meaning and could only smile admiringly at her strategy to bring him back to himself. Her compassion was equaled by his gratitude to her.

'Let's incandesce together. Let's become the light,' she suggested, winking saucily.

First she held him; caressing the back of his neck, she nestled him in her arms and stroked him for a long while. Their curtains were opened wide and the moon bathed them in her milkiness; afterwards, they felt themselves lift out of their bodies and drift towards it. Their beings atomized into oneness with the universe.

Gladdie became far more important to Megan. They loved her. Eagerly, and using her considerable intelligence, she tried to find out more about her birth mother, the mountain woman, but there was no way to trace her. Louise built a stockade of canny, massive immovability. Megan became obsessed with the idea of adopting Gladdie. There was nine years' difference between Benjy and his half-sister. Benjamin, as an only child, went to a pre-school crèche from an early age. She ached, she yearned for Gladdie and desperately longed for Benjy to have a sister. She hoped too to ameliorate her sadness; the attrition of heavy sorrow was milling her spirit down.

CHAPTER FIFTEEN

•

They were on their way to the school when Abigail next saw Roberto and she was looking and feeling at her very best. She had recently returned from a visit to a health spa in California, where she had taken a video on sign language, the better to communicate with Gladdie.

What was it the holistic doctor had said to her? 'Be thankful for your great good health.' Since she had entirely given up the idea of catching Roberto, she was more relaxed then she had been for a long while. She was at ease about everything, including ageing.

'Roberto,' Abigail said, 'growing old is not so bad.'

'I haven't thought about it,' he replied, his eyes still on the road.

'That's because you're young.'

'I'm not that young,' he replied diffidently. 'Not that young at all. In fact, I'm rather old. I grew old relatively young.' They were about to pass a truck that had a bumper sticker proclaiming: 'Life's a bummer, but if you rear-end me, you'll know just how bum life can be'. Relieved, they both laughed at it. She told him her favorite sticker was 'Life is a beach and then you die'. This gave way to further laughter.

After a pause, in a low voice he murmured, 'Sometimes, sometimes I can't wait.'

She flinched. She could feel him moving towards something he wanted to say, but she couldn't help him. She didn't know how and felt useless. The road curved up the mountains and they came upon a clearing that was a small cemetery. They stopped there for a few minutes, the immutability of the modest burial ground instilled a measure of peace. Wordlessly, they continued their journey. They traveled in the companionable silence of old friends until they reached the school. There was a quiet peace between them. There was the pleasure of the present again – this was nothing short of revelation for Roberto. Once more, the American ash greeted Abigail. She got out of the car and patted the tree's trunk as if it were her faithful pet. She was proud to show it to Roberto.

'It looks like elephant's hide,' she said with a proprietorial air.

She noticed that, though pleased to see them, Megan had to make an effort to deal with the importance of their visit. Abigail greeted the children energetically, puzzling over Megan's preoccupied, distracted air. The red Ferrari had inevitably gathered a crowd of excited children around it. Its gleaming surface was quickly covered in smudgy fingerprints. Roberto swallowed an instant's fastidious dismay as they pawed and explored it. Jake said that today was Louise's day of the week when she did extra special house cleaning and offered to take them to her. Savoring the tide of envy, which followed him up the street like green smoke, he showed them the way. He couldn't wait to tell Gladdie. How often had he heard about the sin of envy, of covetousness, from his father? But something that felt this good couldn't be evil. He ran in at Abigail's prompting to tell his mother that she had guests.

Louise's face shone as though oiled by the same substance that caused her entire house to shout out its spotlessness. She seated them, her eyes furtive. She guessed why they had come. As soon as they were seated in uncomfortably upright chairs, she left to make coffee.

Louise was frightened, but firmly resolved not to tell them a single thing. Although previously she had been inclined to persuade Hester to meet these people – a church for worshippers of the Lord was a mighty thing – she dared not allow them to find out what Hester had done to their Pa! Restlessly her mind scurried through all the possibilities. What if it all became known to John Jacob? What would he think of her? Her heart pounded, that dreaded word 'patricide'. She began to feel faint and dizzy; her hand tapped against her temple. Pat-ri-cide. She had to lean heavily against the wall.

Roberto and Abigail could hear all her movements and gazed dazedly at one another, wondering why they had come to this odious little house. The comforting friendship they had just formed began to founder as Louise panted and sighed; they felt it wheezing away. Bearing thick, steaming coffee mugs, they noticed Louise crook her little finger and they exchanged secret smiles, their complicity resuscitating their friendship.

'Mrs Boardman, what site would you choose for your church?' Roberto began. Louise started trembling and had to put her coffee down on the pretext that she needed more sugar. Ignoring the question, Louise launched into a sermon on the evils of too much coffee leading to smoking.

'The inventor of cigarettes was inhabited by the Devil.' Each of Roberto's appealing efforts to get Louise back on track was brushed away. 'Cigarettes cause cancer. People die without being Saved.'

'A good reason for your church,' Roberto slipped in.

'And drinking and smoking usually go together. Do you know the evils of drinking?' Louise enquired, earnestly searching for further subjects.

'May I have a glass of water?' Abigail hurriedly interposed.

'Adultery.' Louise heaved herself out of her chair whispering, 'Thou shalt not commit. It's one of the Commandments.'

While she was out of the room Abigail quietly said, 'Louise has either gone crazy or is scared of something.'

'It's both,' Roberto replied.

They heard the water running into the glass. They felt unequal to the task – they could not deal with unreason. In the habit of being listened to, they couldn't negotiate with her, but they were both confident she would eventually run out of gas. They had to be patient. They had to wait.

'We thought,' said Abigail, 'that you, your husband and his congregation would be uplifted if you all had your own church to pray in.'

'I know what you want,' snorted Louise, her face slanting craftily. 'Our folks are taxed too highly. It keeps them poor. There is malnutrition among the elderly. I make them hearty soup. I bake corn bread.' She spoke with relentless monotony. 'I give them plenty of potatoes so they can put some meat on their bones.' Her eyes, that had been darting around endlessly, focused meaningfully on Abigail.

Louise felt trapped. Frenziedly she preached on and on against the worshipping of the Golden Calf and worldly goods – anything she could think of. Her body was as substantial and stiff as her words and eyes were furtively swift. Her worry was suffocating her.

'What,' Roberto inquired quickly, 'does your husband think about a church that would have enough room for all?' This finished Louise completely; besides gasping, she didn't respond. She couldn't move. Her eyes were stilled and her tongue stuck to the roof of her mouth. They realized that she had told nothing of it to her husband.

They rose to leave, unconsciously rubbing their backs, and started for the front door, at which point Louise forced her rigid body to follow them. She grabbed the large box of chocolates with roses on it and thrust it out to Abigail.

'But I brought them for you,' protested Abigail. It was the most beautiful picture Louise had ever seen.

'Thank you,' she said, remembering her manners. When they said their farewells and thanked her for her coffee, she relaxed and something slipped out – 'She shoulda done it sooner,' she said.

'Done what?' they said in unison.

But Louise quickly put her hand in front of her mouth.

As they got into the low-slung car Louise muttered from behind her hand, 'Good to meet you,' to Roberto and, 'thank you for coming.'

Roberto prepared to pull off then, leaning casually out of the window, softly asked, 'What should have happened sooner?'

'She shoulda done it sooner,' Louise replied, unable to stop herself. An expression of cunning, and then of exultation crossed her face. She grinned gleefully. Neither of them asked who the 'she' was. Louise clamped her fist across her mouth. They waved to Louise and when they looked back they saw she was clasping the chocolates to her breast.

They came across Gladdie and Jake returning home. They stopped the car and Jake couldn't believe that he had ridden in it. Gladdie smiled at them happily. Roberto recognized her from her floppy hat.

'How would you like to play the piano in a big concert hall one day?' asked Abigail. Gladdie smiled radiantly.

'She would like that a lot,' Jake answered for her.

'How do you know that?' enquired Roberto.

'She tells me everything. We belong to a club and we've got our own secret language.'

Abigail started to use the sign language that she'd learnt from the video. The children looked at one another in amusement, it meant nothing to them. They couldn't help but laugh at Abigail, Jake loudly making up for Gladdie's laughter, which was all breath without sound. They waved at one another as the car purred off, Gladdie dropping a perfect curtsey whilst taking her hat off with a wide flourish.

'I wonder if she could become my ward?' mused Abigail.

'Where did you learn sign language?' asked Roberto with a strange sound in his voice.

'I'm just a beginner,' apologized Abigail, and Roberto found himself deeply moved by this paradoxical woman. They continued their journey in silence.

• •

I gave nothing away, Louise reassured herself, but what, oh what, would happen when they came back and spoke to her husband? Louise knew she had to go to Hester to work out a campaign. There was also the matter of their mother's tombstone to be discussed. Between them they would find a way to work it all out.

Louise prepared more carefully than usual for her trip. She chose the foods she knew Hester would most appreciate and she took two dresses that she had finished making for Hester's daughters. She used fabric from two of her own tent-like dresses, and took the trouble to trim them up in a way of which she herself disapproved, but Hester would figure was a demonstration of sisterly love. She had to soften Hester up for their mother's tombstone. When she reached the house and puffed her way in, she was surprised to find Hester sitting cross-legged on the floor and not leaping up to greet her in her usual exuberant fashion. She sat looking at the stove, gazing sightlessly at a few dying embers. Almost with reluctance she uncurled herself and started absentmindedly to feed wood to the ever hungry stove.

'Are you ill?' Louise asked unbelievingly.

In reply, Hester slung her arms about Louise and gave her a tight hug. Hester's strength was as dependable and unwavering as their mother's had once been.

Hester's eyes glinted in appreciation. She's come about Ma, Hester guessed, and something else. Great cumulous clouds veiled the sun. Something else, Hester's bones told her. Something else.

'The sky looks whitish,' Louise worried. Hester touched Louise on the upper arm with the palm of her hand, as though testing her body temperature and comforting her at the same time.

'It's getting ready to storm,' she said, gently propelling her sister to the door. 'We'll go now in case it rains.'

She always knows, Louise marveled, as hand in hand they went to their mother's grave. As they walked through the forest Hester didn't push away the leaves from her face as Louise did, she liked the feel of their gentle caress. Now and again they stooped to pick a wildflower, Louise for her mother, but Hester stuck hers in her hair. When they reached the shadowy place, Hester immediately sat on her mother's grave in a friendly way, gesturing Louise to rest beside her so that they could commence negotiations. Louise hid her exasperation as best she could by pretending not to notice. Her few wild flowers, by now crumpled, she strew about where she thought her mother's head lay. Closing her eyes she began to recite the Lord's Prayer.

When she opened her eyes, she saw with shock that Hester was lying on her stomach along the full length of the grave, her arms spread as though to embrace the earth covering their mother with her ear pressed to the ground. The sight made her lose her voice. Hester, signaled by her silence, sat up and said unexpectedly, in a quiet flat voice, 'Louise, you can put up the tombstone, but not a large one.'

With her hands she demonstrated a height of about twenty inches and width of eighteen. Poor Louise immediately acquiesced, a little disgruntled that she couldn't argue the case she had thoroughly prepared.

'Let's talk here,' insisted Hester, who was quite at peace sitting cross-legged on her mother's grave. Louise sat down beside the creek, after careful inspection for snakes.

'Tell me, tell me what the matter is,' Hester invited.

'They want to give a church building to us. But they have to meet you. They think that after they meet you they will be able to help Gladys to talk again. You've told me, Hessie, that she can and that someday she will, and I believe you. But Hessie, I've not heard her make one sound. I've never told John Jacob that you said she will speak. We all believe it is a punishment from the Lord, whose Ways are not our Ways. We've all prayed for her, we've got down on our knees and we've borne witness. All we ever hear from her is her breathing, and even that seems softer and quieter than most.'

Hester was still and for a short while Louise seemed to lose her sense of purpose. The sky appeared to darken and Louise sensed the glow in her sister's eyes, which somehow encouraged her to continue.

'But I'm afraid, Hester. I'm afraid they'll find out. About Pa. What he did. About you and what you did.' At this point Louise lost control and a low moan issued from the very bowels of her being, not unlike the sounds she gave during childbirth. Her sister neither intervened nor questioned.

'Hush up, Louise and come and see what landed on my hand!' Hester's tone enthralled, exhilarated. Louise slowly quietened down and tried to see from where she sat, but only made out a darker shadow on Hester's hand, but as she moved closer she saw, just as it began its flight, a large butterfly. Brief its flight, unique its glory.

'That was Ma,' whispered Hester. Then she brought her mind back to Louise's anxieties.

'I don't mind them meeting me, whoever they are,' she said. 'You didn't want it. Now you've changed your mind. That's OK. Don't worry about Pa. He's in a good spot, they cain't find him. What he did cain't be undone, but it cain't be repeated.' The sympathy pain Hester felt between her legs was as sharp as she remembered it had been whilst she had mopped up Gladdie's young blood.

'Don't worry yourself about it. Them city slickers don't know about our lives on the mountains. Pa was like a bear with a sore head; you never knew if he was gonna just hit you or rip your guts out. He was the bad part of the mountain. They cain't understand that. Sometimes, even nature goes crooked. It goes savage. It don't take no prisoners. That was the way he was made.'

It had started to rain as they talked, and now they were wet through. Hester felt her heart ache, looking at the waterlogged mass of her older sister. She's like a snail, thought Hester, without a shell. A slug, trailing silvery slime. Tears squeezed past Hester's eyelids, joining the rain. The earth on the grave grew quite muddy; it was no place to be buried, Curt had told her. But that's where her mother chose, what she had wished for. They stayed in the purifying thunderstorm and made no effort to leave.

'They do a census,' Louise started to sob. 'They have to know when people die. It's the law.' At this, Hester began to laugh.

'Since when – since when did we pay any attention to the law? Pay it no mind, Lou. Don't worry yourself. They won't find him.' She caught her breath and tried to stop laughing. Finally the storm exhausted itself and they strolled back.

'The children will wonder where we've been.'

They arrived sodden and muddy. The children thought they looked hilarious. Jewel had donned her new dress and the stove was warm. On it bubbled the hot soup.

'We went to see Grandma.'

'My wreath was the best one,' Emmett said – he was the one who had used feathers and chicken bones. They had eaten all the crunchy peanut butter. Louise was annoyed that they hadn't saved any for her; then she smiled at herself, thinking that she would have eaten it all up too. When Louise got into her car, empurpled shadows were merging into darkness. She hadn't the nerve to tell Hester that although heartened, she was still worried and muddled.

'They want more,' Hester warned. 'They want Gladdie. Switch your lights on.'

'Gladdie is mine,' Louise angrily retorted. 'You gave her to me. The Lord took mine and then He gave me yours.'

'Be careful, Louise,' Hester cautioned as the car pulled off.

What, Louise thought with irritation, would they want her daughter for? Anyway, they couldn't have her. She thrust the idea from her mind, judging that this time Hester was wrong. She began to think of ways in which she could word the news to John Jacob about the possibility of having their very own church. Hester watched the last of her sister's car lights thread down the mountain and felt her lower butterfly lips smile grimly with the exact knowledge of whose child Gladdie was. And always would be. When starless night comes, she thought she would plan what to do. She turned her attention to Jewel's wedding.

CHAPTER SIXTEEN

•

Tom didn't know how or if they could succeed in adopting Gladdie. He tried to submerge his hopelessness; he had to do his best for his daughter, otherwise he couldn't live with himself. He needed a little hope even if it was, he suspected, illusionary. He decided to contact an old friend, now an attorney, David Talbot, to find out what the legal position might be. His blood knew Gladdie was his, but what rights did he have in law – if any?

David Talbot was blind. He told them that it was essential to contact the biological mother; it was, he thought, a difficult situation. John Jacob, the religious fanatic uncle, had even to be persuaded to allow his son to have medication; the mute child most certainly wouldn't be tissue-typed, as this would be blocked. David felt great sympathy for his two friends and wanted to help them.

He had an idea he thought might well help them and suggested that he meet with the aunt. He felt, listening to their story, that his blindness would assist her to unburden herself. People tended to confide to the blind what they would not tell a sighted person. It provided a kind of mask and, as a result, a sense of free openness.

Tom and Megan were touched by his generous offer. They thanked him profusely and Megan kissed him.

Waiting for a chance to arrange the meeting was hard. In the meantime, they decided to make a quick trip to the mountains in search of Hester again, taking Benjy with them, so that they could get some enjoyment out of the excursion.

'Look,' they said to him as a red flash rose in front of their car, 'a cardinal. The national bird of Kentucky.' Canadian geese squawked by, a munificent flash of blue flew through the trees, a mountain blue bird. They marveled at the profusion of pin oaks, maples, black pines, and stopped to admire a perfect hemlock framed by sculpted rock outcroppings.

'Makes nonsense out of a lot of contemporary art,' sniffed Tom. Nature's gigantic hand had squeezed and scrunched the mountains together, so narrow and steep were some of the ravines that there was scarcely enough room for the road. They were pleased about the new blacktop roads because that meant accessibility for snowbound hillbillies. They admired some of the architect-designed houses that nestled in large acreage beside rundown and over-housed farms in the broader hollows. Each new home had its own lake, as municipal water was unavailable. Farmers divided and subdivided their land to give to their children, which made farming uneconomical. Some of the marginal farmers made moonshine which, when properly, as opposed to poisonously brewed, has a mule kick and a strong aftertaste. Nobody tipped the cops off. The boot of a car scraping the road provoked knowing glances; it was usually dragged down by the weight of sugar. If someone was busted, people never suspected the grocer, who sold the sugar. You couldn't buy large quantities from a supermarket unless certain the assistant was known and wouldn't squeal.

The smooth blacktop gave way to a dirt road, which was increasingly bumpy, with nerve-testing curves, S-bends and sudden inclines. Tom concentrated on his driving while Megan sang nursery rhymes to Benjy.

As their Jeep rounded the last bend towards Hester's home, Hester saw it and melted into the forest. Her children recognized them and, aware of their mother's wishes, continued with whatever they'd been doing. Hester climbed a dense oak and watched. Benjamin had grown well and she would have liked to hug him. She idly wondered how she would feel if they took her Gladdie; the plexus of her blood vessels and capillaries answered her. Her flesh burnt redly. Something coiled inside her, her upper lip raised itself revealing the shine of an incisor. Not a muscle in her body moved as she opened and stilled herself, until she and the tree became one. A luminous calm transfused her as the tree recharged her power; trees never failed her, sap from the tree's heart flowed to her heart. She watched them leave, observing their brave disappointment. They left and she shook her head, there was nothing wrong with them and Gladdie would come to no harm. But she did not belong to them. One accidental particle of sperm did not make a father.

'She was there,' Megan told Tom, 'I sensed it.'

'I didn't,' he said, thinking perhaps Megan was right.

'She was watching us. She was watching Benjamin.'

'But how could she see us?' he asked. 'The forest is thick, except for the vegetable garden, and the road there has no clearing, no vantage point.'

Megan acknowledged this, reluctantly nodding her head. 'You know she's wild – she climbed a tree!' Megan exclaimed.

Tom's faith was instantly restored. 'How,' he asked mischie-vously, 'would what we've just said sound in court?' and they laughed, which made Benjamin laugh too.

After careful consideration, Abigail decided it was still a good idea to have the children participate in her Spring Ball. She had to stay in contact with Louise and any excuse would do. She duly received, with the expected reluctance, permission from Louise. A donation to assist a parishioner who had black lung was the key which allowed John Jacob to praise the power of prayer. Meanwhile, although Roberto appeared to go about his business in his pleasant way, he became increasingly involved in the drama surrounding this beautiful and gifted child. Who should have done what sooner? Why was Louise so determined to keep them away from Gladdie's mother? He suppressed the degree of his interest, kept his feelings undisclosed but he was developing a strong desire to play a pivotal part in Gladdie's life.

The evening of the long-awaited spring ball arrived at last. Mandy had excelled herself. Abigail inspected herself and smiled at her reflection in the mirror. If she could help gifted Gladdie realize her full potential, her life would have more meaning, more purpose. And Roberto's respect for her would grow. This purpose had already begun to steady her and give her a confi-dence more real than that provided by her wealth.

All was readied. Ice sculptures of dolphins surrounded with oysters and ice seagulls nesting on gulls' and quails' eggs adorned the tables, large ice octopuses cupped beluga caviar in each alluringly-curved tentacle. The first band was playing fifties classics which alternated with one that moved from rhythm and blues to Latin. Champagne flowed, guests smiled appreciatively at the decor. Vast swathes of silk hung from the ceilings looking, as they were meant to look, like billowing clouds. Abigail was pleased that her interior designer had worked with an artist to hand-paint it so effectively. Long white damask cloths rested sumptuously around the guests' ankles, chairs had been draped in palest blue cloth and on them were painted dolphins. The chair backs were folded into the shapes of fins, slung over the chairs and tied with silver cords were gifts for each guest.

They stood around for cocktails, everybody looking to see who was there, who was wearing what, who wore new jewellery. Estimates were made as to the value of the gems; many of the men were as interested as the women. All Abigail's usual guests were there, some of them to admire, some to be admired, some to scoff, some to disdain. Some told themselves that they were there merely to observe the circus; but they all came.

In the past, if any man arrived with a partner who was dressed in too brazen a fashion, she would be handed a little black jacket. That had happened and now no woman ever wanted to be 'black jacketed', as it became known, nor did any escort permit his date to be dressed in an unseemly manner. Wives would ask their husbands if they looked respectable enough, to be assured that yes, yes, they looked wonderful. Couples reaffirmed their partnership simply by being there; together their social prowess was reconfirmed, their lives validated.

The night was a remarkable success, with young and old dancing until three in the morning. The guests had been pleasantly startled when just before midnight the floor which covered the swimming pool rolled back to display mermaids and mermen swimming in a carefully choreographed routine. Underwater variously-coloured lights illuminated the pool and overhead lights were dimmed. Those who thought of it tried to work out where the swimmers had been before the performance began. When the show ended, each mermaid was helped onto a moving belt that seemed to appear from nowhere. Their long tails, complete with shining fins, made it impossible to walk; they lay like odalisques, with their long hair wet and their bare breasts gleaming. The assembled crowd, waiters, bar tenders, guests, musicians all applauded wildly. Abigail had done it again. Once in their motor cars, the guests opened their gifts. There were crystal dolphins for women and, for men, mermaids balancing on their tails. The date of the party and the words 'The Seamen's Rescue Mission' were discreetly sandblasted. It was impossible that the exorbitant price of the tickets could have covered the cost of the party. Everyone went home satisfied and satiated and never knew that a part of the extravaganza had been missing. The Boardman children did not appear.

Just before the party began, Abigail with Buffy, her hairdresser, had joined the children and Jake told her she looked as good as Christmas, whilst Gladdie smiled at her in admiration. Jake stepped into his merman costume and was zipped up by the two women. Gladdie, as a mermaid, was happy to put silvery green slippers on and she particularly liked her tail. Jake allowed them to put a crown made of shining beads on his head. The instant the luxuriant red wig was placed on Gladdie's head, she began to tremble violently and fiercely tore it off. Tears squeezed past her tightly shut eyes.

'She doesn't like it,' Jake explained, looking every bit as perplexed and dismayed as they were.

'It's only a wig. Please, won't you please let me put it on you?' pleaded Buffy. Abigail was dumbfounded. Buffy picked it up and gently put it back on the child's head. The little girl opened her mouth to scream, and she did in her soundless way, and again flung the hated wig to the floor. Jake, seeing his cousin's state, threw his headdress off. It made tinkly sounds as it crashed into a chair leg.

'She doesn't like it – and if she doesn't, I don't,' he explained, looking at once defiant and bewildered. The cousins clasped one another. 'It's alright,' Abigail said, trying to calm them down. She had meant them to stand with Roberto and herself to receive the first of the guests. It would have been a nice touch, and Roberto suggested that if the little ones were unwilling or bored they needn't stay.

'You don't have to wear it,' she pacified the little girl, who was still trembling but had tightly shut her mouth and covered it with both hands.

'It was so frightening,' she was later to tell Roberto. 'That little mouth wide open, those soundless screams. Her face was bright red and her eyes tightly closed. She looked like a baby that had a difficult time being born. She was unrecognizable! She's afraid of long hair. Terrified. There must be more to it. It's valuable information.'

She had wanted to put her arms around the child; instead she touched her lightly on the cheek.

'Nasty old wig. What a bad idea,' and now lightly Abigail stroked her untidily cut hair.

'Buffy is a hairdresser. Would you like her to trim your hair?'

At this, the two children exchanged quick glances. Gladdie bobbed her head up and down affirmatively and clapped her hands together.

'She's not allowed,' Jake started to say, but was silenced by a vitriolic look from Gladdie. Jake was worried when Buffy, with the finest, most shiny scissors Gladdie had ever seen, began to cut her hair. Gladdie was the happiest Abigail had ever seen her, Jake looked anxious. 'Don't cut too much,' he mumbled. He then busied himself with a slim box of matches, lighting one, blowing it out, then another.

'You're going to look lovely. Don't you think Buffy is a good hairdresser?' Abigail spoke to Gladdie as though she could answer her. She put her arm around the dejected boy and told him that Gladdie could always wear her hat, at which point he brightened up.

'Roberto – you know, my friend with the Ferrari – is here. Why don't you run downstairs and fetch him back up here? He's at the front door. Do you think you can do that?' Jake dashed away and Gladdie hardly noticed.

Buffy thinned and layered the cut, and by the time Roberto, whom Jake had found without difficulty, came it was almost finished.

'Doesn't it look lovely?' she trilled to Roberto, and then whispered: 'I'll explain. Find a way to distract them. The party will be too much for them.'

'Miss Gladdie Boardman,' Roberto picked up the child's hand and lightly kissed it, 'may I call you Grace, because you are full of grace – would you and Jake like to come for a ride with me in my Ferrari?'

Jake jumped up and down with delight, while Gladdie's eyes were fixed on her face in the mirror. They waited for Buffy to finish snipping away; when she finished it looked as though Gladdie was wearing a feathery cap. Roberto and Abigail smiled at one another.

The three raced off to the car to go for a long ride through the darkening landscape. The car swooped up and down almost deserted roads and Jake whooped with excitement; every now and then Gladdie touched her head pleasurably. Abigail received her guests alone and without her co-host by her side, something the society columnists keenly recorded. This could be juicy news.

Their headlights rocketed tunnels through the road, silhouetting leafy lanes, speeding the children into a realm even they could not have imagined. They seemed the only people in this world, they were released and freed into the moment. Roberto looked at Gladdie in his rearview mirror, he had turned on the interior lights to heighten their sense of intimacy and intensify their closeness. She looked like a little boy who had entered his own reverie.

'Are you having a good time?' he asked, catching her eye in the rearview mirror, hoping that she might actually answer.

She nodded her head emphatically. He wanted to break her sound barrier, tried to exploit their shared intimacy; hoped, in short, for a miracle.

Awaiting the children were two generous ice-cream sundaes in pretty bowls that they were to keep. There was a long rolled-up parcel for Louise. It was the proposed plan of an appropriately simple church which was coloured a subdued red. As usual, they had picnic baskets for the return journey. Abigail censored her idea of sending chocolates to the Boardman's Senior. Instead, for Louise she sent a large jar of honey complete with honeycomb.

'God's work,' she'd told Roberto dryly. The children had enjoyed themselves. On the way home they agreed that they liked Roberto. They thought Abigail was good and kind because she gave Gladdie two extra hats to wear, similar to the one she had. Gladdie sensibly plucked the floral trimmings, feathers and bows off them and left the remnants in the car.

The party was over. Abigail lay on a chaise longue, her languid posture belying her sprinting mind as she reviewed the evening. Roberto sat on a chair opposite her, leaning forward to capture every word. The evening had been an unqualified success: half a million dollars had been raised for the 'Seamen's Rescue Mission', for which Roberto smilingly thanked her. They were more involved in Gladdie's reaction to the wig; there had to be some dreadful reason for her reaction. Abigail related what glorious long tresses the child had when first they met, that she'd worn one long thick plait, hanging like a molten rope down her back. But the next time she saw her, when she had played the piano having lost her voice, she hadn't recognized her.

'I doubt very much that the cutting of hair is allowed. The aunt won't be pleased with you for instigating the haircut.'

Abigail knew this. 'But Roberto, if you had seen how happy she was! I couldn't help myself – and Buffy was right there! Do you think it might set our case back a little? I've a feeling that Gladdie will be very careful and disguise her hair cut. And I gave her two more hats, a pinkish grey and an olive green. I don't anticipate that they'll notice; she keeps her head covered all the time.'

They had been sitting like two old friends keeping easy company, when a degree of disquiet insinuated itself as both became self-conscious. They were sitting beside her favorite artfully lit fishpond. They looked for goldfish, they listened to the sounds of the night, a whip-poor-will called. It was as though a spell had been cast upon them; and, in truth, one had. They themselves cast it, together with the events of the evening. Unspoken came the knowledge that they had to speak with complete honesty; too much was at stake.

'I never had a daughter,' Abigail began.

'And I, I once had one; but she was stillborn.'

The word 'stillborn' hovered on the cool night air and they worried that their budding closeness would be lost to them unless they forced themselves to continue. Stillborn. A gloved silence intruded. Abigail's insecurity paralyzed her; she wanted to encourage but didn't know what to say. They stared at their blurred reflections, as if these might help them. Something nascent began to swim into being.

'She was my only child, although I had one other who was sometimes like my child. She who was my lover, my sister, my mother, all my women, all my life; she was my wife.'

Abigail made a reassuring murmuring sound.

'I felt betrayed. I called her the little traitor. How could she leave me... like that'.

Roberto knew that survival without meaning is nothingness.

'I have to start living.' They were still and quiet for a while. 'I've asked myself why I'm so involved with the little one's silence. My daughter' – and his body shuddered – 'would have been a little older.' He paused, then continued in a clearer tone. 'You told me she could sing, could speak, but is now silenced. Has she been... muzzled by something unspeakable?'

'I've heard some bad things about hillbillies,' whispered Abigail haltingly.

'I'm amazed how deeply I care for her, how much I think about her. There is something magical, charismatic even; I'm surprised by the depth of my involvement,' said Abigail.

'Yet Gladdie's disposition is so sunny it refutes suffering. Always quick to smile, to laugh, albeit soundlessly.... Perhaps it is organic – diseased vocal cords, or scarring caused by trauma,' Roberto said.

'Did I not tell you,' Abigail asked, 'did I forget to tell you; she's seen a doctor? He found nothing wrong. Perhaps we should try different specialists.'

'We have to find the mother.'

Abigail and Roberto stayed beside the pond. As dawn added milk to the night sky, blotting up the stars, they strolled hand in hand back to the large house, its lights still lit. They had to find Hester.

CHAPTER SEVENTEEN

•

Tom and Megan met with persistent obstruction in their unsuccessful efforts to communicate with the mute girl's mother. Each person they sent had been easily spotted by the mountain people. They instantly recognized the agents as authority, the sort that they were honour-bound to keep in the dark. They closed ranks.

Outsiders had no idea of how loyal these folk would be towards their own. They figured out that maybe Curt had done something bad whilst he'd been a drunk. A good few had been to jail and they didn't want Curt to be sent back inside. Prison added another dimension of brutality into their lives. No jobs, no money, no opportunity. Discrimination operated against them even as it united them – they took pride in keeping themselves to themselves.

Megan was waiting for David and she gave him a hug and a quick affectionate kiss. Early in the morning she had prepared a bouquet of flowers from her garden, and the night before she baked a chocolate cake. She was ready to meet Louise. She'd sent Jake home during school recess to ask if it was convenient to bring a friend. It was.

Louise waited in trepidation. She had no idea what lay behind Megan's visit; vague suspicions, yes, but the whys and wherefores were unknown. Hester had warned her to be careful. Turbulent anxieties inundated her mind. She hadn't worked out a plan yet; be careful, be careful, she repeatedly warned herself. John Jacob was not home to assist or advise her. She couldn't quite decide whether that was a good or bad thing. Louise and her children watched Megan and David emerge from the vehicle – the moment Gladdie saw his wooden walking stick, she rushed away and hid in her closet.

The introductions were made and the excuse given that David had heard how well Gladdie played the piano and wanted to meet her and her family.

'What I would like to do is make a recording of her playing. I have friends who could perhaps assist her,' said David. Louise was flabbergasted. The Lord had seen fit to afflict this man with blindness. This Mr Talbot had heard about her Gladys and had traveled all this way to come and meet her! Louise felt genuinely sorry that she could not permit him to help Gladys. 'We allow Gladys to play the piano because she can't speak, we made an exception. Our religion strictly forbids frivolity or entertainment of any kind,' she lectured him loudly.

'My hearing,' David interrupted her, 'is no way impaired. I can hear very well.' Louise, somewhat mortified, nevertheless continued in the same vein. 'We do not offend Our Lord. We pray, we give thanks, we give witness to His greatness. We pray for His mercy that He may redeem us, we pray to Him to save us. Through Him, and only through His love and Sacrifice, can we enter His Heaven and the life hereafter. My husband, Brother John Jacob Boardman, baptizes all his parishioners. We are steadfast. Our Lord died for us. How dare we insult Him with entertainment?'

David allowed her to continue and waited for her to run out of examples of what could befall a person who committed entertainment.

'We follow His commandments,' Louise faltered and seemed to bite her wart. She eventually managed to start up again, to Megan's relief, she didn't think a decapitated wart was something she wanted to see.

'Music –' began David, only to be interrupted.

'In this sinful and sinning world we believe that levity in the sight of the Lord...' Louise floundered again. Overly sensitive, she was embarrassed that she had used the word 'sight'. David took full advantage.

'Music means so much to people like me,' he said.

Louise was now at a disadvantage. 'The lame and the halt are especially loved by the Sweet Lord in his merciful loving kindness,' she reassured.

'Yes,' David replied, 'which is one of the reasons that He created music.' Here David allowed a mournful note of melancholy, which Megan thought he did to perfection. 'Did not David of the Bible, he with the same name as me, play a musical instrument when he wrote the psalms? Tell me,' he asked softly, 'tell me about your children.'

Louise gave him the fullest account of Jake's life, including his epilepsy and the cure, that the doctor with the Lord's help had effected. How he did at school, how he helped her around the house, what a good boy he was and how she hoped he would follow his father into the ministry. Jake could hear every word and when he again heard his mother's oft repeated dream he rolled his eyes.

'Tell me about Gladys,' David enquired gently. 'Where does she get her musical talent from?'

'Don't know,' Louise had to admit, 'we've got some good whistlers in the family. Jake can whistle very well. That's allowed,' she told David, 'because the birds whistle.'

'Yes,' agreed David, 'so does the wind.' Megan thought that David was about to get sarcastic.

'It's very thoughtful, very kind of you,' David continued, 'to let Gladdie play, as she, like me, is handicapped.' Megan was breathless with admiration and her opinion of David went up. She knew he didn't regard himself as handicapped.

'Gladys is a happy little girl and I couldn't live without her. We will hold a prayer meeting for you, Mr Talbot,' Louise said emotionally. 'Where are the children?' Megan asked. Before Louise called them, Jake appeared.

'Hi, Jake,' Megan said, introducing him to David, who stuck out his hand to be shaken.

'Where is Gladdie?' Megan asked.

'She won't come now,' Jake said assertively, pointing to David. 'She's in her room. Resting... taking a nap.'

Megan had never seen Gladdie tired; on the contrary, she was even more energetic than most of her peers. Megan was startled and confounded. She'd never heard him lie before.

'Can I take Mrs Burns to see our vegetable patch?' he asked his mother, who assented with a nod of her head. Louise was still afraid to say the wrong thing, so resolutely said nothing as David promoted his cause.

'Although I can't see you, I sense you're compassionate. Although I can't see you, my heart feels that you're a good mother.'

'Yes,' Louise allowed, 'I am. I'm a good mother.'

'In that case,' David said in sympathetic tones, 'you must be very sad that Gladys can't speak. How difficult and painful it must be for you that she can never join in, must always be on the outside looking in.' David pressed on ruthlessly. 'What will it be like when she grows up? What will she do? Will she get married? Will she have children?' Here David sounded dubious.

'Hester says she will talk,' Louise comforted the poor man, whom she felt she could confide in.

'Who's she?' asked David, sotto voce.

'My sister.'

'How does she know?' he asked.

'I don't know; but if she says it's so, it's so.'

David disguised his excitement. 'Do they spend a lot of time together?' he murmured, barely asking, barely breathing.

'After I lost my last baby – Jake is the only one who has lived longer than a year – Hester gave Gladys to me. It was the right thing to do. It was her Baptist duty that she followed, although Hester didn't know that that was what she was following. Don't get me wrong – Hessie's a good person, even if she isn't a proper Baptist. She won't go to church. I didn't have to argue with her about our mother's tombstone. In the beginning she didn't want one, but now it's all arranged.' Louise felt she could talk to this man, who couldn't see her, forever.

'Do they spend time together?' David insisted quietly.

'Not a lot. It's quite far away.'

'Kentucky has built many new roads. Doesn't that make it easier?'

'Roads,' hissed Louise. David didn't respond, startled by her tone. Suspicion flew through her and she began hyperventilating. Why did he ask about roads – did he know anything? 'Roads,' she moaned.

'They built roads so that more children could go to school, people could get to work, or get to a hospital in a hurry if they needed to.' David sought to mollify her, wondering if something in her religion prohibited the building of roads.

'They are a necessity. I'm thankful that they did, otherwise I wouldn't have met you,' he added, his voice kind and friendly. 'Your sister sounds like a nice person,' he calmly prompted. He doesn't know anything, Louise thought and relaxed. Nobody does.'

'Hester is my closest friend. I respect her more than anyone I know. She was the brave one and I was the coward. She took all the punishment, because she knew that I could not bear it. The Good Lord gives burdens to those who can carry them. Hester carried mine for me.'

Out in the garden Jake showed Megan the vegetable patch. Megan couldn't contain herself another second.

'Where is Gladdie?'

'She's hiding in the closet in her bedroom.'

'Is she afraid of blind people?'

Jake laughed. 'She's not afraid of people,' and he added, in an embarrassed way, 'It's the walking stick. She's afraid of walking sticks. Don't ask me why, I don't know.'

It was Megan's turn to be astonished.

'I want to see her,' she said wretchedly. She wanted to get the little girl out of the closet. Jake could see how unhappy she was. 'If you take the walking stick back to the car and put it in the trunk and lock it, I'll tell Gladdie, and maybe then she'll come out'.

They re-entered the house.

'David,' Megan whispered urgently, 'may I have your stick?' and not waiting for an answer she whisked it away.

David felt naked. Up until that moment he hadn't realized just how much he needed it. Louise saw how disturbed he was, although she had no idea why. 'I'll fetch you some fresh coffee and cookies.' She left him to go into the kitchen. What was Megan thinking of, he fumed to himself, sitting in the dark, feeling helpless.

Gladdie lay with her body clenched, her knuckles pressed hurtfully against her lips and her eyes tightly shut, sharing a far blacker shade of darkness. David heard Megan and the boy returning, heard the large woman's body brushing against the furnishings, heard the kettle half smothering the sound of her heavy breathing, and he asked himself what he was doing here. He felt a surge of fury against himself for being a sentimental fool, a sentimental blind fool. His anger fatigued him and he heard the boy say: 'The stick is locked in the trunk. You can't see it. Nothing to be afraid of.'

He heard Louise's click of vexation. 'She'll grow out of it.'

'You can come out now,' the boy said. Louise loaded the tray as the smell of cheap coffee wafted across the drained man. He heard the boy again say in dulcet tones, 'You can come out now.'

Then he heard Megan, as the closet door opened: 'My sweet little Gladdie!' she exclaimed, as Louise added another mug to the tray and carried it in.

'She'll grow out of it', Louise repeated.

David sat there so silently, so still. Megan and the two children came in, the girl pulling her hat on more firmly. Megan sat next to David and held his hand. He looked haunted. 'I'm late,' he explained, indicating his Braille wristwatch. Louise added extra milk to his coffee to cool it down; somehow the big woman's presence prevailed and David drank the loathsome milky coffee. He again pointed to his wristwatch, and as they took their leave he mumbled, 'I'm very pleased to have met you, and I hope to meet your sister someday soon. I'm sure she is as hospitable as you are.' He extended his hand, and was surprised when an unfamiliar little hand took his.

'Gladdie?' he asked, and heard the boy answer, 'Yes. Thank you for coming.'

When Louise took his hand she put something in it. It felt like a chocolate wrapped in foil.

'Thank you,' he said.

Louise, he thought, smelt ripe, like game that had been hung. Venison, he thought. Megan led him back to his car, and as he sat down in the coldest tone he could summon up he began to say,

'And now I –' only to be cut short by an even more determined Megan: 'Later,' she said.

'I'm sure your pupils don't cause you any problems,' he said, as the car pulled off, in what he hoped was not too sarcastic a tone. He didn't want her to know how much he needed his stick, how defenseless he felt without it.

After a while he could hear Megan breathing rapidly and then he heard the first sob. What, he once more asked himself, what am I doing here? He heard another sob as Megan struggled to gain control. Why am I here? How did I let myself in for this?

'You can stop here,' Megan said, tapping the driver's shoulder. 'Please fetch Mr Talbot's stick.'

She breathed in deeply and slowly.

'Gladdie is afraid of walking sticks, petrified of them. She was curled up in terror in a closet. Perhaps she had been beaten.'

'Louise told me that Gladdie is her sister Hester's child.' David produced his bit of news. They pooled the information they had assembled. Recalling the feeling of the little girl's hand in his own, knowing of her terror and part of her story, David too felt himself caught up in the hunt to find out more. He told himself that being a sentimental fool wasn't the worst thing to be. Find out, and with the cause of her voicelessness exposed, explained and understood, he felt certain the power of speech would return to the child.

CHAPTER EIGHTEEN

•

Hester felt awkward and shy about going in to choose the dresses for Jewel's wedding. These were unfamiliar and unwelcome reactions. She reminded herself she had ripped her father's walking stick from his vulture claw and beaten him almost to death. When he lay unconscious she had moved his arms to systematically break his ribs. She broke his right hand. She wanted him to remember never to rape any child again. He had almost succeeded with Jewel. And when he forgot his savage beating and raped her Gladdie, she killed him. Put him down like a rabid dog. She felt no guilt, only regret.

Hester was furious with herself for being afraid of entering a shop. She thought she'd go down into town after she finished some tasks but then decided to leave immediately because she knew she was procrastinating. On her way down she bathed in the creek drying herself with her shirt. Instinctively she wore the clothes that the nurse had given her that day she took the children to the emergency centre. On her feet she wore ancient sneakers.

She stalked into the dress shop, hoping that her brother-in-law John Jacob didn't see her attire. The shop assistant was a young woman with several earrings in each ear. Hester was thankful that her girls didn't do that.

'I've come to look for a dress for my daughter's wedding.' As she said this a curtain opened at the back of the shop and a woman with pink hair came forward.

'Can I help you?'

Hester felt outnumbered. 'My older girl is getting married,' she explained again.

'How nice for you. Formal or informal?' Hester looked at her blankly.

'Day or night?' offered the Earrings.

'Cocktail-wear or day-wear?' continued Pink Hair.

'We haven't worked out what time yet,' Hester hedged and added, 'I want it to have flowers on it.'

'Ah,' said Pink Hair, 'a print. I think I have just the right thing for the mother of the bride,' she gushed, and with an imperious sweep of her head made it known to Earrings that she would handle this one.

Hester was near the doorway, like some wild animal near an escape hatch. 'What size are you?' enquired Pink Hair. Hester offered no reply. 'You're an eight of course,' Pink Hair answered herself. 'Your size is over here,' she pointed.

Hester saw the one she wanted in a trice. Pink Hair pulled out three dresses, one with small sprigs of flowers, one with oversized roses and one with small daisies embroidered along the yoke. They were garnished with frills.

'Come and try these on in the fitting room,' Pink Hair urged her.

'This one too,' Hester said, lightly touching it. It was a verdant green dress with leaves scalloping the neckline. She went into the fitting room to try them on. She took off her clothes.

'You're lucky to have such a slim figure,' Pink Hair said from behind the fitting room curtain.

'Are you ready?' she asked.

'Yes,' Hester said. Pink Hair was disgusted when she saw Hester standing there naked.

'I depend on you to tell me which is best,' Hester said. The woman averted her gaze and handed Hester the dresses. She tried one on and walked out.

'What about this?' Hester asked. Never in all her years, Pink Hair indignantly told herself, never had she had a customer like this to deal with.

She pulled herself together. 'Looks pretty,' she said.

'But you'll tell me, won't you?' Hester pleaded.

'Oh yes. Pretty.'

Hester could not imagine what had shocked Pink Hair. One by one she tried them on, leaving the best till last, the green forest one. Hester had to admit as she looked in the mirror that she looked good.

'What do you think of this one?' she asked, although she already knew.

'Oh yes. Pretty.'

'I'll be bringing my daughter in,' she told Pink Hair.

'Does she also go without underclothes?' Pink Hair asked in scandalised tones. That's why, Hester thought, and couldn't help smiling at Pink Hair.

'Only when it's hot, 'less it's her time of the month,' Hester said. Pink Hair looked upset and Earrings could not muffle her laughter any longer; eruptions could be heard as Earrings dashed out the back of the shop. That, combined with Pink Hair's reaction, made Hester flush with humiliation.

'This,' she appealed to Pink Hair, 'this is my first daughter to get married.' She looked at her reflection in the mirror and it renewed her confidence. 'This is the one.' Then she remembered to ask about the price of the dress. Pink Hair's sanctimonious repugnance for the hillbilly was overcome by a rare feeling of compassion. She remembered her grandmother came from the mountains. And Hester's eyes reminded her of a favorite tomcat she'd had to put down. She wanted to get rid of old stock anyway.

'Twenty-seven dollars,' she said.

Hester felt her blood drain away as she pulled the dress off and quietly handed it back to Pink Hair. Her nude body disappeared into the dressing-room. 'I can take the price down for you,' Pink Hair cajoled.

Hester felt cornered.

'We're the same size, my girl and me, I like the one with the little flowers on it.'

'With the sprigs,' Pink Hair corrected.

'With the sprigs,' the defeated Hester echoed, her voice hollow. 'How,' she began to ask, 'how mu...'

'It is twenty-seven dollars too, but I can lower the price for you.'

'To what?' Hester asked.

'To seventeen dollars apiece. They're on my sale.' Pink Hair surprised herself with her own generosity. Although she would still make a profit, it wasn't the usual way she did things.

'We might have enough,' Hester said, 'for the one with the sprigs. Hold it for me and we'll get back to you.'

As Hester was leaving, Pink Hair felt obliged to tell her that she would require new shoes.

'Also,' she continued remorselessly, 'you must wear underclothes for the wedding. A woman must wear a brassiere,' she added forcefully.

Pink Hair felt that she had performed her Christian duty to help the poor woman. Hester fled.

Since she was in town, she elected to get everything done. Altogether too many people were making enquiries about her. She had to go and work it out with Louise. She went into the hardware store.

'Tell Louise that I'm ready when she is,' she told her brother-in-law, who was outraged by Hester's dress and bemused by her message.

She looked in at the fire station to make up her mind about the wedding party and saw there would be plenty of room if they drove the two fire engines out. One was an old, seldom-used model; it was kept in good condition, the firemen were sentimental about it. The open plot beside the building was attractive, lined with hackberries, black locusts and tulip trees.

'Mrs Howard,' one of the men enquired, 'wouldn't you like to say hi to Curt on our short-wave?'

'If you want me to,' she said, shrugging her shoulders.

They located him and Curt's eager voice crackled onto the line. 'It's me,' Hester said. 'I've been to a dress store.'

'What? What?!' a clearly astounded Curt shouted.

'A dress store,' she said, her voice dull. 'The dresses cost seventeen dollars each, but I don't have one; only Jewel wants me to.'

Curt was taken aback because Hester sounded a bit tearful.

'We can make it,' he said firmly. 'We've got money. Now –' meaning now that he was no longer drinking, meaning he was deeply sad for all the years of affliction and deprivation. He was saving up to buy a generator to ease the lot of his family's life. He had succeeded in repaying most of his financial debts. Alcoholism had cost his family too much: he fought against being flooded by bitter heartbreak; he must never allow himself to lose his footing, no matter how strong the tide.

'Thank God,' he quietly told Hester.

She couldn't utter a word. He had told her that he had found God through AA. Hester didn't know how, or even ask. She felt gratitude because this had helped her family. It was not the kind of religion that Louise had found and she was grateful for that too. The line hissed and splintered.

'You can buy both dresses,' he assured her. 'This is our Jewel's wedding and it is gonna be great,' he told her. 'The fire station will be great, won't it? You'll see, Hester, we'll have a high ole' time.'

Hester roused herself apathetically. 'Thank you Curt,' she said, and disconnected.

She waved to the men and ascended the mountain. She took off the sneakers and held them, walking back up the mountain, the earth beneath her feet restored her to herself. She glimpsed a flying squirrel and her spirit flew anew. She was back in her element and laughed raucously at herself. She felt like dancing; she sang wordless songs, she patted tree trunks, branches, caressed leaves as though she had been long gone from them.

She rejoiced in herself, in her mountain, the mountain to which she belonged and yet was uniquely hers. No one owns land, Hester knew; it belongs to itself.

The vegetation constantly growing or decaying had long ago been decoded by Hester. Death and life co-mingled as crows' feet, forest mushrooms and other life forms grew, nourished by whatever was decomposing. Hester's fearlessness grew directly from her knowledge about death and its value. She knew that some day it would be the lover she had never known. A trace of the shame she felt when she'd been humiliated by the store assistants intruded into her profound sense of oneness. Don't be a fool, girl! she castigated herself. You've never bought ready-made dresses in your life. Her mother appeared before her and she heard her mother say that she, Hester, had done well. That she was the bravest of her children and that she was proud of her; and then she vanished. Hester was calmed by the apparition and wished she'd stayed longer, had told her more. But then her mother had always been frugal with words. If only she had heard her mother laugh, just once. Just once. Her smiles had been rare and radiant. Hester fancied that her mother's laughter would have sounded like Gladdie's piano-playing.

'Jewel, Jewel,' she called out even before she got home. 'I've found you a dress and, oh Jewel, you will be the most beautiful bride I ever saw,' she cried triumphantly.

Hester considered men to be an entirely different species. Even as her own sons grew up, she realized that the two sexes were as different as bluebirds and groundhogs. She tried to teach them right, but felt from the outset that her efforts were wasted. She thought that, as members of the breed, her sons and even, in his way, her husband, were better than most but still it was foolishness to trust them. She knew why Tom Burns wanted her daughter, but why did the skinny woman's man, whose name she didn't know, why did he want her too? And they wanted her badly. They were offering a church for her, a bribe they knew Louise couldn't resist. Idly she wondered if the two couples knew about each other's schemes. She thought not. She was intrigued that Megan had craftily brought a blind man to weasel things out of Louise. She saw that people might think Louise silly because of her religion, and slow because of her size, and obstinate because of her ways. Hester understood that for Louise, religion was a sacred haven, that she ate because she thought she was hungry, and that she was tenaciously vigilant because of her fears. Hester understood that her sister could not change because, as long as she lived or whatever she did, she could never forget. Even, Hester sadly reflected, even now that the reason for her hunger and fears no longer existed, her remembrance of the feelings was too powerful to be erased. They were corrosively etched into her being, relentlessly her memory outlawed forgetfulness.

Louise knew the outsiders found Hester frightening, strange and unpredictable, but she knew her sister was strong, dependable and deeply kind. She had tried to explain to Hester the joy, peace and exalted glory that being a hard–shell Baptist gave her. Tried to explain that it cleaned her; made her shine, but to no avail. Hester just grinned at her, as though to placate a child boasting about an imaginary good deed. She was saddened that she couldn't share this blessing with her sister. She had longed for Hester to feel the light, the pure white light, as she did when the Spirit entered her. Once she'd dashed outside to search the heavens at night to look for a space without stars, she felt as though a gigantic pitcher had poured stars down into her. She had felt herself shining.

CHAPTER NINETEEN

•

After the party and subsequent revelations, Abigail and Roberto experienced a surprising shyness. He had tried to bury his pain. Now her knowledge of his long-hidden agony bonded them. Eventually, she broached the subject. There were two priorities. Firstly, there was Gladdie and their need to play a more important role in her life, to feel significant to her. The second imperative was understood but unspoken.

They had to make it known, in some delicate yet definitive way, that Roberto's wife had died, but it was essential that the date and place of the joint funeral of mother and stillborn daughter be kept unsaid. Their conviction was absolute that Roberto's associates, acquaintances and friends, except for the very few who already knew the awful truth and who would corroborate the version of events which they chose to reveal, were incapable of understanding his long silence. In all likelihood, even if they did not mock him openly, they would think him ridiculous, would laugh at him. Abigail wanted to spare Roberto further anguish. She knew that in the telling had come some healing and was determined that he retain every precious drop of this elixir.

But first the question of Gladdie. She telephoned Megan, who answered the phone, amazed that it was Abigail, whom she had been just about to call.

'It's telepathy,' she exclaimed.

'I have vital information about Gladdie,' announced Abigail importantly.

'Me too.'

'Me first,' countered Abigail.

She related the story about putting the wig on Gladdie's head, how she had torn it off and how happy she'd been made by the haircut.

'You cut her hair?' Megan sounded alarmed. 'Louise Boardman doesn't allow that.'

'That's exactly what Roberto predicted. Don't you think it's a breakthrough?'

'I have something to tell you too,' Megan replied, and she described how terrified the child was of walking sticks. 'Walking sticks and wigs. She doesn't like long hair and walking sticks.'

The unbearable conclusion, they agreed, could only be that someone must have beaten the child badly.

'Louise told our friend David Talbot, a certified attorney, that Gladdie is her sister's child. We knew that, but he's convinced that if I hadn't come into the room when I did she would have told him her sister's whereabouts,' Megan reported, both triumphant and chagrined.

'Louise is going to tell me anyway.'

For a moment, antagonistic rivalry sizzled down the line, to their mutual astonishment. Then they both consciously switched emotional gears and chose to be charming to one another.

'That is most promising,' Abigail said. 'I will tell Derwent Fox, who is an expert investigator. Roberto picked him to discover the identity of Gladdie's parents.' Megan could not bring herself to tell Abigail that her own beloved Thomas was the father. They ended the conversation agreeing how helpful it was to share information, even if at present it didn't really elucidate matters. But it was now becoming impossible to ignore or hide from the dark possibilities of what had happened to Gladdie. Tom couldn't bear to think about it.

When Abigail telephoned Roberto, ostensibly only about the news concerning Gladdie, she also suggested to him that he leave things to her. Roberto nervously said he would, and knew what she was referring to.

'Have faith in me. Trust me.'

'I do', he replied gravely. Abigail would see to it that Eve's death would no longer be kept secret. Eve could rest in peace. Finally.

While he was calling Derwent Fox, Abigail was calling a close friend of the social columnist Ben Bellamy, who conveniently, as it turned out for Abigail, had been unwell and unable to attend the party. She telephoned him allegedly to find out how he was. He was touched by the call, yet another example of how caring Abigail really was, hard as it was for others to believe. He had no idea that her call was a pretext. They chatted about the party, the guests and the Seamen's Rescue Mission. Somehow he found himself agreeing that of course, he knew that Roberto Albuquerque was a widower of several years.

As expected, her own tame society columnist telephoned her to tell her of the proposed contents of her column about the party. She too was obliquely reminded that Roberto's wife had mercifully died some time ago. Abigail had only one more call to make, to a very good friend who had flown down, together with her miniature schnauzer, hairdresser and general entourage, for the spring ball. Mrs. Newton Ball-Green was beyond reproach and a doyenne of New York and Washington society. She held several honorary doctorates. She was on all the right cultural boards and made the necessary substantial donations. Several hospitals nationwide were recipients of her unstinting philanthropy. Whenever Abigail received a request from one or other of this woman's foundations, she gave her standard ten thousand dollars. Newtie, as Abigail called her, after first admitting that she had forgotten, remembered that Roberto's wife had died some time ago. She thought she'd even been to the funeral. She was going to check with her friend, a famous society columnist. There was nothing further Abigail needed to do.

When Roberto telephoned her the next day, Abigail told him that if ever he wanted her to accompany him to place flowers on the sacred graves, she would come with him.

'Violets, I thought,' she said reticently. 'You can take them and I'll wait for you in the car, if you like.'

They both knew that he would never take her, but he understood her meaning and said that Eve had liked violets. He thanked Abigail. He hung up and put his head in his hands.

'Rest in peace,' he told her. 'I'm so sorry I disturbed your dust for so long. Rest in peace. Rest with your beautiful baby girl. Rest my beloved, rest.'

Roberto felt like crying, he felt like singing. He'd served his time, his self imposed sentence. As he drove to the bank that day he enjoyed the feel of the car, of its wheels hugging the road, enjoyed the power of the engine and its precise steering. To his surprise, he even enjoyed the envious glances at him in his car. He knew he would love Eve and mourn her for the rest of his life, but, for the first time in over a decade, he was vibrantly glad to be alive. And felt neither guilt nor betrayal.

When Megan eventually tracked down the doctor who had dealt with Jake, she found him curiously distant. Dr Jergens remembered Megan the second he saw her. He had broken the law. How could he explain that night to anyone – that he had been terrorized by a mountain woman, and then mysteriously entered into a pact with her? That he further compounded his guilt when he acquiesced to what he imagined was a small girl's imploring gesture? He had deliberately witheld the truth when first he saw Megan. The apparent goodness in bright, blue-eyed and dutiful Megan would have anyway made the telling of the dreadful tale impossible. He enquired after Jake's health and seemed satisfied to hear how well the boy was doing. He had left the clinic, he told the young teacher, because he had become more interested in laboratory work.

'He is so cold,' she later reported to Tom, 'he doesn't like dealing with people. Specimens are more his line.'

The doctor threw no light on the subject of Gladdie's muteness. He appeared uncaring. As Megan left he watched her from his window, well aware of her unconcealed dislike and disappointment. He took a calculated gamble that she wouldn't find it necessary to look for records, she would not have found them, as he had shredded them. He had done his best for the two injured children. From what the caring and conscientious teacher told him, he deduced that although Gladdie couldn't speak she was a happy child. She had forgotten it. He judged it entirely probable that one day she'd become a talkative little chatterbox. When Megan explained about the wig and the walking stick and the probability that she may have been beaten, he smirked at her, indicating that she was taking up his time. This was when she'd turned on her heel, exasperated and disheartened. To Doctor Jergens it was obvious that the man must have had a walking stick and grabbed her by her hair; it was so blatantly obvious. The teacher's naïveté both irritated and comforted him. He sat down at his desk again and stroked it lovingly, so grateful to be away from that place and those people and their distressing suffering. He remembered the whole episode with clarity, but would not permit a momentary lapse to jeopardize his future. He shrugged his lanky frame in an effort to eradicate the entire event and his shrugging body sloughed off the remnants of the compassion that had almost drowned him.

When Louise and Hester met to discuss Gladys, they judged that there was nothing to fear from outsiders. They were of one mind about Megan and Thomas Burns. Hester was not so sure about the thin woman,

Mrs Dunstable, whom she recognized as being the woman she'd seen the time she went down to listen to Gladdie playing the piano, but what she wanted with Gladdie was something Hester expected soon to find out.

Hester's curiosity was boundless and she wanted to see

Benjamin, to see if instinctively Gladdie would be loving towards him because he was her half-brother; so she decided, much to Louise's confusion, to invite Megan to Jewel's wedding. Jewel loved the dress her mother had chosen and was dimly conscious that it had not been a simple task for her to accomplish. The service would be conducted by Brother John Jacob after a civil marriage. The party was to be at the fire station, or, if the weather was clement, the lot beside it. Somehow she and Curt had contrived that all the children had new-looking clothes and shoes, so there was no way that Jewel would be anything but proud of her family. Megan and her husband would add a touch of class and what could be more innocent a time for them to meet the mother of Gladdie?

Astonished, Megan unhesitatingly accepted this unexpected falling away of Hester's evasiveness. Surely that must mean that soon they would be able to add to that meagre little collection of facts about Gladdie; that she was terrified of walking sticks and wigs; that she lived with religious zealots and that she had a happy disposition. And also, of course, that she was a musical prodigy. Megan occasionally took the time to listen to her practicing, which Gladdie did with pleasure and diligence; Megan surprised herself as tears of awe filled her eyes. Francesca went as far as to believe that even the composer of what she was playing would be enthralled. At long last, Megan was to meet Gladdie's birth mother.

Megan telephoned Abigail to share her amazement over the unexpected invitation and to discover as she did so if Abigail and Roberto would be there too. The moment Abigail finished talking to Megan, she telephoned her farm manager to make arrangements to move the barn that was already painted a warm brick red. The church was the price of their ticket to the wedding. All that exercised her mind was whether Roberto had already bought the plot of land where they planned to situate the church. They had to pour the cement soon. Perhaps they had already done so.

CHAPTER TWENTY

·

On the day of Jewel's marriage, Hester took her first-born out into the forest at dawn. Leaves rippled and dimpled like water singing with light in the creek. They had both awakened earlier than usual, Jewel began to feel premonitory snippets of nostalgia. Intermittently, throughout her life, she would long for the mountain and the shack where she was raised, the shack which was as humble as the mountain was magnificent. There was no polarization as the shack belonged on the mountain, and when it disintegrated it would be of the mountain. This morning volatile, disturbing emotions shook her; she was stepping into the unknowable and the path was perilous and invisible. Hester half-expected her daughter to be overwrought.

Skimmed milky light slanted through the leaves and, smiling, Hester walked her fingers through the shafts to her daughter; Jewel skipped her fingers as though up a staircase. They smiled deeply at one another. Hester wanted to say something momentous, give sensible advice, protect her first-born from inevitable suffering, yet she knew that whatever she said would have no effect on her child's fate. Still, she made an attempt.

'Don't trouble yourself about us, we'll be OK,' she reassured. 'Visit us when you can. Don't let him beat you. If he does, don't wait for a second time. Call your brothers and they'll thrash him raw. Then come home. Don't go back – this is still your home. It always will be.'

Hester put her arms about her and stroked her hair with tenderness, as she had done when her daughter was small. Jewel half wished to stay in her mother's embrace forever. Holding her, Hester found herself once again startled by the power of her love for her children.

Jewel and Davis planned on living with his sister Patti Jo, who had a spare room available on the outskirts of town. The chief route for young people from the mountains was to apply for a job in the healthcare field. There were several education outreach programs and Patti Jo had seized the opportunity. Many hillbillies came from large loving families and were familiar with caring for the aged, infirm or handicapped. It was natural for them to give assistance to those who need it.

Brother John Jacob Boardman was in a froth of exhilaration as he prepared to perform the first marriage in his church. He fussed about. The chairs didn't arrive on time and so they borrowed bales of hay to serve as pews. Hester's children cut branches of pine, juniper and hemlock and decorated the aisle. John Jacob was particularly proud of the fine lectern that would serve as his pulpit. He considered his House of Worship pleasing in the eyes of the Lord. The only real disappointment was that, once again, Curt Howard had quietly told him that there was to be no sermonizing, just the service and a brief blessing. He knew Curt was passing on his wife's instructions. How dare Hester interfere with his first marriage service? After all, the benefactors, Mrs Abigail Dunstable and Mr Roberto Albuquerque, would be coming. The school teacher Megan Burns and her husband Tom would be there. They had never attended one of his prayer meetings or, he piously suspected, any properly devout Baptist service before. They had never been to a hard shell Baptist prayer meeting, he was certain of that! It was a golden opportunity for converts, a golden opportunity being denied him. He thought it wicked of Hester, but he quailed at the idea of disobeying her. Yet, he argued with himself, who was Hester – a mere woman, his wife's sister – to tell him what to do? He was, after all, a sixty-four-year-old preacher. He stood waiting, his over-starched collar reminding him of his importance and of how he loved his Saviour and how his wife loved him. Suffused and bolstered by these loves, he heard footsteps as those who had congregated for the wedding entered his church.

He scarcely recognized his niece. Jewel was like one of those fancy-looking girls who drove by the hardware store. Curt looked handsome and proud as his daughter walked beside him. Jewel's young man, Davis, took her father's place. There was a radiance about the family; the sun shone through a skylight directly upon the group. There were, John Jacob noted, several elegant ladies. He recognized the teacher and the thin lady who had donated the church. He was bedazzled by the illustrious gathering and found it impossible to give up the divine opportunity of making a sermon. He began in a harsh stentorian voice exhorting his captive congregation to love the Lord. Between deep, hasty breaths he blasted out the truths of the Saviour, the Evils that could befall those who did not obey, the Sins of Alcohol, the Flesh, Tobacco and not attending to Prayer, which pleased the Devil.

He was in the midst of explaining the pathway to the Devil when he could not resist looking closely at a stylish lady in a green dress. He gaped when he recognized Hester and her mocking eyes locked with his. He left the Devil dangling and performed a brief marriage service as he'd been told. He pronounced them man and wife and added a flourish that, inasmuch as the young couple were now united in marriage, they too were united with the Lord. He blessed the couple, telling them that they were exalted because they were the first couple to be married there.

Everyone filed out. The spare old and well-kept fire truck was awaiting the bridal couple, and all those of their family who could squeeze onto the balloon-festooned fire-eating chariot went along for the ride. In a flurry of noisy excitement they arrived at the fire station. Disused halves of sorghum drums had been converted into barbecue pits. A feast awaited the guests. Hamburgers, steaks, macaroni, cucumber, potato and tomato salad welcomed the guests. The dessert was jam cakes.

Roberto and Abigail raced after the fire truck, illogically afraid of losing the wedding party, without exactly knowing what they yearned for or what to expect. Roiling dust devils trailed the fire truck, powdering away the Ferrari's shine. They tunneled through greenness; impudent leaves fingered the Ferrari as it sped along the dirt road, spitting gravel. Their faces flickered with mottled shadows and they were cosseted by the smell of sun-warmed leather. An expensive smell. The fire truck roared and clanged ahead, strung with laughing faces. Abigail and Roberto felt outsiders. The way they dressed and spoke was different, there was this uneasy sensation of wanting to be part of a group they normally looked down on – if they thought about it at all. Abigail observed miniscule indentations on the palms of her hands. She thought she must have pressed too hard on the bales of hay. She was still tense.

'The Preacher –' she began.

'– will become an entertaining conversation piece,' he chuckled.

'Won't people be curious why we were there?'

'Because you, my velvet-eyed one, donated a church.'

'How very good of me,' she said dryly.

'There wasn't a need for a church. John Jacob's voice can blast through concrete pilings.'

'Well done! You expedited the plot of land with ease and skill and speed,' Abigail congratulated him again, smiling to herself, well-knowing what kind of currency Roberto had employed. They arrived and sat waiting in their car, not wanting to be the first to get to the celebration, and needing time to assess the party and work out how they would fit in.

'The bride and her mother are uncommonly good looking. Except for Gladdie's colouring, it's easy to see where her beauty springs from,' Abigail said.

'They're a good-looking family, with those high cheekbones and dark eyes,' he agreed. They watched two mallards crossing the road. They almost missed a purple finch. A green lunar moth landed on their windscreen for an instant of breathless beauty. He saw it, she didn't.

'The mother is somehow more groomed than I anticipated,' Abigail commented. 'Her bearing is regal, mesmerizing. I have seen her before. She is the wild woman who walked into the remarkable little concert I told you about. Her eyes are eagle's eyes. She unnerves me.'

He took her hand in his hands, unsure what to say to her, aware that if there was battle to be done for Gladdie, it would be between Abigail and Hester. He depended on her. Curt would be easy; he would make him his ally. They wanted to be certain that they would have ready access to give the child whatever opportunities they deemed appropriate.

The party was in full swing. Potent homebrewed moonshine had been provided by one of Curt's friends and Clay's wife brought blackberry wine. After all, what was a party without a drink? Curt could only agree but not partake. Oh no, not partake. Ever. He sweated a little. The Boardmans had considered it unnecessary to ban alcohol; they had assumed there wouldn't be any, John Jacob sniffed reproachfully and his joints fused in fury. Louise pretended not to notice. At least Hester had allowed a conventional church wedding. She had been worried that her unpredictable sister wouldn't want one, oblivious that Hester did what pleased her child. Hester had no quarrel with any church; it simply wasn't her way.

Megan watched Hester as a predator watches her prey. Her protective maternal instincts kindled red orange. Her body pointed like a gun dog. This woman had conceived Gladdie without any difficulty. Accidentally! She had used Thomas as an unwitting donor. She wasn't worthy of Gladdie; that casual coupling meant nothing to her. Thomas was a victim of this heartless savage, who, registering Megan's laser-beam stare, sauntered up offering her a hamburger. Megan, who had so much to say, could only nod her head and clench her fists. The woman put her hand on Megan's arm, as though to steady a frightened beast. She tried to shake it off, but Hester tightened her touch to a grip. Megan's rage heightened, but looking into Hester's face she saw on it an expression of gentle compassion, at odds with the strong fingers digging into her arm.

'If my Thomas is Gladdie's father then he has a right to his daughter,' she was horrified to hear herself say.

As though Hester hadn't heard, she slowly loosened her grip, which long afterwards Megan could still feel. Days later when she looked at her forearm she half expected to see those strong brown fingers gripping it. Hester strolled away, talking to other guests between bites of her hamburger. A finely-webbed veil wove itself over Megan's vision and comprehension. She couldn't let Thomas and Benjy down, and attempted to compose herself.

She went on automatic pilot when some deep-rooted assumption in her was attacked. Never assume, her father had taught her. She had come to meet a woman who repulsed and disturbed her, but whose daughter she wanted for herself. For her own family. She totted up all she had to give Gladdie, she could make sure Gladdie could continue with her music. She had studied psychology and a bit of anthropology and she was, she knew, a gifted teacher. She was even aware that too much knowledge became excess baggage! She knew that she taught with an intuitive heart. And now that same intuitive heart was perceiving that Hester might possess qualities and gifts as yet unexplored by herself. She began to waver in her enmity, almost collapse. Then she roused herself, remembering that without her encouragement Gladdie would not have been able to develop her musical talent. She had stopped hoping that she could restore Gladdie's speech. Music was her voice. And she could help this voice to be heard in concert halls the world over. She could rescue the child from those religious fanatics, it would all work out well.

Roberto befriended the broad-shouldered Curt. Abigail never left his side. They were viewed as a couple and this eased them into what was something of a social ordeal; although both prided themselves that they could mix with anybody from a duchess to a dustman, they laughed about it. Unused as they were to bribing their way in, they had wangled their invitation from a gushing Louise. Their discomfort was suavely veiled by their need to help the little girl – to become, at the very least, Gladdie's patrons. Money could move mountains. Why, it had cut the very road they drove on through the mountains. They had no qualms about the many things money could do; they saw no reason why theirs should not purchase Gladdie.

The child couldn't express herself verbally, so they took it upon themselves to decide what was best for her. Abigail and Roberto's needs, fantasies and wishes became unrestrained. Abigail imagined herself with a young charge, which would make her younger. Gladdie was to be the child she had, the one that she and Roberto would bring up together. If Gladdie didn't quite make it as a pianist, she would to send her to Barnards to study whatever she wished. But of course it would first be discussed with Roberto.

Abigail scrutinized Hester from those observant corners of the eye, while Roberto told Curt how much they could do to assist Gladdie's music and probably help her to talk again. Curt was willing to do whatever was in his daughter's interests. It was plain that these people had money and it was possible that, through them, there could be work for at least one of his children. Maybe, he hoped, a job for more than one.

Roberto saw himself applauding her at concerts, and felt how proud he would be. He visualized himself being dragged off to stores. But willingly. Willingly. To choose her clothes. He saw himself reading bedtime stories, not too much TV. He would tuck her in at night and she would smell of the soap and shampoo that he would buy for her. He wondered what he should buy for her first car, nothing too flashy, he would impart all the love a sensitive yet quietly firm father should.

Megan was determined to bring out all Gladdie's brilliance. All that exceptional ability she showed right from the start. She could wear her hair anyway she chose. Megan would make absolutely certain that she had the greatest possible music teachers. She would support her individuality. She, together with Thomas, would help her live by a well-developed ethical code. By example – it could only be done by example. And Benjy would have a sister and they would have a daughter. Her family would be complete, they would be a foursome. She never doubted the justness of their cause and Jake could visit whenever he wanted.

Tom put it down to destiny. Gladdie was his daughter and should be with him, not that preacher nutcase. She should be snug as a bug in her own home. His wife was her teacher; was it coincidence or fate that events transpired to bring his beautiful daughter back to him, where she belonged? Why, his own mother, her grandmother, gave her piano lessons. She would be with her own loving family, who would make sure that she had everything of the best. He tried to put Hester out of his mind, she was the black cloud that spat lightening, that same vivid crackling re-ignited his erotic first lovemaking experience. Then he couldn't help remembering her body, dappled in shadows, lying on pine needles. He thought of that indelible sex whenever he walked on drifts of fallen brown pine needles, though he quickly stamped out that unwanted memory. He would redecorate a room for Gladdie with Megan. He dreamt about colours, fabrics and where to put a piano. He would read to her, then tuck her in and give her a goodnight kiss.

Louise's belief in the Lord was validated even further. God gave her Gladys. He was rewarding her because He knew that she deserved to be rewarded. He took her other little flowers because He only took the best. Gladys was the just replacement who would be brought up fearing and loving the Lord. She would be good and kind, learn to help folks in need. Louise couldn't think of a better or more secure way of life than that of a hard-shell Baptist. Perhaps Gladys would someday know the same ecstasy as she had. But more important than anything else – she would be welcomed into Heaven! What joy and peace for Louise never to have to worry. Gladys would have a Place, a very good Place in the Hereafter.

John Jacob was gratified that Louise had someone to help with the household chores and that Jake had someone to play with. Taking her in demonstrated what a good preacher he was.

Abigail could tell Curt was a pushover. Unconsciously she took in a deep breath and thought to introduce herself to Hester.

CHAPTER TWENTY-ONE

•

It was at this moment that a hush descended on the guests. Suddenly Hester began dancing with Jewel. Their arms waved as though gracefully pushing away unseen clouds, their bodies swayed and undulated. They were as supple as billowing willows. Hester tapped her foot and, as though rehearsed, they raised their knees and brought their right foot and arms down and then their left foot. The beat quickened. Their bodies whipped like young trees before a storming wind.

The two women danced in silence. Gladdie very briefly played an imaginary piano before curtseying deeply, gracefully extending her arms in invitation, then joining in. Abigail's body answered before she was aware of it and swooped into an unchoreographed invocation to propitiate long-forgotten gods. Megan, feeling Hester's bright gaze upon her for an instant, as if hypnotized, seamlessly linked in. All the women were dancing in a daze of the most intimate rapture. It was something of a sensual waltz, somewhat sexual as their bodies weaved through atavistic rhythms. Hips swinging defiantly, flinging all inhibition to the wind. They pointed their toes, came down on their heels; their bodies shimmied, twisted, twirled, limbered – smooth and entirely at one in this passionate lyrical dance. They clapped their hands, slapped their thighs and snapped their fingers. Their steps and moves flowed, carrying them further. Unheard drums throbbed through unknowable time. The women danced, gyrating, to a pulsating tempo, stretching their arms as though to touch the sky; then describing melodic arcs, fluttering their fingers, they drew to a close and the watchers heard their lilting laughter. How long this dance lasted no one could remember. It had been mesmerizing.

The men had wordlessly been excluded. They neither noticed nor cared. They had been surprised, then shocked because although the dance hadn't been explicitly sexual and there had been no invitation, several men perceived an unexpected reply in their loins. Not one man moved. They had become like a frieze on a shard of ancient pottery. During those frozen moments it felt as if they had been denied oxygen. They breathed in great gulps of air. Some felt as if they had just engaged in high-voltage sex. There were others who suddenly remembered

143

how they had felt when they had just been baptized. There were those who felt both sensations. The men had been conscious of their blood as the women's energy flooded into them, for once and for a brief time they had become one organism, heart one heart, body one body. Then, with the women's laughter, they were back in normal life.

Spontaneity bestows inalienable truth. The bride and her little sister plucked flowers from the bouquet, presenting with smiling dignity a flower to each of the dancers. Jewel gave one to her stunned mother-in-law. Abigail gave hers to Roberto; putting the stem in his hand, she enclosed his hand in hers. The group had been spellbound and now found themselves a tad embarrassed, covering up with overly loud laughter. The Boardmans didn't know how to react because both of them had noticed that Louise too had swayed, had rhythmically moved her body. Had in fact danced. There had been nothing the ear could hear, yet there was no doubt that all the women present had heard Hester's music and their bodies answered it.

'Ah,' said Curt aloud. His heart sung. When Hessie danced there was magic afoot. She dances so seldom, my Hessie. The other woman all followed my girls. My wife. My beautiful Hester. She commands – they obey. Then he sighed to himself, if only she danced more often. So beautiful it was, hauntingly beautiful. He was so proud that his three beloved friends from the AA had seen his wonderful wife – and witnessed her dancing. They had only just met his family, as there had never been an occasion before. Then he smiled widely. What, he wondered, would the Boardmans think?

Later, Megan tried to explain what had happened, as much to herself as to Thomas. 'Possibly I could hear my pulse throbbing. Perhaps we were all in tune. Perhaps our hearts all beat as one.' She sensed that they had all been swept back in time – yet her intellect insisted that she didn't believe in any of that. She was baffled and afraid. 'She is a force of nature, as you warned me.'

The woman she wanted, needed, to regard as an enemy had enfolded her into the beat of her heart. She felt wrong-footed and the active accomplice was herself. She felt that she'd let Thomas down, let Gladdie down. She had entered into an unspoken covenant with Hester. Everything had gone awry, she wept tears of self-recrimination. Tom, unable to comfort what he found incomprehensible, reasoned that Benjamin would accomplish it for him. His son slept all the way home while his bewildered wife cried. At last she regained herself, only to lose it again when Tom told her how beautiful she looked when dancing. He was acutely concerned about the effect Hester had had on Megan. He asked himself if a mountain could subdue a hurricane anymore than a hurricane could subdue a mountain. He kept his sadness to himself.

'I was kind of hypnotized. We all were. Why?' she asked defeatedly, more of herself than Thomas, and sunk her head in her hands.

Driving home, Roberto did not mention the dance to Abigail because he was of the opinion that the sacred should not be diluted by analysis. What he had just witnessed was quite outside of anything he knew of.

•

'Do you think my multi-purpose food mixer a good choice?'
asked Abigail. 'I didn't want my gift to be different from the
rest – newlyweds need practical things. I didn't want anything
too expensive. I tried to choose appropriately...' She prattled
on, discussing the party in detail. 'I sipped a little moonshine
and liked it. Curt drank nothing; he had a hunted look when he
gave it to me. Probably a recovering alcoholic. I could tell he
liked you. Megan didn't take her eyes off Hester. Her behaviour
was odd, unlike her normal self. Tense. She's hiding something.' It was not the first time she had surprised Roberto with
her perceptive observations. Bothered and mystified, she spoke
of everyone except Hester, of everything except the dance.

When finally she quietened down, he said: 'Now that
Gladdie's mother is located we can take all necessary steps. Curt
Howard will be no trouble. I find him sensible to his children's
needs. What a lovely little girl she is.'

'She has her mother's light greenish tawny eyes, but she's the
only one with that deep chestnut hair. The only other person I
saw with that coloring was Tom Burns, Megan's husband.'
Abigail recollected hearing from Megan that Tom had once been
a social worker in the area. Then she remembered how Hester
had walked in on the concert, how Hester's eyes had darted
around the classroom that unforgettable day when Gladdie
played Mozart so brilliantly.

Abigail's eyes slitted, suspicion flaring into and then taking
possession of her. But if she was right then the Burns couple
had an infinitely greater chance than they had. She knew that
unless Hester willed it, they would never even have guardian-
ship of Gladdie. Hester could be as unbending and ruthless as
herself. She was alien, the most mystifying woman Abigail had
ever come across. A small pool of silence developed between
them, into which Abigail dropped a peculiar thought.

'I've an idea that she's a witch – I mean a good witch.' He had
no chance to reply. Abigail rushed on, asking and answering her
own questions. 'Did I dress appropriately? What do you think?
I had nothing to go on. I suppose this was acceptable.' She was
speaking her thoughts out loud rather than talking to him, not
expecting a response. 'Do you suspect that Tom Burns is her

father? I think he is – and that has a decidedly negative impact on our case.' Abigail didn't stop to think about how her remark would affect Roberto.

He was shocked. Until this moment he had not realized how much he had been fantasizing. His self-awareness had shut down. He had thought he had come to terms with the loss of his wife and child. His disappointment at finding that he had been deluding himself in dreaming of being a father to Gladdie cut him to the core. For an instant he doubted Abigail's observation, but instinctively he knew that what she said was the truth, though how she had reached her conclusion he didn't know. He was disgusted to find he had been, as it were, competing for a little human being. He struggled for breath, but his esophagus was blocked by a sob. He sobbed three times; the sobs came from the depth of his bowels.

The immensity of his grief appalled her. He pulled the Ferrari over to the curb, got out, and she slipped behind the wheel to drive. She drove on without a word. Roberto never allowed anyone to drive his car. Strangely, he didn't care that Abigail heard him; he lost all need for pretence, yet he didn't cry again. His body felt fatigued. He hadn't known how positive his iron certitude had been that Gladdie would be a daughter to him. His immeasurable yearning to love and protect her was to be denied. Foolishly he had taken it for granted. Abigail, horrified by his devastating need, was powerless. I can't help him, she panicked. I can't.

She drove fast, straight to her home. He got out of the car as though his entire body ached, as, in truth, it did. His muscles bunched in anguish. She affected not to notice how disabled he had become and strode towards her small private sitting room, stopping to wait for him at the top of the stairs. She poured two stiff bourbons and when he lowered himself into an overstuffed chair she presented him with one. They sat together quietly.

Finally Roberto said wryly, 'I sounded like a Great Dane with indigestion.' They contrived a ragged chuckle. Silently, they acknowledged his grief; nobody can alter the past; his wife and child had died; nothing could ever restore the happiness he once knew. Nothing. Accept the void, he told himself; accept it, accept emptiness.

'Roberto,' said Abigail quietly, 'we must think clearly. Gladdie is more than a symbol of what you so tragically lost. She's a little girl who loves her mother as you loved your wife and child.' Accept the void, he ordered himself. 'Your loss is a vicious irony. So many are born into this world with none to love them.'

Accept, he commanded himself. 'You've done well to survive. We won't get Gladdie. We will do all we can for her, but that must be enough. We can only speculate as to how much the Burns see as their right to the child. Then what about Louise Boardman? My dearest, she too has lost her newborn babes. I begin to see what Hester has done, and why. It is only to Hester, her mother, that the child belongs. Perhaps she can still become our ward. We must be grateful for that.'

Abigail spoke with solemn passion. Feeling the bourbon warming her, she took courage. But in truth, it was the dance that had emboldened her. The dance that bound them all together with its silent music, its sacred moves. She stretched out her arm to Roberto and he took her hand. With supple strength she drew him to his feet and they stood face to face. She stared into his eyes.

'I humbly,' she stumbled, 'offer you my love.' She led him into her bedroom and took off his clothes as though she was his loving nanny. She slipped off her own and they lay together between her silken sheets. She stroked his face and hair and then put her arms about him.

'Sleep, my sweet Roberto, sleep.'

And he did. He fell like a child into a sleep of grace.

In the morning Roberto woke. He could see the phosphorescent numerals on the bedside clock. He slipped out of bed and went to Abigail's bathroom. For the past ten years an agency had supplied him with skilled professional women. It was as unsexual as physiotherapy. His father insisted, for the sake of his health, that he express his sexual energy. His father first arranged it and then exacted a promise from him. He would do this for his father. At first nothing worked but in the end it became a glum twice-weekly mechanical exercise that sufficed. He saw rows of cosmetics and then found a shelf with several toothbrushes still in their wrappers.

The dance was a primitive ceremony of innocence. She had melded in as though rehearsed by the Great Choreographer. There was a subtle shift in her breathing and he knew she was awake. Like him, she slid out of bed and went to the bathroom. He turned onto his back and lay waiting. She glided back into bed, and he could smell her and the coffee that was percolating in the minute, fully-equipped kitchen that she'd installed beside her bedroom for privacy. He felt her brace herself.

'Roberto,' she whispered, 'I'm scared... I haven't done this in a long, long while.'

'Neither have I,' he said.

She hoped it would be all right. But it wasn't alright, it was magnificent. Their bodies were rendered boneless, their muscles toneless. For a moment Evie became a vanishing shadow and his past was blurred, then expunged.

'I once pretended that I was one of Monet's water-lilies, but now,' Abigail said, as she opened her eyes, 'I feel I am one.'

He thought of the flesh of a water-lily. When he was a child he remembered probing one and cutting half moons, with his thumb nail, even leaving milk teeth indentations in its petals.

What they had found in one another was so fragile that they were afraid it would be destroyed; that its very beauty ensured its destruction. They avoided talking about it and couldn't figure why they had been singled out for the distinction of another chance. Like all lovers they felt unique, and like all lovers they were unique.

They focused on Gladdie.

Derwent Fox, the investigator Roberto had employed, came up with some details that were missing from the puzzle. Gladdie's grandmother's grave was located and with his customary thoroughness Derwent photographed it. The modest tombstone was engraved 'Webb. Ellen-Agnes'.

'No date of death, possibly because they didn't know her date of birth, or because there wasn't the room on the stone. It is a small stone. She was buried in an old family cemetery where the land sloped down to a creek. If there was even slight flooding.... The grandfather, husband of the deceased, has disappeared. His reputation is of a vicious, mean old codger.' Derwent saved the most important piece of information for last.

'Old man Webb sustained an injury to his leg while driving a truck under the influence. He used a walking stick and had a disability pension. This has not been collected. It transpires that a young girl, a minor, had tried to cash his disability check in, but ran off when questioned. Nobody knows who she was, but I ascertained that Mr Webb lived with a succession of young girls, most of whom were runaways, homeless. He is known to be a vagabond. It is unusual that nobody is collecting; it makes me think. Talk about from the fat into the frying pan, those kids winding up with old Webb,' he'd smacked his lips expressively. 'But there is no report of a death or a crime or of a missing person. His shack is about to disintegrate. Raccoons have made a den there.'

Derwent felt he hadn't brought sufficient information to earn his generous retainer. He produced photographs of the grave, and of the remains of the abandoned shack, copies of the grandmother's death certificate and proof that the disability pension was no longer collected. No one had seen Mr Webb for a long while and no one missed him. Apparently he frequently took off, went on the road, wherever and whenever it took his fancy.

'It's a funny case,' he pleaded with Roberto. 'To find out why a little girl has lost her voice. I'm sorry we haven't had much success – but my operatives and I are doing our best. I know Gladys Howard is afraid of walking sticks, you told me that yourself – but did you ever think it is a virus?' asked Derwent Fox.

Roberto smiled wryly, interested to note that Derwent's integrity was intact. Derwent handed Roberto his typed report. While Roberto perused it, Derwent scanned Roberto's office, which was like a living-room, spartan, masculine and minimalist. Short of facts though the report was, it left Roberto so sure of what must really have happened that his face went grey and he had difficulty getting words past his teeth.

'It is essential that you track the old man down. Even if, as you suggest in your report, he may have taken to the road and become a drifter, I want him found. It is plain to me that he attacked our little girl. He grabbed her by her hair and beat her with that stick. You may have thought the wig and the walking stick whimsical, but I regard them as evidence. I suspect they are linked directly to her grandfather, and I must insist that you find him.'

Derwent was taken aback by the ferocity of the usually cool and collected banker, thinking privately that his Spanish – or Puerto Rican – temperament was showing. Latinos were not types he liked. But he bit back his resentment, and left sounding more confident than in fact he was, as he promised to do just that.

The next day Abigail considered the other women who wanted Gladdie: Louise, who probably knew the truth but had clothed it with religion; and Megan, who had wanted to uncover the untellable. Only Hester knew and would speak the unvarnished truth. By now Abigail knew that if she asked her straight out she would give an exact and honest answer, so she planned to go to her. That night, as they lay in bed, Abigail told Roberto that she was convinced that both sisters and Louise knew what had happened, and that she wanted to confront Hester, but the cautious banker side of Roberto prevailed upon her. 'Let's find the barbaric pig first'. Abigail had to be patient. They had waited this long.

CHAPTER TWENTY-THREE

•

'Thou shalt not kill' kept going round and round in Louise's head. They had all been trying to find her sister; she had hidden her, protected her, saved her. And then Hester goes and invites them to the wedding! Hester always confounded her, and now her belief that Hester could overcome calamities was under threat. She worried that her sister had gone too far. What about Pa? What if they found out?

A seizure twisted Louise's body and flung her to the floor. She was terrified of the electric chair. Terrified. She lay on the floor like a large petrified mummy, her gaze vacant, her breathing slowed. She lay, a clumsy mass, putting her hands together but unable for the moment to pray. But fear the Lord she did, in full and absolute measure.

Unusually, everyone was in good health, which deprived her of 'visiting the sick'. More time to pray, she was silent as she prayed and implored the Lord to forgive Hessie, to be merciful to her and save her and allow the brilliant light of her sister's life to shine on. Abruptly she stopped. Her imagination eclipsed her prayers and she saw the highway, a slick thick black snake; and on it, directly over her father's body, stood the symbol of justice: the electric chair.

She loved the Good Book, loved the Ten Commandments. But she was happy that he was dead. She struggled to her feet. Her glee escaped and she giggled and shouted in joyous triumph, spreading her arms and pumping the air. 'Deeaad, deeaad.' Blessed relief. 'Deeaad.' She was as guilty in her thoughts as Hester and couldn't bear it. She struck herself on the head to punish herself. What horrified her most was the question of Hester's soul. What would happen to it? Where would Hester go? Afterwards. Please, Lord – don't let Satan get her. Her mind was uncontrollable, no matter how many times she smacked her head.

If only she could talk to someone about it. Keeping her fears and terrors stuck inside her made her feel as if she was drowning in her own gelatinous blackberry jelly jar. She gasped for breath and felt viscous jelly stop up her breath but somehow she could swim. She pushed aside her suffocation, swam out, and found herself in the placid lake of forgiveness.

She would tell her husband. Once she told the appalling truth she, and by association her sister too, would be absolved. Patri-cide, she retrieved the word from her scudding memory, thinking it an impressive word. She could use it when she told John Jacob about Hester. He would be gratified that she had learned her new words so well.

That night, after her duties were done and the children were asleep in their beds, she told her awful tale.

He wouldn't believe her! He told her that she imagined the whole thing. Patronizingly explained to her that she was jealous of the wedding, jealous of Hester's dress. Jealous. Louise was stunned, then angry. She demanded to know why, why he didn't believe her? He didn't deign to answer. How could he even think she would make up such a story! She wanted an answer, he gave no reply, his manner contemptuous. Then she started to beg him to reply; her breathing became rapid; she licked her wart, her eyes leaking miserably. She beseeched, she implored but he turned away, his stiff back remonstrating with her.

'I am disappointed in you. When you get over this stupid nonsense, I will forgive you.'

She was sinking back into the jelly jar, felt her body shrinking to fit in, saw a large hand tighten the lid. Her own hand. He saw her posture slumping into the foetal position, saw her struggle with asthma, and felt the full force of her helplessness. He studied her.

'I will,' he said, doing her a favour, 'check it out. If, and I say if, you have told the truth, and not uttered a falsehood, then I will act in the Lord's name. He has graced us with our beautiful church. He hears our prayers of thanksgiving and supplication, He will not abandon us,' he said complacently, patting her on the shoulder. There are times, he thought, when you have to put them in their place.

Despairingly, Louise understood that it didn't suit him to believe her – it would spoil the image of his church, his own wife's sister a murderess! Even worse, patricide – he would be dragged down. But she worried – what action would be taken in the Lord's name?

Brother Boardman paid a circuitous visit to the area where his father-in-law lived, no one missed the curmudgeonly old man, there was only rumour and gossip. He must have taken off, as he often did, John Jacob satisfied himself. For some unfathomable reason, this strange idea had come into the mind of his pure and saintly wife, who, according to his teachings, was the living example of how a wife ought to be.

Louise wept a lot. She tried not to cry in front of her children, but when they were safely out of the way she howled and vented her disorientating and jumbled emotions. She didn't want anyone, least of all her children, to witness her lack of faith. Her somber melancholy hunched her. She remembered going down an animal trail on the mountain that Hester showed her when they were little. It descended past elephantine boulders and there, hidden, was a cave. It was narrow and they crawled in even though Louise was afraid of rattlers. Hester took her by the hand and a little further on the cave opened up into a large space. Hester promised her that she had explored it, Louise was afraid of bats and Hester got annoyed because she didn't enjoy this secret place. It was pitch dark and the air seemed thin. It smelled unused and fetid. Now Louise longed to be there and she tried to recapture it, but it was hard for her to concentrate because she was so preoccupied. If only her husband believed her... or if someone, anyone, would believe her. She tried to put her misery aside, it was clogging up her mind. There she and Hester would be safe, safe in that dark, dank cavern. Louise's memory fallaciously drew the cave into a velvet starless night, cozy and warm – now she saw it the way Hester did. The air sweet and moist – the air that Louise longed to breathe. Again the breathlessness squeezed her throat, bruising and compressing her lungs, her hands clutching her throat. She had to tell someone. Someone who didn't care about their church, someone modern and educated, someone like Megan Burns.

'I am absolutely determined to work it all out.' Megan said to Tom. 'Some things, well, just happen, and perhaps we should accept them as such. A happening not meant to be understood, but experienced,' Tom suggested. Trying to lighten her load, he added: 'I envied you your rapture. Watching you dance bewitched me. Your arms became like the limbs of a young tree, beckoning and swaying in the wind, a tempest and then a gentle breeze. It's hard to describe. You looked... beautiful. Damned sexy too!'

Looking into his eyes, Megan realized that for him it was phenomenal, and winced as something of the dance chimed through her. She decided to work rigorously on it, without inflicting her frustration on her Thomas. She found his description touching.

But Megan was floundering. Despair swept over her, through her. She couldn't work out why she was saturated with sadness. Briefly she wondered if it was some sort of long delayed post partum depression that afflicted her. Typical, she thought angrily, they haven't performed any extensive tests on the complicated biological changes women endure. If only Gladdie came to live with them then she would be in a pretty house filled with music and books; she would have Benjy and barbecues instead of bigotry and barbarity. Hester was remarkable – even unique, Megan admitted to herself. Perhaps she should try to meet up with her again. She had gone to Jewel's wedding consumed with loathing for the woman whose act of casual sex had conceived Gladdie, then abandoned her to her extremist sister and her nauseating, self-righteous husband. Yet it had to be true – it was true that mother and daughter loved one another.

She became withdrawn. Only Benjamin could cheer her up. She hoped for a violent storm to break the oppressive atmosphere, the humidity seemed to sop up the oxygen. She wanted to close the shutters but the sky was invariably blue, the air unforgivably crystal clear. Her energy became depleted, she couldn't go to school and instead rode a medical merry-go-round. Megan, a born optimist, until now had enjoyed overcoming obstacles, disappointments and even heartbreaks, but now her intelligence became non-operational. It was like a slippery tool that she couldn't grasp. How, she asked herself, could she be miserable when she had Thomas and Benjamin, when she did the work that she loved? Was it all because of Gladdie?

Thomas was beside himself when Megan told him she hoped something would be diagnosed, whatever it was. She had lost weight and was distraught when they could find nothing wrong medically. It seemed she'd been invaded by depression; shame-faced, she went to a therapist and almost invented interesting past problems – she felt guilt because she was one of the few who came from a balanced and loving home. Obediently she took tranquilizers, and life dragged on, at least her crying jags abated. Benjamin was spending more time with his grandmothers. She had magazines to read through and somehow the nights faded into days.

'If only a storm,' she said to Thomas, gesturing to the cloudless sky, 'would break.'

There were other storms when Megan gently massaged her temples, half expecting her fingers to come into contact with electrodes. Lightning had zigzagged into her head and white-hot bolts of electricity seared her brain. Her head crackled with agony. They didn't give electric shock therapy any more – why was this happening?

On the bed, she lay with the side of her head pressed into her cushion. She opened one eye and was momentarily startled by an unfamiliar dark shape; she stared at it and began thinking. An extremely powerful microscope would make visible the fuzziness of where her nose ended and the cotton covering of her pillow began, molecules would mingle and merge. All things merge and coalesce, from her nose into the cushion, into her night stand onto the floor, out of her window into the maple, segueing into the sky, covering the town and all its trees. Her small breath cleansed by the trees, giving it back to the environment. On and on. Floating. Gliding. A cloud moving towards the mountain. A cloud laden with tears. The boredom of continuous self-analysis drained and exhausted until, finally, a shallow sleep gave her respite. Sleep, her only escape.

She woke up with her fists in her eyes. She lay trembling and started to cry softly, too exhausted to sob. She heaved herself out of bed, pulled on her jeans and, without combing her hair or changing her pajama top, slipped into her Jeep and headed for the mountains obeying a subconscious command. She felt strange, she wasn't at first sure where she was going – she certainly didn't know why. She felt as though she lived in the cracks between seconds, as though there was no time, as though there was no sequence or continuity.

Megan got out of the Jeep, took the path to the shack, and Hester saw by her movements that something was very wrong.

'What is it?' she asked.

Megan stood looking at Hester, gulping.

'Coffee?' asked Hester.

Megan looked around and felt she was slipping off a cliff. She held her arms out for balance. Hester fetched her a glass of water.

'We'll go for a walk,' Hester said.

She turned her back and Megan followed her. They walked for a while without speaking and then Hester increased her pace. She led Megan to her sacred place. It was the small family cemetery.

'This is my mother's grave,' she said, and sat down on it indicating that Megan could join her, but Megan remained standing. Hester didn't ask again what ailed her unexpected visitor, she simply waited, Megan was not yet ready. A mockingbird, flicking its tail up and down, watched them alertly.

'Ma, she never laughed. Had the laughter beaten right out of her. She worked hard. Work was her only pleasure, from work came our vegetable garden, our food. Food for us 'n her. She planted rhubarb, green beans, cucumbers, potatoes, turnips, spinach, peppers, cabbage, tomatoes, all from seed,' she said. She paused, sticking grass between her teeth.

'A man come up here and took a picture of her grave,' she told Megan.

'What did he do that for?' she asked rhetorically. Megan made no reply, however she was calmer.

'Ma chose the right spot. Look what it's done for you.' They didn't speak for a while and saw a plane in the distance, heard a cricket shrilling, watched a breeze rifling the leaves, gentle as a lover. The clean pungent smell of the earth surrounded them.

'My daughter died,' Megan said.

'I heard you lost your girl baby,' Hester said. 'You went straight back to school. You didn't give yourself time, see. You've gotta take time off for grievin'. Even if learnin' is about the most important work there is.'

'But I've got Benjy!' Megan cried out.

'Don't matter how many you got. You lose one, you grieve. But you gotta do a good job of grievin'. Otherwise it stays in you and it grows there. My mother learnt me that. After Louise and me, none of her girl babies lived. They all died in their sleep, she told us. But I've wondered why,' Hester added darkly. 'All of them. They was five. And between Jewel and Gladdie two girls died. But I can have more. I heard you cain't. That's sad. You grievin' for them too, the ones you cain't have no more. It's the hardest work, the grief work.' A peace-giving silence followed.

'I've lost my smile, too.' Hester smiled at her when she said that and, to her surprise, Megan smiled back.

'Maybe you're right about me; I didn't give myself time.'

'And you feel bad about Gladdie too,' prompted Hester. Megan hung her head.

'I cain't give her to you. I hope you see that. I kinda gave her to Lou already. But she is really mine. She got born kinda special, see.'

Megan looked at her, imploring her to tell why, whether Thomas was the special reason. The slight possibility of gaining some relief existed – if Thomas was not Gladdie's father....
Hester deciphered her questioning eyes and shook her head. She

157

explained how this was the one time when her mother hadn't been her midwife. How she'd had her all alone, up on the mountain at the river's source.

As the two women were walking back to Hester's house, Megan thought of asking if Gladdie could have a blood test but she chastised herself. It would be insensitive.

'We can give her a very good home, with many opportunities.' Hester nodded her head in assent. 'We can see that she goes to the best music school in the country. We can provide her with the best education possible,' added Megan miserably. 'But you already know all this.' Hester made no reply but looked thoughtful.

'I think that Mrs Dunstable and her friend also want to give her these chances,' Hester told a disconcerted Megan.

Hester embraced Megan as she had embraced Jewel the day of her wedding. She pressed Megan's head against her shoulder and stroked her hair; crooning wordlessly, she stroked her back. They held one another. The two women stood for a while and Megan felt Hester pouring strength into her.

'Thank you,' Megan managed. 'Thank you.'

Megan accepted her suffering and grief for the baby girl she'd carried beneath her heart and the other little ones she would never have. Hester had comforted her, had understood her entirely natural responses. Hester knew the difference between grief and depression. Gratitude, like delicate rain, softly soaked her. Megan's intelligence reasserted itself; she thought Hester's mind was clear and uncluttered. Hester didn't set out to be compassionate and kind; she was made that way. Her way of being. Megan had wanted, needed, to hate Hester; instead, the strength of sorority infused her veins like additional red blood cells. She respected and loved her. Her instinct sent her to Hester for help. Gladdie was of Hester's blood, she rejoiced, and the power and goodness that flowed from Hester flowed in Gladdie. An elated Megan trusted the child would sing again. Megan went back to school and began the difficult attempt to reactivate her life.

It was a long and arduous task. Megan found out about a group of people who gathered together to deal with the loss of a child. She joined and went to the meetings. Thomas came with her but only once, he felt gauche and somehow out of place. He urged her to keep attending. She had to keep going to the weekly meetings; her equilibrium depended on them. Her sense of isolation was somewhat assuaged; she heard at one of the meetings that time helped but did not heal.

She went to her philosopher father and discovered that he was a fatalist. He carefully wrote out the sayings that, as he told her, he sailed his ship by.

From Euripides:
How dark are the ways of God to man!

From Sophocles:
Fate has terrible power.
You cannot escape it by wealth or war.
No fort will keep it out, no ships outrun it.

He folded it up for her and she put it in her purse. They smiled bravely at one another, their eyes shining too brightly. Megan's mother sat alone in a darkened room; she, who hardly ever prayed, was praying that God would help her daughter.

One morning before school began Louise was waiting for Megan, looking haggard with worry. She asked Megan if she could speak to her. Privately. As soon as Megan arranged with another teacher to take her class, she left. Mrs Boardman looked ill. Her ubiquitous coffee was steaming and ready when she walked into the parlour. Louise sat down and waved Megan in the direction of freshly-baked jam tartlets.

Louise vacillated between the danger of telling and the dire necessity of unburdening herself; she had to put her trust in Megan. But was it possible, she asked herself yet again, that Hester would be found out if Megan wasn't the sort of person she thought she was? Louise recalled the many mistakes she'd made in the past; it wasn't a good time for such recollections. Her breathing became laboured as she struggled to contain herself and quell her rising panic. Her eyes darted about as though demanding escape from her skull. She pushed against the arms of the chair; she tried to extricate herself, tried to stand, then gave up and slumped back into the chair. Megan sipped her coffee, concealing her bewilderment at Louise's travail. She made several comments about Jake and Gladdie, how well they were doing at school, what good children they were.

'It's about Hester,' Louise eventually succeeded in saying. 'But first you must promise me, in the Lord's name and in the sacred memory of my dead little ones and for the sake of Jake and Gladys, that you will never tell a living soul what I'm going to confess. I have to tell, because it's like a boil on my soul and it's burning me up. Only I shouldn't tell anybody, but if I don't, it's likely to burst!' Louise pummeled herself hard on the breast and belly. Megan waited. 'You mustn't tell,' Louise begged. 'You mustn't tell.

'I won't tell,' said Megan.

'Pa is dead and Hester did it.'

Louise put her fist against her mouth and bit against it to stop herself blubbering, but didn't succeed. Megan believed the woman was telling the truth. Hester, her rival, who had bound her with swirls of dance into an unwanted sisterhood, who had comforted and strengthened her, was now at her mercy. Her mind slipped into traitorous bedlam – how to use this valuable, terrible information against Hester and have Gladdie with her family, where she belonged? The treachery of her thoughts demolished her, her unworthiness paralyzed her. She couldn't utter a word.

Louise was aghast because Megan didn't even reply. She visualized the electric chair waiting contentedly on the carless blacktop just above her father's body. Waiting for Hester to be strapped in. Louise fought for breath and her gasping stopped Megan's spinning mind. Loaded with sympathy, she attempted to comfort the shuddering mass that was Louise. She stood up and tried to hold the heaving woman, but succeeded only in clasping Louise's upper arms.

'You won't tell!' Louise exploded out. 'You won't tell!'

'Why,' asked Megan, attempting to calm the woman, 'did she do it?'

This had the opposite effect, as Louise seemed about to choke for want of air. Megan rushed to the kitchen to fetch a glass of water. The clean tidiness of the room struck her with humility. She noticed that an old square tin that had once possibly contained cooking oil had been shone up and looked like silver. Louise slowly sipped the water.

'Hester must have had a good reason,' Megan suggested.

'Thou shalt not kill,' Louise wheezed, pressing the small silver cross that hung from her necklace between her thumb and forefinger.

'True,' admitted Megan, 'but then what made her do it?'

'He was bad,' answered Louise. 'He was the evil side of the mountain. I worry about Hester's soul. I can't bear to think what will happen to her when she gets to the Other Side.'

Tears mingled with the sweat on her face and dripped down onto her pure white collar. Louise was wearing her best dress, had hoped it would somehow help Megan respect her as a God-fearing woman and, by association, her sister too. Hoped that Megan could somehow ease her rabid fear. Megan stood holding Louise from behind the chair, not knowing what to say. She put her cheek against Louise's head, then stood erect.

'I do not believe in a God that punishes,' Megan said forcefully.

'But,' shouted Louise, 'Thou shalt not kill'.

'I believe in a loving God,' Megan said, conviction surging through her.'Hester must have felt it was the right thing to do. She knows what she's doing. She's not a fool.'

Louise felt a smothering weight lifting off her chest and her breathing became easier. She became almost calm.

'Hessie is clever, Mrs Burns. She know lots of things. So you won't tell, will you?'

'Your sister is a remarkable woman. I wouldn't do anything to hurt her,' Megan said.

'Thank you for complimenting Hester. She is younger than me,' said Louise.

'I don't understand what you mean about the evil side of the mountain,' said Megan.

'Someone like you can't understand,' said Louise, sounding a little patronizing.

'If things are properly explained to me, I generally do understand.'

'Mrs Burns, what do you think about the Devil? Do you know he wants to get Hester?'

'I must hurry back. I'm late,' Megan quickly exclaimed, to avert a diabolical theological discussion.

Relieved, Louise let her go, got out of her chair and on examination decided to polish it.

That night Megan told Tom, which was like talking to herself and therefore not breaking her vow. Told him, her tone soft, her heart aching.

'Now that we know everything about Hester, we have more choices. Perhaps it's our duty to help Gladdie escape the Boardmans.'

But she did not tell Tom that she went to Hester and received help, understanding and freely-given kindness. Her clamorous feelings drained and exhausted her.

Tom listened intently. 'There is nothing that Hester does that can shock me,' he said. 'But how will Gladdie react if she finds

out that her mother murdered her grandfather? If Hester obeys
any rules, they are her own rules. No doubt he was evil so she
took the law into her own hands. She is governed by herself
alone. She could be dangerous.'

'Dangerous?' echoed Megan. 'I don't think she is dangerous –
not to us anyway,' she murmured.

'I think you're right – not to us. And she may have had her
reasons. Before we use this information against Hester, we
should check out the facts. We needn't rush.' Tom spoke gently, afraid she might sink once again into a quagmire of depression.

That night they lay in bed clasped in one another's arms, each
trying to soothe the other. As Tom lay there, his impotence over
unfolding events gritted his teeth; they held one another close
and tried to sleep, Tom was mystified by his wife's puzzling
ambivalence towards Hester.

'Go to sleep, Megan,' he pleaded with her. 'Go to sleep.' She
turned over.

Megan couldn't sleep. She felt deep shame – how could she
even contemplate action against Hester? Hester, whom she
respected, honoured and was indebted to? Yet what about her
husband's rights? What was best for Gladdie? She tossed and
turned as her ceaseless questioning beat her about. She crept
out of bed to the liquor cabinet and poured herself a vodka. Her
indecision was driving her into madness; she couldn't afford
madness.'I'm the sensible, well-balanced teacher. Parents
depend on me because I am dependable. Can this wreck be me?'
she whispered out loud. Tom slept on.

Hester had restored Megan to herself with infinite compassion and understanding. She knew if she betrayed Hester she
would inflict an even greater betrayal on herself. Her first pri-
ority was, she knew, to keep her sanity intact. It was, she admitted to herself, flimsy.

CHAPTER TWENTY-FOUR

•

Abigail called the fire station to find out when Hester could visit her, the Chief relayed the message to Curt in his lookout and a date was arranged. The key to what action they took lay entirely with Hester who fascinated Abigail and Roberto. Something of Hester was in Abigail too – did anything exist between the two women that were similar? They supposed that it was their strength, both knew that the dance linked them profoundly, yet they didn't speak of it.

The day came and they took the Range Rover, thinking to pick up Curt to show them the way but Hester was waiting at the fire station. She was dressed in her green dress and, with the splendid dignity of an oak, stood barefoot. In one hand she carried her sneakers and in the other a paper sack containing pinecones and pone bread studded with bits of dried apple. Before Roberto had time to open the car door she had slipped into the back.

'This is gonna be interestin',' said Hester. 'I ain't never been to your part of the country. Wasn't never no reason, nor time.' As the car moved forward she leaned towards them.

'Gladdie is mine,' she told them. 'Always will be. Maybe sometime she needs extra dollars, I'll let you to give it to her. How, I dunno, my other kids won't like it. Louise needs her. Can we have some music? You got some tasty music? I reckon we'll hear it. The rain is light, just a drizzle.'

Whilst they drove it rained and rained, gentle, soft and soaking; the trees, the grass, everything was awash in mists of greens and grays. Neither of them mentioned her damp hair and her dry dress. She smelt a bit like a wet day, of pines, of earth and of baking. These pungencies overcame their fragrances. The two sitting in the front were disconcerted by the altered atmosphere; the upper hand that they unknowingly expected was lost to them. Haphazardly Abigail put on a CD. Hester leaned back and Roberto could see her eyes in the rear view mirror. They briefly became unfocused and then seemed to widen; she leaned further back, her expression blissful. Roberto gestured to Abigail to look at Hester. The tawny stare had left her eyes and Abigail felt that she was looking into the half-open eyes of a mildly sedated lioness. All three enjoyed the music.

The sun came out again and the earth had the freshness of a small baby just lifted from the bathtub. The leaves shone and the shadows were newly laid. Everything seemed possible, even a friendship between the three of them – particularly between the two women. 'Good man,' Hester told Abigail, as though Roberto wasn't there. 'Don't usually like them. Men.'

'Thank you,' Roberto said.

Hester saw a red-tailed hawk sitting on top of an electric pole, lazy now the road always brought fresh slaughter.

The leaves were not yet out on the walnut trees, their trunks and branches stood out like antlered sentinels. Always the last to come into leaf and the first to drop their leaves, like a guest afraid of overstaying her welcome. Admire me while you may. The sycamores arched the driveway, creating a cathedral corridor.

'Nice place,' Hester said.

They had stopped and eaten hamburgers on the way because Hester was hungry. The delicious and carefully-chosen luncheon would now be eaten by the cook and her family. Naturally Hester was enchanted by the trees, a few species were like strangers to her, but she didn't tell. The flower gardens had no vegetables. Nothing to eat. She wasn't particularly interested in the house as Abigail took her through it. It was too large and, she could tell, would be difficult to keep clean. There were pretty pictures on the walls.

'These are called Impressionists,' said Abigail.

'Well, whoever they are they know how to catch light,' Hester said as she opened and quickly closed her hands, as though she had caught a ball.

Abigail and Roberto exchanged a delighted glance. In the dining room there was a still life by Hans Holbein.

'Good eatin',' said Hester. She was awed by a pair of Antique Lusters complete with tall unlit candles on the dining table. The afternoon sun shone on them and refracted crystal lights onto the wall behind them. Hester sighed, enthralled by the prisms. Observing her, Abigail tapped them lightly with her long nails and prisms danced across the wall, the ceiling and over the paintings. It seemed as though the entire house was alive with them and the tinkling music that they made as Hester tentatively tapped them with her fingers. The three stood in silence. Arrows of light flashed over them, further uniting them. 'Please take them as a gift,' offered Abigail, stretching and picking one up.

Hester, who had earlier given her gift of pone bread and collection of carefully-chosen pine cones, thought for a moment.

'Yes, thank you. I'll take one, then you will have the other.'

'But they're much more precious if they are a pair,' said Abigail.

'Right,' agreed Hester, 'you'll have one, and so will I.'

Abigail agreed, surprising Roberto yet again. They had fresh lemonade out of crystal glasses. Roberto flicked his thumb against an empty glass to watch Hester's expression, as expected, she quivered and smiled. He was pleased to contribute to this proud woman's pleasure. Later on they had strong espresso.

'Smells good, tastes awful,' Hester said. And then they strolled around the gardens, Hester plucked a few fan-shaped leaves off a ginkgo tree.

'Jethro collects leaves, he hasn't got these. He presses them in an old school book then puts rocks on top.'

Abigail and Roberto were amazed to see turkey buzzards stubbily pouncing about on the grass. 'Your creek flooded, that's what's left of a carp,' said Hester. They saw another fish skeleton.

'Tell Jethro that ginkgos have grown since the Jurassic period. That's about eighty million years ago,' he explained. Then they walked to the fish pond. They looked around for Hester, who had disappeared. She dropped out of a bur oak, smiling impishly at them.

'Couldn't resist that one. It opened its branches and in I went.' They sat at the pond in quiet intimacy. They watched a brilliant turquoise dragonfly and gazed at pond skaters, goldfish and waterlilies. Hester reached out her long sinewy arm, plucked an open lotus blossom and gave it to Abigail. To Roberto she gave an engorged bud.

'This one,' she told Roberto, 'is you; the other one is your wife.'

She gave a quick, naughty smile. In a subtle, unknowable way the garden was hers and they became her guests. She pointed at the purple black shadows and told them she had to leave.

They listened to more music on the drive back, nobody wanted to talk. Some way before they reached the fire station she asked them to stop.

'I'll take a short cut. I like to walk. I'm invitin' you to my mountain. Sometime soon.' she said. 'Rob, you can come. If you want.'

She got out of the car, the luster firmly held in her grip. She waved goodbye and was gone. Roberto made a U-turn and they headed back.

'She must have left her wet clothes somewhere... I can't wait to visit her mountain,' said Abigail. They drove home weary and contented, their fervent curiosity about Hester somewhat satisfied. Somehow Hester had consecrated their union beside the fishpond and they decided that this was all the ceremony needed.

Hester enjoyed the day. It was quite outside her experience and had inspired her enquiring mind to find out what sort of people those two were and see how they lived. The ginkgo leaves were as sensational as the lusters. She climbed the mountain like the mountain cat that she was, carefully carrying her light-capturing gift which she couldn't wait to show to her children. There was a ferment of storm clouds and tree branches thrashed and twisted as though seeking to harm, to hurt. Turbulent earth aromas rose up; a typhoon was brewing, then ominously, every-thing stilled. The sky darkened as vast grey cumuli thundered and struck out their threat of a torrential downpour. The grey deepened to the right of the clouds and Hester paused to sur-vey it. The sun sent two long rays past the clouds, as though drawn by the promise of a distant horizon. The leaves left their stillness and their susurrus enlivened and made Hester smile, as if hearing the voices of beloved friends. She knew the storm would bypass her, but still hastened her pace to join the last of the streaking shadows home. The children would see the luster by morning light. Once her work was done, she would fetch Gladdie to see it; of all her children, her little girl would most appreciate it. Jethro would love the ginkgo leaves and the story behind them, even if he wouldn't understand the length of time they'd been on earth. Children don't understand time. Eighty million years – Hester didn't understand it either.

Megan still told no one, not even Thomas, of her visit to Hester. Megan's ineffable gratitude was to be with her throughout her life, even though she didn't like owing anybody so much. The magical dance troubled Megan constantly. The unexplainable made her uncomfortable. Facts, facts, were the meat and veg-etables of her approach to life. She granted the reality of instinct and intuition, but valued knowledge above them.

Two weeks later, her contradictory doubts became a loud uproar that Megan could almost hear and she was again having disturbed nights. Tom suggested that she go back to Louise to talk through her story once more.

'We can't allow you to go on like this. Use your prodigious logic. Get the truth,' he told her, firmly utilizing the one form of persuasion he knew she couldn't resist.

But truth is an opaque, sprawling panorama, filled with unforeseeable hazards. Her father had taught her that nearly all facts should be contested because they depended on a point of view. She felt sympathy for Louise. She realized how damaging her words would be. But how could Louise be trusted? She was an hysteric. She believed in the scaly devil and in a punitive God. She believed in heaven and hell. Megan considered Louise superstitious, slow-witted – against all modern thought. Megan outlawed compassion and remorselessly went to rob Louise of her cherished yet delicate peace of mind. Wasn't peace of mind usually frail and brittle for any thinking being anyway, Megan asked herself.

'I've been thinking....' Megan paused looking through the steaming coffee at the unsuspecting Louise. 'I've been thinking that what you told me was probably a bad dream,' she said with careful tact, adding: 'I've had some pretty bad dreams myself and they seemed so real at the time to me.'

Louise sat stolidly, inwardly flinching. She could feel sweat starting to slide down between her arms, beneath her breasts. She was numbed.

'I understand how you feel,' Megan said.

At this glib impertinence Louise boiled over. Her perspiration sizzled on her hot flushing body as righteous anger took precedence over despair.

'What do you know about the mountain?' Louise coldly asked. 'Nothing! You know nothing. If you think it was a nightmare about murder then why don't you ask Hester yourself? Ask her. Why don't you? I told you about the evil; I warned you about the Devil; that he is after Hessie.'

'You're right, I don't really know the mountains. I've driven around in my Jeep and I've taught children from the mountain, but I don't know it the way you do.' Megan paused and, clasping her hands prayerfully together, earnestly said, 'I must ask you to please forgive me.'

Louise did her duty. She forgave. She waved to the young teacher as she left and looked down at her foot to find an ant crawling over it. She remained standing at the gate because she couldn't move. A column of ants marched across both her feet.

Her body trembled as misery and betrayal overwhelmed her. She stared down, unsure if the ants were real or not, afraid to brush them away in case they weren't really there.

Megan thought she might discuss it with Abigail. After all, Abigail was Hester's friend.

Whenever Hester arrived unannounced to collect Gladdie, Louise repressed her envious resentment. John Jacob was right. She was jealous of her sister because, when she saw the two together, their happiness shut her out. She remembered how beautiful they looked dancing at Jewel's wedding. She did everything for the girl; nothing she did was enough. Still the little girl loved her mother more. Louise felt left out – it was a repetition of when she and Hester were with their mother. 'Thou shalt not covet,' she silently reprimanded herself. She knew they were impatient as she fussed about, making them sandwiches of thick slices of bread with wedges of cheese and jelly. She wasn't going to let them go without sustenance. Was not bread the staff of life? Well, they'd remember her when they sank their teeth into the sandwiches, she cheered herself up – she saw more of Gladys and could not blame or compete with Hessie. Gladys rejoiced in Hester's company – did not Louise herself feel strengthened and full of laughter when they were together? The small ritual of self-castigation over, Louise watched the two depart without regret. They would soon be back.

Hester and Gladdie hitched a ride to get up to the shack quickly. Soon after they left the road, the sounds of the traffic receded and the mountain played her melody of interconnectedness. They heard the imperious call of a carolina wren, a loud call for its tiny size, a blue jay laughed harshly, a phoebe sang honeyed notes. Phoebe, phoebe, it called its name. Smells of the greenness surrounded them, scents of moss, of damp rifts of leaves, rock pools, salamanders, wild rose and honeysuckle. They almost danced up the mountain. They swung from thick sour grape vines and heard a train whistle in the far distance.

'I wonder where the people go, what lives they lead, what sort of work they do,' Hester said. 'Try to imagine.' They sat on a rock and ate their sandwiches as they watched a flickering of butterflies, the flight of a chickadee. But Gladdie wasn't interested in the passengers on the train, she was restoring herself. They reached the shack then Hester made Gladdie close her eyes for a big surprise. Hester quickly decorated a log with leaves she'd gathered on the way and carefully placed the luster. 'Open them,' Hester sang out. Gladdie was transported, bewitched but Hester was disheartened. Secretly she'd hoped that her daughter would exclaim out loud.

'Ain't you gonna talk?' she reproached, vexed, arms akimbo.

Her daughter burrowed her head in her mother – love enveloped her as she embraced her child. A yellow finch darted along its way.

'When you're ready, you will,' she reassured. 'When you're ready. Don't let anything ugly dictate to you. There's lots ugly in life and we mustn't let it beat us. What happened to you happened to me, and I'm OK. So will you be.' Gladdie cried in her mother's arms. But what, she wanted to ask, what happened to us? Finally she wrote with a stick.

'What?' Hester looked blank.

'Happened to us?' she scratched out.

Hester was silent for a while – perhaps Gladdie had forgotten. Is that good or bad, she asked herself. 'Most snakes,' she answered, 'are harmless; they won't hurt you, but you don't go making friends out of them. You let them pass on by. We'll let this one pass on by too. Maybe someday I'll think different; but for now, we'll let it be.' Gladdie nodded agreement, thinking it must have been just terrible 'cause Mommy's afraid to talk about it. And Mommy's not afraid of anything.

For the first time in her life she felt her mother undependable, not the rock she could rely on. In her very core she understood that her mother was mortal and fallible and that she too would die one day, just as her grandmother had done. Just as she herself would… And she cried in her silent way as though all was lost.

Hester held her shuddering little body and judged that right now everything would be too tough for Gladdie. Shock still protected her. Then Hester knew, with the crystal clarity of the luster, that when she remembered, she would speak. Worn out and spent, Gladdie calmed down and with her eyes questioned her mother about the beautiful object.

Hester told her about her visit with Abigail and Roberto. Her eyes glinting expressively as she shared her amazing day, they started about their chores just as though they worked side by side every day. 'Hon, everything's gonna be just fine. You've got Granma's blood in you, and great-granma's, goin' way back. Our womenfolk is strong. Come and give me some sugar.' They kissed and hugged. Whenever it rained the air, hot and humid, reminded Gladdie of her mother's body.

When Jewel married, Hester longed to see more of Gladdie, her elder daughter had been her only feminine company after her mother died. She couldn't count Louise because, although she was of the mountain, she'd moved to town. Clay's wife Minnie always lectured the same parts about their history; she had never really liked her, they were too different. There were never-ending chores, the washing hung permanently on the line. Curt constructed a frame to stand before the stove in winter; it made the room dank and musty, but there was no other way. The family wore the same clothes for as long as possible and in as many layers as they had. In summer Hester liked to see her work waving like triumphant flags; the children all did their bit to help, Hester's strong hands worked hard on the washboard. The secret to repetitive work was to dream.

'It's free time,' she taught her brood. 'You can go anywhere you want, think anything you like, grow as tall as a black pine, see as far as an eagle.' They developed their imaginations. The mountain, a vast breast, fed all of their needs.

They weeded the bean patch after they had done the carrots; Gladdie sensed that her mother felt lonely just as she herself did. She yearned to tell her mother but, when she tried to speak, the words were without sound. Hester quickly noticed her facial movements and bade her stop weeding.

'I'll try and understand what you're saying by watching your lips.'

'I'm lonely too,' Gladdie mouthed and put her hand on her chest.

Hester couldn't get the middle word. She knew that Gladdie mouthed 'I'm', but was uncertain about the next word.

'Scratch it out,' she said, giving Gladdie a stick that was lying nearby.

On reading 'lonely too' she asked Gladdie to say it again, and this was how Hester began to lip-read her daughter. Fair was fair, she couldn't take her back from fragile Louise; but she was determined to see her daughter more often.

'Honey, don't be lonely; so many people love you and want you to stay with them. Sometimes I am lonely, I suppose, but I didn't know it till you told me! I guess it's hard 'less there's folks to keep you company.'

Hester was not given to introspection; she coped with difficulties as they arose, external events interested her, other people's feelings – seldom her own. Early in life she expected to handle whatever came her way, and that was how she lived. This loneliness thing happened and she would deal with it. 'Are you happy?' she mouthed and then uttered aloud.

Gladdie caught on.

'Yes,' she nodded. 'Today, with you.'

'Today' and 'with' she then scratched on the ground.

'Yesterday?' Hester mouthed and then said aloud. 'Yesterday?'

'No,' Gladdie mouthed and shook her head.

'You know why?'

'Yes. I have bad nights,' mouthed, and then the words scratched out.

They kept up their new means of communication.

'What happens?' asked Hester.

'I think things are not what they are. I think my coat is a burglar man. I think that iris bleed, stuff like that.' Hester was thunderstruck. For once she didn't know what to say. She simply sat down, pulled her daughter into her arms and rocked her.

'It'll pass,' she pacified Gladdie. 'It'll pass. We'll see each other more often.' She felt her child's dainty skeletal structure and she bitterly reproached herself for not killing her father sooner. She swallowed bile that filled her mouth. She began to croon her own lullaby, repetitive words of love. 'Lu lu lu love you, Lu lu lu love you. It'll pass. This sort of thing always does.'

Sitting there, holding her daughter, she summoned up her mother: she saw her mother and was quickly relaxed and put at ease.

'Later,' said her mother. 'Choose your time carefully. Today is not the time. When she becomes a woman, if she hasn't spoken, you can tell her. Tell her when you think the need is there.' She was strengthened by her mother's advice; it was over in an instant, she continued rocking and crooning to her Gladdie, her baby girl.

'Lu lu lu my baby. Lu lu lu love you'

'Life goes on, like spring and summer, the golden time and then winter.' Hester comforted. There were still faint traces of anxiety about Gladdie, even though she was entirely safe in the glow of her mother's embrace. Hester scrutinised her keenly. A lump formed in her throat.

Louise began to fret about the ants. Had they crawled over her feet or not? Were there ants at the gate? Were they still there? She shuffled down to the gate, taking her time. The ants had gone and taken her confidence with them. Surely there was someone in the world she could tell, someone who would understand and accept that the terrible story she told was the truth. There had to be one person, not of their parish, not too close, that she could unburden herself to. There had to be one, just one.

Louise knew that her anxiety was driving her precarious sanity away. Where had the ants gone? Why did it matter? At this rate she would land up in a crazy hospital. 'Thou shalt not kill.' She feared for her sister and herself. If only Hester had not told her...She thought of talking about it all to Hessie. She winced, imagining Hessie's response, her usual safe place was blocked. She would grin that Louise was happy when she first heard and insist that no one would ever find out. Hadn't she laughingly mocked Louise and her religion in the past? Any commandment was not something that bothered Hester.

Louise knew Hester would be concerned if she knew of her suffering, but, the cause would be foreign to her. Hester was so strong, ordinarily she would have gone to her, Louise was frustrated, everyone knew she was truthful but no one believed her. John Jacob disliked Hester, yet he chose not to believe his own wife, even though he agreed that she had never lied to him. It was not her imagination. Now the teacher Megan didn't believe her. Her honesty was her only precious source of self-esteem. She felt betrayed; they didn't trust her; trust was what life was about. If you didn't have trust, you had nothing. Trust in the Lord, she commanded herself.

If only there was somebody strong like Hester. The name Abigail Dunstable sailed into her mind. All she had to do was to figure out a way to get to her. Trembling with apprehension and hope, she turned to the telephone book.

CHAPTER TWENTY-FIVE

•

Abigail and Roberto were at the swimming pool. He chose to leave the bank before three on Wednesdays. They had just got out of the water; he swam twenty-five laps and she ten. They lay on white toweling chaise longues in agreeable silence. Roberto preferred swimming nude. The telephone on the side table rang. 'I should have this removed,' Abigail said lazily. Mandy had answered the phone and put it through to Abigail.

'Sorry to disturb you,' she said in her pleasant tone, 'but I think you'll want to take this. It's that Louise Boardman woman. She sounds very nervous.'

Abigail jerked up, immediately pushing the conference button so that Roberto could listen.

'Hi Louise. What a lovely surprise to hear from you.' They could hear Louise breathing.

'How are you doing?' Abigail asked. Louise tried to wrap confidence around herself, but it was like a wet cloak in a windy storm.

'Are you OK?' Abigail quietly questioned. 'Is something troubling you?' Abigail continued, allowing her concern to be heard in her tone.

'Yes,' Louise breathed, 'yes, something is.'

Abigail, the seasoned negotiator, employed a small silence. More heavy breathing. Louise grasped her frayed self-confidence and finally said, 'Mrs Dunstable, I would like to meet with you.'

'Where and when shall we meet?' enquired Abigail. This set up another storm of breathing and gasping.

'Tell her the church,' Roberto whispered.

'We can meet at the church tomorrow.' Now they heard a hurricane of breath. 'I can fetch you on the outskirts of town, near the fire station. I would like to see you again,' cajoled Abigail. 'If I can help you, I would be honoured.' The breathing became less laboured. 'Tomorrow at noon – would that suit you?'

Louise got herself under control.

'Yes. Near the fire station. On that side of town.'

'We can have a picnic. See you tomorrow'

'Until then,' Abigail confirmed. What, they wondered could be the meaning of desperate Louise's request?

As the car reached the designated area, a figure emerged from the trees; Louise opened the car door, squeezed in, then looked agonized. She pointed an accusing finger and Abigail hurriedly switched the music off. To make amends Louise attempted to whistle, but was too nervous.

'The birds whistle, so that's allowed,' she explained to Abigail. 'Sometimes, though not too often, when I'm with Jake we both whistle. They say I whistle very sweetly. I don't know that they're right.' But Louise knew that she could whistle better than anyone – even better than Hessie. 'Hessie can imitate quite a few birds and they answer her call.'

Abigail waited for Louise to confide in her; she parked beneath a dappled green canopy for their picnic – wholesome and simple, nothing fancy, Abigail had instructed her cook. She had provided peaches, plums and delicate portions of baby chickens. Louise then brought out her offerings. She brought bread, fried pieces of chicken, peanut butter, honey, homemade jelly and four apples that had been so polished that they looked like rounded Christmas ornaments, Roberto was told later. Louise was scared and frightened. She noticed with distaste the minute chicken portions and thought it was no wonder that Abigail was so thin. She poured hot, milky coffee for her companion from a flask that she had bought for this occasion, and then summoned up her courage and began her tale of woe.

'I know someone who did a bad thing: she broke a commandment. I'm afraid for her, terrified, because when she dies Hell's fire will be waiting for her... the thought is murdering my mind.'

Abigail remembered Louise saying 'she shoulda done it sooner.'

'Perhaps if you tell me about it, I can help.' Abigail encouraged. Still the woman hesitated and added sugar to her coffee.

'You have to promise me that you will never tell anyone ever,' said Louise.

'Talking alone helps,' Abigail said. 'A burden shared is a burden halved.'

'But you'll give me your promise,' insisted Louise.

'Yes,' answered Abigail, holding up her right hand.

'Hester, my sister, did away with our pa.' At last she forced her words out. Abigail didn't say anything.

'She killed him. Dead.'

'Why?'

'Because he was buddies with the Devil. He was one of the Devil's own.'

'How? How?' Abigail wanted to know both how he was, as it were, related to the Devil and how the deed was accomplished. Louise had never asked her sister how – she hadn't thought to ask, didn't want to know anyway how the grisly job was accomplished.

'I dunno. But I know where his body lies, where his body rots.' Louise was afraid that again she would not be believed.

'I know the exact place – maybe not exactly, but nearly,' she added. Abigail couldn't wait to tell Roberto. 'How do you know?' Abigail asked, thinking, I knew from her raptor eyes that she was capable of anything.

'Hessie told me,' she sealed it triumphantly. 'She made me drive on the road and we both laughed.' Her voice became muffled. 'I am glad he is dead. He can't do the Devil's work no more.' Abigail realized that Louise needed absolution as much for her laughter as for Hester's deed.

She attempted further questions. 'Why was your father like the Devil?'

Louise looked surprised.

'But I told you he did the Devil's business,' she answered, her arms supplicating.

'Please believe me! He is dead.' They were sitting on a blanket Abigail had brought, the picnic baskets opened, the food ignored. Louise maneuvered herself onto her knees. 'Please believe me.' Instinctively Abigail stood, like some ancient priestess, and placed her hand on her supplicant's head.

'God loves you and understands your unhappiness,' Abigail intoned, surprising herself. Louise clutched her about the legs and wept.

'The Good Lord will protect you from harm and he will save Hester. He can do all things. You are such a good and righteous Baptist, because you feed and clothe the poor in your community; because you are so very, very kind, the Lord in his mercy will help you. Your house shines with cleanliness. And godliness. You don't smoke or drink and you allow your children to bring happiness to others,' Abigail concluded, hoping that she'd sounded as sincere as she felt. Everything that she'd said about Louise she knew to be true. She was unused to the feelings of genuine compassion that swept through her. Louise snuffled, her terror slowly abating. Something heavy, squat and dark lifted off her lungs; a darkness shaped like her father. Once more she felt the blessed relief of confession.

Finally, gathering back her loving spirit, Louise sat down and began to serve from the picnic basket. Louise far outshone Abigail in the hostess department and in the interest of friendship and politeness, Abigail ate more than she intended.

'What will happen to Hester?' Louise worried.

'No one knows, and no one needs to,' Abigail replied.

'That is just what Hessie would say,' an elated and relieved Louise exclaimed.

'You two are just the same,' she continued. 'I saw it when you danced. Although it is against the Lord's wishes, I also sort of moved a little. I don't know why I did that.'

'Neither do I. It was spontaneous and glorious'.

In a jagged about turn, Louise's white hot terror detonated. 'Hester won't be sent to the electric chair. She won't, will she?'

'She will never be convicted because no one will ever know. There will be neither sentencing nor executing.' Louise stopped hyperventilating. 'We don't have to worry. Anyway, I don't think they use electric chairs any more. I think they give them lethal injections.' said Abigail, trying to assuage Louise's ghastly fear. She felt safer and was too courteous to correct Abigail, although her ignorance surprised her.

'Then everyone will wear an injection needle,' said Louise.

Abigail lost her moorings.

'If Jesus had died now,' explained Louise, 'then we'd have a needle instead of a cross on top of churches and graves and hanging from our necklaces.' Abigail couldn't utter a word.

'I've often wondered how the electric chair would look,' said Louise.

Abigail's body stiffened.

'It would look funny!' and she couldn't contain great bursts of laughter.

'Electric chairs are not funny for the people in them. I am afraid that my own sister will be fried in one.' Louise reproved her. 'They fry in Kentucky.' She began licking her wart, as though to remove it along with her doubts.

'Nobody knows. Nobody must know. I will never let them do that to my sister. Never must anyone find out. Never. Never.'

'You have my sacred word of honour,' Abigail solemnly promised. 'I admire Hester. I couldn't bear such a terrible thing to happen to her.'

The unmistakable ring of honesty in Abigail's tone allowed feelings of security and safety to course through the large woman's body. Her trust was regained. She wasn't going crazy and cried briefly with relief.

Their rendezvous over, Abigail dropped Louise off and returned to High Wings.

Louise walked home, jauntiness in her step. She started whistling. She was happy. Happy that at last someone – and someone clever, someone who drove a big limo – believed her, even if she was wrong about the needles. But, she thought proudly, I told her the way. The sheer joy she felt overcame her and she found a wall to lean against. It was reminiscent of her religious ecstasy. Her happiness vividly reminded her of her 'beautiful light times' as she called them. It was similar to the brightness she experienced when her husband had baptized her. The sky, seen through clear creek water, shone silver. It was the first time she saw the Lord's light; her lungs had screamed for air and when she came up, her husband had held her tightly. Her husband. The man who married her, saved her and didn't mind about her wart.

Now she had to sit down as she became dizzy. Tears flowed down her cheeks. 'Yea', she whispered, 'my cup runneth over.' John Jacob had been a little anxious. She was the first he baptized. I can do it, John Jacob thought. I can. With the Lord's help, of course.

Infrequently, in fact rarely ever, something wondrous happened to her. Her body became infused with spirit, with inner radiance. Her breathing became rapid, her heartbeat quickened even as her body flushed. She briefly fainted and would find herself lying on the floor soaked in sweat.

'Can you tell what happened to me? Did I shine like a big big light bulb?' she would ask John Jacob. It was all he could do not to fall on his knees before her.

'I can't describe it. I thought the stars came down again and shone inside me.'

CHAPTER TWENTY-SIX

•

Abigail decided to give Megan a quick call. There would be time before Roberto came home.

'Is it a convenient time for a quick chat?' Abigail asked.

'I meant to phone you, Abigail, but I haven't gotten around to it yet.'

'Why not?' asked Abigail then, without waiting for a reply, rushed on: 'I want to talk to you about that amazing dance!'

'You dance beautifully,' a careful Megan replied.

'I was a ballerina once upon a time.'

'I didn't know that – now I see why you move so superbly.'

'You dance very well yourself. But what made you dance? And, for that matter, what made me dance?'

'I don't know, and I'm uncomfortable not knowing. I am something of a dilettante anthropologist and I've been trying to, to... get to grips with it.'

'Tell me more.'

'It's interesting that no less an authority than Leakey found that Neanderthals displayed concern for the human spirit.'

'How so?'

'Well, for instance, flowers and pollen were placed with bodily remains.'

'Ah, flowers. I love flowers. In every way,' she said, thinking of Mother's Day and her highly profitable flower imports from South America.

'There are skeptics. Some say the flower residue is accidental. Anthropologists occasionally tend to argue among themselves. For example, Neanderthals were buried lying on their sides as though sleeping. Others claim that the bodies were tied with thongs into the foetal position. This early in time there was evidence that man cared about his fellows.' The teacher in Megan couldn't resist an eager pupil.

'Why does it seem that something in us needs to express itself – perhaps through the medium of dance?' asked Abigail.

'It is by observing preliterate societies' need to dance that we may infer that group dancing instills a feeling of unity, a oneness. Dancers connect with one another, and perhaps the universe!'

She had embarrassed herself by saying this and rushed on,

'It's a sort of language, a ritual, with spiritual or religious connotations. I intend studying all the available evidence.'

'I see that you are even more interested than I am!'

'It's the Internet; I'm wedded to my computer, I need to understand in order to dissociate myself from the whole damn thing,' a disgruntled Megan replied.

'That's because you're afraid something witchy happened,' Abigail laughed, 'some sorcery. But why dissociate yourself? It is something to marvel at. Hester called us up there, made some potent mystical movements that kind of radiated out and then drew us in. Like a tidal moon pulling.'

'I dislike anything lacking a reasonable, logical explanation, happening to me,' Megan said, a note of hauteur insinuating itself. 'I am researching the subject.' Pedantic Megan stuck to her position.

'Dance is a process of communication and can aesthetically project emotions', said Abigail. There was a short silence. 'Roberto will be home soon,' Abigail said, sounding happy. They were both reminded of the men they loved.

'Benjamin is waiting for his dad and so am I.'

'He really is a cute kid. Have you heard anything about Gladdie or her family?'

'I had a weird conversation with Louise. She has a surprisingly vivid imagination. I had to promise her I wouldn't talk about it.'

'It must be about Hester killing her father,' Abigail calmly stated. 'Am I right?' For a moment Megan was speechless.

'I don't believe her. I discussed it with a friend of mine, who said it must have been because he...', she hesitated, 'he attacked Gladdie. That he had a walking stick and her hair was long and he pulled her by it. He's the lawyer I told you about.'

'You have broken your promise,' said Abigail derisively.

'I know,' said Megan, running her hand across her hair. 'But you see this whole thing has been driving me crazy, and he is a friend, and there is a code of secrecy between a lawyer and a client,' she defended. 'How do you know about it? I still don't think it's true,' Megan flatly asserted.

'I've spent the afternoon with Louise and she told me. She worships Hester and is incapable of making up a story that could hurt her. How do you know?'

'Louise told me too. She said it was like a boil on her soul. I decided not to believe her. I have strong doubts about her sanity.'

'I can't agree with you on this. I think that she is an authentic innocent,' said Abigail. 'I didn't realize she told anyone before confessing to me. We mustn't let this story out,' Abigail said warningly.

'We won't,' agreed Megan.

They promised to have a coffee together soon and hung up.

When Roberto heard that Megan had spoken to a lawyer, he thought it probable that the Burns couple wanted to bring a case against Hester. They concluded it was vital that Hester never went to court. Megan had been vague. She had said that they just wanted to sound out the situation.

'The thought of her imprisoned makes me shudder,' Roberto said. 'Her wings ripped off.' Abigail, realizing selective memory at work, did not remind him about the death penalty. Or about a gold chain with a pendant shaped like an electric chair. She saved that hilarious morsel for a time more conducive to laughter.

'Megan wants Gladdie as her own. Hester was right about that,' said Abigail.

'Try to win Hester's confidence and find out anything you can – we have to see that she remains free.'

They made an appointment for the following week, via Curt.

On the seat beside her, as she drove in her Range Rover, was a cashmere and silk shawl with a leaf design she, together with Roberto, had bought for Hester. She had been touched that Roberto took time to help choose it. The unending chore of washing clothes must wear the ligaments of one's personality away, thought Roberto. His ideas had been an electric generator and washing machine as future gifts. Mustn't chase her away by being overly generous, she had told him. Later, she had said, maybe we can send those later.

The day was raw with fecundity; green shoots thrusting, growing and thriving, trees growing lustily, fields spreading succulently. Momentarily saddened, Abigail was reminded that she could no longer bear children. She was smiling when she saw Hester waiting for her with a cup of coffee. Hester led her up the mountain. They stopped to admire roots tenaciously snaking through rocks. Hester pointed out a possum, unusual to see in the day time, blue birds, explaining that they lived in holes in trees, flying squirrels, and all things she thought beautiful. Textures of bark, leaf, stone: she made Abigail touch them and smell their perfumes. Abigail was a novice and Hester inducted her into her mountain. Hester showed Abigail the way to gently hold the leaf of a pin oak between the thumb and fore-finger, asked her to stroke it, and then told her that this was the feel of how she loved her children. A young ash leaf in spring was the exact feel.

Before they left, Hester had proudly shown off her vegetable garden and caressed some carrot tops to coax their growth. There wasn't time to talk. She did her best to keep up with Hester and found that Hester paused every now and then, prob-ably for me, thought Abigail ruefully. She was relieved to be wearing her snake-proof trousers. Finally they reached the place that Hester had chosen for their meeting. It was where Gladdie had been born. Hester baptized Abigail with the story of Gladdie's birth.

'I was real glad. Her real name is Gladdie but for my moth-er's sake I called her Gladys.' Hester was the only woman she knew who could have given birth on her own. Pausing by the spring, they watched the light-giving water and gazed deeply into one another's eyes.

'The lusters,' said Abigail.

'Nearly as good,' Hester said. She stretched out her long neck and she drank the water, suggesting with a gesture of her body that Abigail do the same. They crunched on their apples after first washing them in the stream. Doves were cooing. 'We've got lots of wild flowers here; we've got iris, violets, golden coreop-sis with cheeky little faces. Sometimes, but not often, we see a ladies slipper. We've got plenty of different flowers, and in early spring there's trilliums.' They sat on their haunches and Hester complimented Abigail on her fitness for a woman of her age.

'I s'pose you eat onions,' she said. 'Good for the heart.' Abigail said she didn't especially.

'We do what the old folks did. They learned from the animals.'

'Like what?' Abigail asked.

'If we get a fever, we don't eat, just plenty of water, and we lie where it's shady and cool. We don't eat berries 'less we see birds eating them. Things like that. But for poison ivy we use Clorox. Listen, can you hear the woodpecker, can you see his red head?' Abigail listened, Abigail saw.

They followed the stream until it became a brook. Hester stripped off her shirt and britches, which she had worn in Abigail's honor, and lay in the water.

'Come in,' she invited. 'It's cool. We've got good fish, blue gill, bass, carp and the ole catfish.'

Abigail couldn't bring herself to get into the creek. She was scared of what might lurk in the water. Hester came out, shook her body free of water, the sun at her back, and stepped into her clothes, her body still wet.

'The funny thing is,' Abigail later told Roberto, 'I'm shy about being naked.'

'Not with me though,' he had smiled.

They continued down the mountain and Hester persuaded Abigail to swing on a wild grapevine. Then Hester became solemn as she took Abigail to her mother's grave.

'You the only other person not kin I've brought here,' she said. Abigail was deeply moved. Hester, unbeknown to Abigail, took her to introduce her to her mother. Maybe her mother knew, maybe not.

'I'm honoured that you brought me,' Abigail put her hand on her heart.

Hester sat on the grave and Abigail crouched nearby. With a start, she recalled why she had come.

'Tell me about your father,' she ventured.

'My mother chose her time to die. There was nothing wrong with her. She felt she'd lived long enough.'

'And your father?' pressed Abigail.

'He's dead.'

They sat in companionable silence and Hester, with sweet clarity, realized that Abigail knew what had happened and was non-judgmental.

'You saw Louise, didn't you? What she said is true. I waited too long,' she said bitterly, self-recrimination throbbing at her temples.

'He tried to rape Jewel. I caught him. I almost beat him to death with his walking stick. I bust his ribs, his arm and his right hand, thrashed him black and blue. I didn't think he'd touch my Gladdie. When he did, I killed him.'

'Good God!' Abigail hissed in shock, striking her chest. 'You should have done it sooner!'

Since she'd cried in the bath at the emergency clinic, and later with her sister at this same grave, Hester had not cried. Now her lungs like unused bellows heaved in and out and hoarse gasps choked her. In a trice, Abigail was holding her, both women cried. They cried for Gladdie, for her muteness, and their own helplessness. Hester tried to tell more to Abigail, but only managed a few odd half words through her gut-wrenched sobs. Now, as though they'd shared the same amniotic fluid, salty tears bound them. Both women were entirely unused to the love and friendship they felt for one another. The earth came up into their bodies, strengthening them, the earth which covered Hester's mother's grave. Exhausted, the two women went back to Hester's home. Hester gave Abigail a jar of blackberry jelly and a hickory nut sapling that she had carefully placed in a brown paper sack with just enough earth covering its roots.

'Don't tell anyone about it. Nobody else must know,' Abigail insisted.

To which Hester responded, with her flashing smile, 'What about Louise though? S'pose she's worried that the Devil, with his horrible scaly tail, is gonna come and get me.'

'I've tried to reassure her and I hope I've succeeded. But she's told Megan Burns.'

Consternation flushed Hester's face. 'They want my girl. Oh Lord. They could give me trouble... I ain't gonna tell anyone else.' As if by invitation Hester added, ''Course you'll tell Rob, but that's OK. They want Gladdie. Why cain't Megan be satisfied with her son and the school kids? She teaches Gladdie. My girl will talk someday.'

'You know, Hester,' said Abigail quietly, 'there are trained people who help child rape victims to get over their trauma.'

'We don't need them. She don't remember. When she is ready to, she'll talk again.'

'You're sure, then?'

'I'm sure. My mother told me, when she remembers, she'll talk up a storm.'

As Abigail took her farewell, Hester reiterated that if Gladdie couldn't talk to her then she doubted that she could go over the nightmare thing with a stranger. She promised Abigail she'd give it thought. Both worried that if the story got out, it was bound to follow that Gladdie was raped, and that Hester would be charged with murder, which would be even more tragic for Gladdie. Something both knew in their bones as the only course of action was treated very differently by the law. Hester's only concern was how Gladdie would be affected; the child victimized again and in every way. They wouldn't countenance it. They wanted to make sure Gladdie would not suffer any more than she had already. They clasped one another tightly, promising with their eyes, with their straining bodies, promising to protect.

Abigail told Roberto what had happened to Gladdie and Hester had done. Roberto's surge of raw grief was in full flood yet he still remembered to deal with Derwent Fox and quickly terminated their arrangement, paid what he owed and explained that the cause of Gladdie's voice loss had been found.

Roberto invited Megan and Tom to his home for a drink, it was to be a casual and relaxed. He planned diplomatically to turn the conversation towards Gladdie and her future. He needn't have bothered, he was preempted.

'Why are we such pigs?' asked Tom.

'Perhaps we're made up of positive and negative electrical impulses,' said Abigail.

'No average woman takes the law into their own hands. What we're talking about is cold-blooded, premeditated murder, and patricide at that. No one denies that most people feel murderous rage at some time – fortunately, it fades away,' said Tom.

'How sure can you be? Perhaps it lives and even grows?' said Abigail.

'Think about it,' said Roberto. Each thought of when or if they had experienced rabid, homicidal rage.

Trifling though it had been at the time, Megan had felt like killing a schoolmate who had deliberately banged the top of the piano down on her hands. She never forgot her brutal impulse. More recently, angry and frustrated as she had been by Hester, she'd imagined how convenient it would be if Hester died. She forced herself to stop thinking these unworthy thoughts, she flushed with shame, she loathed being so indebted to her. She was a good giver but a poor receiver, unaware that receiving is the greatest giving.

Tom's skin felt too tight for his skull when intruders broke into his parents' home, trussed up the three of them, and then pistol-whipped his father. He'd felt his skin was on fire, and was surprised when he wasn't covered in blisters. Given the slightest opportunity, he would have shot them down like rabid dogs. He was fifteen years old then. All these years later he still clenched his fists, remembering. Still resented that he'd been denied any form of vengeance or retribution. They were never caught.

Roberto wasn't a man given to rage of a homicidal nature. He had experienced raging grief. But he thought he would have put old man Webb down without hesitation or compunction.

Abigail could quickly become furiously angry. But she acknowledged that the only rage she felt was self-directed. She had allowed her first husband's rejection to almost immolate her and kept that shaming marriage a secret.

'There is a thwarted gladiator of sorts in all of us,' Abigail said. 'Let he who is without experience of consuming rage start the case against Hester.'

'We can't rely on people's inherent good, it's fallacious,' said Megan.

'But Hester isn't people. She's a mother,' protested Abigail, who, as she had never been one, inclined towards romanticism.

'And as such, she is responsible. Being a mother doesn't mean a license to commit murder... why didn't she go to the police?' asked Megan.

'She's unlike anyone I've ever met,' said Tom.

'The troubling question is how to deal with rapists – and child rapists in particular. They are practically all recidivists. The statistics can't be argued away,' Megan said somberly.

'Ever since time began, there are those of us who have tried to make sense out of catastrophes. Socrates himself decreed that knowing good and doing evil was impossible. Yet we see evidence all around us of man's ubiquitous inhumanity to man. My late wife – ' and this was the first time Abigail had ever heard Roberto publicly utter this phrase ' – thought language a key to peace. Her view was that a universal language could defuse the way we observe and interpret one another. That a collective commonality would lead to deeper brother – and sisterhood.'

'When did you loose your wife?' asked Tom softly.

'More than ten years ago,' Roberto replied. 'She died in child-birth.'

'Was it a girl?' Megan couldn't resist asking.

Roberto went white and Abigail answered for him by nodding her head. Immediately all understood his connection to Gladdie. Tom and Megan exchanged disconsolate glances. Gladdie wasn't, as Megan had surmised, merely an engaging project for them. Tom folded his arms and started clenching and unclenching his fists.

'As a teenager I stopped bothering with conventional religion, but while my wife was pregnant I found myself believing in God,' Roberto quietly said.

'I believe that a Higher Intelligence exists only because it is a need of mine. Between the ritual and the superstition, I can't find myself at ease with any traditional religion, even though the philosophy behind them is basically sound. Do unto others, et cetera,' said Megan. Tom was drumming his fingers on the coffee table. That was all that could be heard.

'In a way,' said Abigail, 'if none of us knew of this it would vanish. We wouldn't find a need even to speak of it.'

Unexpectedly, the usually well-mannered Tom lost control.
He jumped up and shouted: 'My little girl was savaged! Raped!
Now she can't even speak!' It sounded as if there was blood in
his sobs. 'She lives with that fat hard-shell Baptist cow. And her
self-righteous husband.' He punched the air in a paroxysm of
impotence. 'And her mother murdered her grandfather.'

He became incoherent and Megan rushed to his side. Tom was
given a stiff shot of whisky and fresh coffee was brought in. Talk
petered out. They were all drained.

'Hester did what she had to do,' Abigail insisted. 'And she
should have put him down the first time.' She told them about
how Hester had beaten her father senseless after his attempted
rape of her elder daughter Jewel.

'He was monstrous. Monstrous.' The women knew, from the
innermost recesses of their hearts, that Hester had been too
kind, or too foolish, the first time. She misjudged him, even
though she knew him well. Possibly she obeyed an ancient blood
taboo that prevented her from taking the life of a parent.
Perhaps she felt that as no life was directly threatened, she need
not kill him. They sensed this. The discussion waned and they
were at a loss. They were unnerved by Tom's raw anguish. None
of them said a word, for they had nothing to say.

Roberto's house was perfectly proportioned. The room, with
its high ceilings and symmetry, reasserted itself and a semblance
of quietude was re-established. The warm autumnal colors
enhanced by the subtle balance of space held them together,
sanctioning and prompting further discussion. It gently roused
lucidity and courage.

'I know that in her place I would have done the same thing.
I would be as guilty as the law will find Hester. If you were judge
and jury, sentence me now,' said Abigail, her steady voice belying her dramatic utterance. 'Knowing the sentence, I would still
do it and I wouldn't care,' she uttered with pale defiance. 'If it
was a crime, who was the criminal, who the guilty? Hester, for
doing away with evil, or the old man, for... I can't think of a
word bad enough.'

'Let's not blame society either,' said Megan, trying to stabi-
lize the situation and give Thomas time to regain himself.
'We're all given freedom of choice. True, he was evil and Hester
exterminated him – but even she couldn't control the consequences. They live on.' They all thought of the girl playing the
piano, locked in her secure silence and seemingly merciful forgetfulness.

'Hester foresees Gladdie regaining her voice along with her memory. I don't know why, but I am inclined to believe her. She said her mother, who is dead, told her,' said Abigail. 'Told her when she was already dead,' her voice strained.

'What we have touched on tonight is unbearable... I trust that we will commit ourselves to leave this matter here. Between these four walls,' Roberto said.

'Never to be spoken of publicly,' Abigail supported. 'Who knows,' she added, 'if perhaps we get together again to celebrate, rather than to "grapple with dark forces". Celebrate a concert of Gladdie's. Something like that.'

CHAPTER TWENTY-SEVEN

•

Louise returned to her role as a sister to all the members of their congregation with verve, her purity visible in her shining eyes, piety and daily good deeds. They accumulated in the Lord's Ledger and it was possible, if she amassed a high enough score there, that by association Hester would also be assured of a place in heaven. The children gave her no cause for concern even though Gladys sloped off to see her mother more often. Sometimes Louise wondered if a bolt of lightning would strike her down because her sister had not been punished. And she hadn't either. Still, every now and then, that commandment would throb at her temples.

Louise didn't know how often Hester came at night and crawled into bed beside her daughter. Hester told Curt that Gladdie needed her. Several nights a week she would come, first making the call of a whip-poor-will followed by the whirring racket of a raccoon. Gladdie leapt to the window, a smile broadcasting the ferocity of her happiness. Hester would quietly watch as Gladdie practiced her piano on the desk in her room before joining her in bed. She would smile as silently her mother applauded her. Lying in her mother's arms she quickly fell asleep, a leaf on her pillow and a comforting smell the only sign that her mother spent the night holding her. One of the main reasons Gladdie wanted her voice back was because she wanted to ask her mother if trees had dreams, if they talked to one another, if they had feelings, if they danced at night when no one could see. It was too complicated to write out. Her mother would know the answers, she was sure. One night, Hester woke her daughter and showed her how to get up the mountain as she was getting old enough to do so on her own.

One of Curt's friends was an all night trucker. Every Friday night at ten past ten, his vehicle rolled past the Boardman house. He opened the throttle loudly before he arrived, and stopped for a few minutes a couple of houses further on and she slipped out and hopped into the cab. A decent man, he had befriended Curt at AA meetings. He tuned his radio into what he thought the child would find pretty music, usually country and western, until he dropped her off. A father of seven chil-

dren, the last two in his current – and only alcohol-free marriage – were even younger than Gladdie. He entertained her by
telling her about them – uneasy being with someone who was
unable to talk. What happened if she needed something? How
would he know? He was relieved when she climbed out the cab.
It was unthinkable to let Curt down.

The night fears lessened and their terror diminished. Unlike
the other girls she wasn't interested in boys. They wouldn't, she
contentedly reckoned, care for her. She was dumb and they didn't
like that. Anyway, she had her music and knew she was very
lucky. Every spare moment she practiced on the piano or on any
surface available. She could hear the notes in her head. Playing
music brought her intense joy; it said everything her entire
being wanted to say. She had told her mother that it was not she
who played, but her soul. It was her music, her necessity, that
made her complete.

Her hormones whizzed around making her giddy, but she didn't
attribute these urgent hot and cool swooning sensations to her
awakening body. Sex, if she consciously thought about it, was
distasteful and to be avoided. But she pretended otherwise – she
was different enough, as it was, from the rest of the girls. She
didn't touch her body more than was necessary; she showered,
dressed and was ready to do whatever was expected of her. She
gazed endlessly at herself in the mirror when her aunt wasn't
home, and carefully studied her features. Her face looked back
at her, curious to see what life had in store. But when her breasts
began to bud, Gladdie became keenly involved in her body's
changes. She stroked them and traced them with her fingers and
cupped her hands over them. She showed them to her mother,
like two tiny baby rabbits she'd found, whose soft ears she liked
to caress. Hester was delighted and saddened, her child-daugh-
ter was going away and a young woman would soon replace her.

One night, while at home with her mother, the moon called
Gladdie into her radiance. Gladdie danced about as the moon
wielded her bedazzling influence. For some days now she'd had
a mild backache and she thought to dance it away. She twirled
and swirled until she felt an ecstasy not unlike that which she
felt when she played the piano. Then she felt a sticky wetness
between her legs. Startled, she stopped dancing and glancing
down she saw darkness smudging her inner thighs. She fell
back, spent and afraid. She lay as still as during her night-time
fears. Finally she could not help but look down at her legs. She
saw blood. Black moonlit rubies. A thin cry slid past her lips.

A louder, thicker shriek, a howling yell, a shouting scream as all came back to her. All.

The first scream snatched Hester out of bed. Quickly she was holding her screaming daughter, who seemed not to know her and struggled to escape her firm embrace. Gladdie screamed on; the night sky was rent, tall trees split down the middle, water stagnated in streams, rocks blasted into sand. Eventually her body exhausted itself. She quietened, although she still convulsed and shuddered. Her tightly shut eyes opened and she lay staring blankly into her mother's face, which eventually she recognized. Gently Hester rocked her, gently.

'It hurts,' Gladdie whimpered, 'it hurts.'

Cross-legged, Hester cradled her daughter in her arms, her face carved granite. Whatever anguish Hester felt was masked, her own feelings extinguished and overwhelmed by her daughter's shock and horror. She wanted to re-establish some sense of normality but the sharp slashing, gashing knife both women felt between their legs silenced her. Hester longed to straighten her legs to lessen her own sympathy pain. Imperceptibly she stopped rocking her last-born daughter and they sat as still as a rock formation. The uncaring moon lit them, her luminosity deepening their darkness. Hours passed. By the process of osmosis the stillness of her mother's body stilled Gladdie. Hester's stone head dissolved as expression flickered across Gladdie's face, animation slowly supplanted inertia. They looked deeply into one another's eyes. Comprehension gave focus to Gladdie's understanding and she recalled with clarity what her mother had told her; before asking, she knew the answer.

'Is this,' she nevertheless asked, 'what happened to you?'

Hester barely nodded her head. They held on to one another more tightly. The physical pain disappeared; first Gladdie's eyes asked, and then she asked the question which Hester had never asked: 'Why?' For a while Hester couldn't answer.

'Once,' she told Gladdie, 'I saw a dead fox. A fox I knowed. His body lay half in a pool that the river had left behind. He stank. I took a long branch to turn his body over; a crawdad slipped through his jaws, maggots were having a feast and flies had found him. I could see a trap had snapped on his leg; he gnawed it off to escape, and it became infected. He forced himself to drink, to stop his pain and quieten his fever but he had no chance. Your granpappy was the bad side of the mountain; he was like that trap, maybe he even set the one that caught the fox. He liked hurtin' people, it gave him a good time. Your grandma canned blackberries and was proud of how many she made. He smashed each bottle into smithereens. He stomped on them. If we ate any, we would eat glass. More than one time after we'd spent a long time gatherin' wood and haulin' it up to our stove to warm us through the winter, he lit a big fire and threw all the logs, branches and twigs onto it. It didn't matter to him that we would all suffer, includin' himself – his own coldness seemed to burn away when he saw us shiverin'. We had to collect wood all over again so that we could eat; it was a terrible winter. We lay on top of each other to stop freezin' to death. He was made that way.'

'Where is he?' a terrified Gladdie gasped out.

'Dead,' smiled her mother. 'Deader than the fox was. Good and bloody dead.' She stroked her daughter's head. 'Gone for ever,' she reassured her child. 'Gone. Listen to me,' she told her daughter, 'we don't have to chew ourselves up to escape. The trap is gone, we mustn't let it mess our lives up.'

'Look,' she said, opening both her hands, palms-up to face the moon. 'Here I'm free, I'm free and I'm real fine. So are you. In time the memory fades; the pain turns into an ache, you live with it then you sort of forget it. You carry on rememberin' but it is like a leakin' bucket – it leaks away. You need forgetfulness to stay alive, so you don't spend too much time rememberin'. You get on and have some fun.'

'Fun!' Gladdie exclaimed with offended disbelief. She looked at her mother resentfully. But then, observing her mother's face, she was obliged to accept that her mother enjoyed life.

'Fun…', she repeated slowly, 'Fun?' The sound suddenly longed for was her mother's laughter.

'Laugh for me,' she begged her unprepared mother. 'Please laugh.'

'Cain't laugh at nothin',' Hester smiled quizzically at her daughter, recalling how rarely she heard her own mother's laughter.

'If I say something funny will you laugh? Pleasc! Please!' and while Gladdie hunted through her mind trying to think of something funny Hester tried to laugh. She sounded patently false and then they both laughed at the absurd fake noise that she had throttled past her throat. And that was when the healing began.

'I forgot what my voice sounded like,' Gladdie said.

'I didn't,' said Hester

'Does it sound…'

'It is lovely as it always was. Music. Music to your Momma's ears.' She smiled a smile of unmistakable happiness, her voice was back.

Louise and John Jacob hailed their daughter's returned speech as a miracle, they bade Gladys address their congregation. She stood boldly before them: 'It was like I had a cold and now it is gone. Like I was cold and now I'm warm. Praise the Lord,' she added, for the sake of her aunt and uncle and the entire gathering of those who had so fervently prayed for her.

'Praise the Lord!' she repeated.

The Lord had heard them…. Their belief was the Right Way, the only Way. They were suffused with joy. Truly their Lord was Merciful and their Path the only Path to Redemption and Eternal Life.

'Praise Him, praise Him,' she concluded, raising her arms out towards them perceiving their naïve happiness and successfully hid her embarrassed guilt. She misled them, but it was what they wanted to hear from her – it was OK if it was the kind thing to do. Secretly, in her innermost being she thought that being able to talk again was indeed miraculous. The Boardmans shone with religious ecstasy.

Abigail, Roberto, Megan and Tom were filled with gratitude yet bewildered by Gladdie's piano playing. The dizzying technique was there and she was still a prodigy but something vital was missing, which confused Gladdie. They were thankful for the gain and mourned the loss – it seemed that her speech was restored at the expense of her gift. Gladdie aspired to be a regular girl.

'You can almost hear a metronome. Her head is studiously bent, her posture perfect, her phrasing immaculate. She has lost her rapture,' a distraught Francesca told her husband Randall. Francesca had kept on showing her granddaughter videos of other concert piano players, particularly young ones and scores of new pieces were carefully left lying around. But she wanted to be like all the other twelve and thirteen year olds – she wanted her concerns to be the same as theirs. She craved pack membership.

Her former desire to play at the Carnegie Hall was but a half-remembered dream. Rather she longed to be an ordinary girl, words like 'average' or 'a regular girl' were the accolades she sought. She yearned to be completely accepted by her peers and, to become one of them, she discarded her uniqueness. Piano playing, especially classical piano, wasn't acceptable to the in-crowd. She pretended to notice boys. It was difficult but a fundamental compulsion if she was to be part of the crowd. It was something she determinedly forced on herself. She didn't want any of them to even remember that once she couldn't talk and that she had played the piano! She no longer liked spending time with Megan and Tom; they were always so tense and she knew they expected her to play on their piano, which her teacher had told her they had specially bought for her. How embarrassing!

She wanted to have her ears pierced. It wasn't too terrible that she lived with her aunt and uncle; at least Jake was normal even though sometimes his pesky teen behaviour made her cross. They kept their club private, but they kept it going. Only he saw her as secretly she practiced on her desk, he knew better not to even talk to her about it especially when he surreptitiously saw tears falling down her cheeks. She felt that she was two people: the new one had to ignore the musical one.

Gladdie's band of supporters respected her needs. They didn't want to foist their dreams of her future greatness, or of the huge contribution her gift could be to the world of music. Yet they wanted her to understand that her gift was too great to abandon; how could they help her utilize her time more effectively so she could continue both her practice and her new-found social life?

Roberto had one last idea. He sent out this invitation.

'In three week's time we have Carnegie Hall in New York at our disposal for one-and-a-half hours in the afternoon on Thursday the twenty-seventh. Abigail and I invite you all to join us in what is to be a concert given by Gladdie. Hester, Curt, Louise and Brother Boardman, Tom and Megan are invited, and we will fly there and back.'

Urbane and unabashedly applying charm, he led them to alter whatever engagements they'd planned. Tom and Megan suspected the plane belonged to Roberto's bank and they supposed Abigail had hired the hall. They looked forward with trepidation. Questions swung back and forth. What would happen if Gladdie couldn't perform? If the whole venture proved too much for her? Could it set her back? Were they being fair to her? Their overriding wish was that by playing in such imposing surroundings, even to so small an audience, Gladdie would catch the 'performer's bug'. Gladdie was to precede them, accompanied by Francesca, Tom's mother. Gladdie had no idea of their blood relationship. The proposed concert and the aspirations it embodied alarmed as much as it thrilled.

Gladdie was excited to be going to New York and at the same time did not want to leave her new friends. Her sense of belonging to the giggling clique of girls needed cementing but because the crowd thought it would be cool to go, she went. The teenager did her best to conceal her resentment towards the adults who were trying to tell her what to do with her life. But she was mollified upon hearing that her parents would be coming too. She didn't think it would be fair of her to deny them the opportunity of the trip.

CHAPTER TWENTY-EIGHT

•

Curt was aware that his wife was occasionally lonely. At Curt's urgings, Hester pushed aside her reservations and joined a group of mountain women who met once a month. The first time she went, she encountered five women, dressed in jeans. She wasn't at all sure what was expected of her and to her surprise she almost fled. Well-seasoned in understanding body language, the women quietly bade her welcome and asked no questions and continued talking about holding a quilting bee. The prospects of acquiring the off-cuts from a fabric manufacturer and various other likely sources were discussed. Two women held small pieces of material. They put them on an outdoor table at the home of the oldest woman, who with her daughter had begun these meetings. They tried different scraps together and smiled at her. All became absorbed as they attempted to work out a design for a comforter. Their ambition was to create their own design rather than use traditional ones and they decided, daringly, to place pockets filled with dried herbs round the edgings. They took these fragments to make of them something beautiful, something that would outlast their lives.

Hester watched, her arms hanging at her sides, unable to participate. She thought that if her mother was alive, or if Jewel hadn't got married, she wouldn't have need of feminine company. Minnie was too preachy. Gladdie was too young – and besides, she had her music. There wasn't anyone. She allowed the friendship of the women to seep into her, like the warmth of the sun on her shoulders. One of them approached her and introduced herself. 'I don't much care for quilts myself,' she murmured to Hester. 'I'm here for something different. I'm here to start up awareness about endangered species.'

Hester looked at her and asked what her name was.

'I'm Eunice Brownbel.'

'Hester Howard.'

'Do you know about endangered wildlife here in our mountains in this part of Appalachia?' asked Eunice.

'Some.' Hester did not allow her bafflement to show. Eunice was excited by a new audience, maybe even a convert.

'Our mussels are on the list. I've always loved them since I was a little bitty thing. The fanshell is endangered and the pink mucket and the little-wing pearly mussels are in trouble too. I draw mussels...' she trailed off.

'Don't see one of the owls no more,' Hester volunteered. Eunice cheered up.

'There's one kind of woodpecker. I think it's the red-bellied but I might have the name wrong,' said Eunice. 'I'm more interested in mussels.'

'The one I miss most is the Bald Eagle. They ain't as many as they used to be,' said Hester.

'I've got a new member,' Eunice chanted, breaking up the quilt of women. 'A new member for our ETSCSS – and that stands for Endangered, Threatened and Special Concern Species Society.'

That was how Hester found a new interest in life – one she could share with Curt. 'Save the Bald Eagle!' became their joined battle cry. 'Save the Bald Eagle,' said the men from the fire station, who initially joined only to please Curt but who, to their own surprise, later became keen to bring their concern to the public.

'People can't get their balls knotted about frogs or crawdads, but eagles – all Americans feel for eagles. If you save one kind, they all get a chance,' said Curt confidently.

'Swans mate for life,' Hester told him. He forgot to breathe; could she love him? Had she ever loved him? She stood by him – was she telling him something? He didn't dare ask, as a feeling of gratitude and tenderness overcame him.

Hester was getting to feel almost as real an affection for Curt as for her sons. Now that he wasn't drinking he was actually quite a fine sort of guy. People want to make something of their lives and it's as good a way as any to save something or someone. Might as well be bald eagles or water dogs – which is what the local people called salamanders – or even, as Curt said, the itty-bitty things Eunice went on about. Hester watched muskrats eating clams and mussels, endangered or not, but she didn't tell Eunice. Muskrats don't differentiate.

Megan, driven as much by guilt as by kindness, introduced Louise to Elsie McNab at the battered women's refuge, Louise wanted to do volunteer work and be generally helpful. She liked the name Peace Place, but suggested to Elsie that perhaps 'the Lord's Place of Peace' may be better. Elsie warned Louise that the women's lives had been hell and under no circumstances was a punishing God to be spoken of. One of the rules of Peace was to leave religion out, unless a woman spoke of it herself.

All that was required of Louise was to be a good listener. Louise could bake, knit, sew and cook for them and teach them how to do these things. She did spice up her cooking with some Jesus talk but, as instructed, she never spoke of the Devil. She could talk of love, but never of revenge; the bony pale brown woman made complete sense to Louise, who understood that her sisters had suffered enough.

Louise felt needed: she hugged, she cuddled and whisperingly confided that she too as a young girl had been tortured and tormented by her father. She stroked the foreheads of the despairing young mothers, comforting them; and lightly, deftly snuck in the sign of the cross on their brows. She convinced herself that when their time came, this invisible emblem, this loving ticket ensured their entrance into the Kingdom. Their souls would be redeemed – they would not roast in Hell – this gave her endless worries respite. They've suffered enough here on earth, she explained to her personal, if punitive, God who understood and forgave her. Forgiveness, she smiled gratefully, was His way.

The women responded to her care. The greater her role at Peace Place grew, the more freedom she gave Gladys. Whatever Hessie had said, Louise was convinced that Gladys' speech was a great miracle, this was one thing she could talk about non stop. The story stitched hope into the hearts of the listeners, it nourished their inner spirit. But all the while, just beneath her practical deeds, she prayed – she prayed to appease – unlike her husband, she wanted no further testing. Praised and prayed; prayed and praised. Praise was kind of like insurance.

The shift of emphasis was off Jake and Gladdie as Louise poured more and more of herself into Peace Place. Jake was sports-mad and took Gladdie's absence in his stride, although he did miss her, especially helping him with homework. The two kept in close contact, using their sign language to keep their club of two as exclusive as ever. They agreed that no outsider should ever witness or work out their secret language. Gladdie told Jake it would spoil it. She didn't want anyone to see yet another difference. Too embarrassing.

Her piano teacher kept leaving new musical scores lying around. A few times, when Gladdie was certain no one would hear her, she sight-read and played one of the pieces – she couldn't stop herself. To her dismay, she enjoyed it so much that she kept playing it. Whether on the piano, a desk or in her mind, she played it over and over. It made her cry.

John Jacob's feelings were ambivalent. He knew Louise was doing Good Work. Young mothers motherless, children fatherless, she chided him when he expressed resentment about her involvement. He didn't like her mixing with women who, he assumed, used blasphemous language. He didn't like her getting too many ideas or thoughts that he might not approve of. He blamed Hester for this turn of events and made a virtue out of his irrationality. He began brooding over Hester, the way she tried to control his life and the unnatural power she possessed. He remembered the dance and shivered: Louise never lied; perhaps she had told the truth. He started wondering about his father-in-law's whereabouts, whether he ought to do anything about the strange, ungodly business. Whom should he inform? He wanted to curtail his sister-in-law's power but without blemishing his reputation or impugning his wife and was at sixes and sevens not knowing how best to go about it.

He began to pave the way. 'I've been cogitating,' he said. 'Maybe you told me the truth about your pa,' he suggested generously. Louise wasn't sure whether to be pleased or not. It was good to be trusted again. But what did her husband intend to do? A coldness went down the sides of her arms and the skin prickled. He watched as she trembled.

'Do you think he could have been murdered by one of the runaways?' he asked, monitoring her minutest movements. 'Then there was that moonshine maker, Bob Bailey, that your father informed on. He may have killed him. It's possible,' he said, his eyes never leaving her.

She made no reply. She could not get her breath; breathlessness was her father's legacy.

Louise wanted to tell the congregation about Peace Place and about Elsie McNab. John Jacob was furious. Only a few years previously the Southern Baptists declared that women were forbidden to preach. He made certain his acute displeasure would be felt as much as a physical blow.

What, John Jacob wondered, what was happening to his wife? Prior to all this she had been obedient and meek. 'Blessed are the meek,' he reproved her: it was all because of Hester. He doubted she believed in anything. Except perhaps herself! She was capable of anything. Anything. He again recollected what Louise told him. It didn't suit him to believe his sister-in-law had slain her own father, much as he despised the old man. But Hester! Hester had the temerity to tell him how to preach, and even dictate the length of his sermons! How dared she, a murderess, instruct him? How dared she! He could taste acidity, his bitterness swelled up, his suppurating bitterness.

For the first time, Louise felt both injured and insulted, in the past, whatever John Jacob had said she had treated as gospel. Now it became a compulsive obligation to speak to him about how much women and children suffered at the hands of men, it was with missionary zeal that she talked it over with Elsie McNab, whose bones were more prominent than those of a woman who had had several face-lifts. She listened impassively whilst Louise vented her disappointment in her husband's strictures. She deemed it necessary to tell Louise what she knew of the Southern Baptists.

'They were a breakaway movement that disapproved of the abolition of slavery. But there is a new fad of repentance and they have issued a statement which goes something like this: "We publicly repudiate historic acts of evil such as slavery, from which we continue to reap a bitter harvest."'

While Elsie spoke, Louise felt a flush burning her own embarrassingly white skin, guilt by association. White skin equaled guilt. She had forgotten Elsie's golden brown colour.

'They apologized to us for condoning or perpetuating individual and systematic racism in their lifetime and they genuinely repent of their racism, which they have been guilty of, whether consciously or unconsciously.'

Seeing Louise's dismay, Elsie put her thin sinewy arms around her and patted her back.

'You didn't know any of this, honey?' she comforted, in the husky voice of a former heavy smoker. 'But, you see, they use the Bible to discriminate against women. Perhaps they always have, anyway, it was written by old men for old men. Don't take it so hard, hon... you just keep on doing your own thing. Remember, they can't take away your pride 'less you allow them. Don't waste your valuable time taking against your husband. Not worth it. A no win situation.'

'You're sure, Elsie?' asked Louise.

'Just pretend you agree with him,' she advised Louise, who all too willingly accepted her advice.

In a way, Louise was relieved that she wouldn't have to fight John Jacob. The profound inertia of the pre-existing marital pattern was too set to break. He issued the orders, and she obeyed. He the leader, she the follower. It would work, as long as it seemed that way.

CHAPTER TWENTY-NINE

•

They all gathered at the airport for the trip to New York. It was a hazy day and pewter clouds predicted a stormy ride. The Boardmans tried to hide their nervousness. Louise whispered to Megan about how discouraged she was by the Baptist way of treating women.

'Patriarchal monotheism has a lot to answer for,' Megan replied somberly.

Louise didn't know what to make of that. John Jacob worried that Louise was getting too many new fangled ideas into her head. He was against the trip, he said, but a kind of greedy inquisitiveness possessed him.

Everyone dressed for the occasion; in her green dress and the shawl Roberto and Abigail had given her, Hester looked elegant and remote. Now, she thought with excitement, I will see what the eagle sees. Curt looked a little uncomfortable wearing a tie. He wore it because he thought it appropriate for his little girl's concert. Roberto and Abigail were dressed in their usual under-stated elegance, she in crème-coloured silk and he in a pale beige linen suit. The Boardmans of course wore their best church clothes, their shoes extra shiny. Megan and Tom chose casual comfort. Megan wore a cornflower blue trouser suit, which showed off her blue eyes and slim figure. She brought a sleek matching parasol. Tom wore a white shirt and navy blazer. Their clothing was their only armour against whatever was about to happen.

Lunch was served on the flight and Roberto, thinking of Hester, chose chicken in a basket to dispense with knives and forks. Roberto and Abigail sat talking to Hester and Curt. Hester quickly tore the flesh off the chicken with her strong teeth, and afterwards astonished the others by crunching, grinding, and then swallowing the bones. She ate rapidly and not a morsel of food was left.

'The way she eats bears testimony to her having experienced acute hunger,' Roberto said quietly to Abigail. 'Chicken bones may be why her teeth are strong and white.' Food for her was not a time for dalliance or pleasantry. They brought her another basket and she demolished it as she had the first.

Hester gazed in fascination out of the window. The swiftly-disappearing earth, the cloud formations (which John Jacob would incorporate into his forthcoming sermon), the wonder of it. They flew so much higher than she thought, way above eagles. The plane reached 33,000 feet and they were above the clouds. She saw another plane below them, which she excitedly pointed out to Abigail. She saw jet streams trailing strings of long white ribbons in the sky.

'Look,' she exclaimed, 'like our lives, half gone.'

The clouds disappeared and she saw the sumptuous quilted landscape below, escutcheoned with lakes and rivers like the veins in her arms. She felt the heat rise up in her blood as she was filled with love and respect for humankind who, even though not equipped with wings, could still fly.

'Ain't humans wonderful?' she said to Roberto.

'Yes,' he answered, 'we are.' He couldn't resist giving her fresh information to watch her reactions. 'Unlike animals, we have imagination and ideas. It all starts out with an idea. Leonardo da Vinci, a great artist who was born nearly 500 years ago, was also a scientist. He tried to design an airplane, even then!'

Hester's eyes grew bigger and each fresh discovery brought her childlike delight. Learning made her feel great. She was surprised that she could walk about in the plane. 'We are higher than our eagles!' she told Curt. He sat drinking his Coke, trying not to wish it was something alcoholic.

The Boardmans were afraid of New York, a den of iniquity. They disguised both their near-prurient inquisitiveness and the shame of possible contamination. Louise's white starched collar and long sleeves with cuffs matching the collar relieved him, her goodness was indisputable. It was in that instant, and with the certainty that thunder follows lightening, that he had his 'epiphany'. He had to do his duty and inform the Authorities about Hester's crime; the Lord's Commandments guided and he would follow them. He cleared his throat as he did before giving a sermon. Louise looked at him questioningly; he gave her a toothy grin.

'Thou shall not bear false witness,' he rebuked her. What had she done, she wondered.

'What do you mean?' she answered.

'Now is not the time,' he said, tapping his nose.

'Why not?'

'When we return I will ask you again about what you once told me,' he said, eyeing Hester meaningfully. 'You were overemotional then, so I ignored it,' he excused himself.

Louise briefly held his hand but his lidded eyes reminded her of a reptile – she preferred the word reptile to snake. 'I make you a sacred promise; you know I always keep my word, I will rectify the past. I will see to it that evil deeds do not go unpunished.' Then dread crept into her. She started licking her wart again.

Hester, cracking and crunching her chicken bones, had recalled old Webb's murder to Roberto and Abigail. Tom and Megan exchanged glances. What made Webb do it? Did he think that he had a right to everything he wanted? To his granddaughters! It was as impossible to understand as to forgive.

They moved about the plane and the four women formed a circle around one of the tables.

'We have a lot in common,' Abigail said.

'Yeah. We're all women,' said Hester.

'We all want what's best for Gladdie,' said Megan.

'Oh, that's for sure,' beamed Louise.

Abigail glanced at her large, square-cut diamond ring. It caught the sun and prisms of light danced like fireflies against nearby surfaces when she slanted her hand. She was about to bring it to Hester's attention but didn't. Hester was staring ardently out the window. Abigail looked at the diamond, thinking that she and the other women aboard were like facets of the same stone. Different elements. Hester is earth. She is basic, strong, the personification of a life force. Megan, she thought, would be fire. Passionate, she wants to burn away ignorance. Louise she supposed would be air; she was the one with the most direct line to Spirit. Abigail had difficulty categorizing herself. I'd be water, she decided: nourishing, yet taking on whatever colour I required. The Hindus say that space is an element too, she reminded herself. Gladdie is that for us. She is all our possibilities and our future.

'What do you think characterizes women?' she then asked, surprising them.

'Back in prehistory we were not competitive; our lives depended on our sisterhood and instinct,' said Megan authoritatively.

'Nature; work; we know things,' said Hester in her forthright manner, having worked out what 'characterizes' meant.

'Motherhood, compassion, nurturing,' added Megan.

'Knowing that we all carry God's light inside us. Knowing that we have God's love, this is how we walk on,' said Louise, glowing with belief.

'Yes. True,' said Megan, anxious to avert a sermon. 'What

would Gladdie say?' she asked. They all began to think of Gladdie. Could the concert fail? Abigail stared down at her ring as though it could comfort her. The men were listening to the women. How they babbled, thought John Jacob dismissively. With rising disgust he watched Megan's hand stroking the leather on her chair.

'Louise,' he called, 'come here. I want to tell you something.' The long cocoon shape of the private plane's interior, the warm colours of birds-eye maple and complementary colours of the leather coverings, formed a cozy intimate space. A place where confidences could be shared. Louise dutifully got up to join her husband, although she wanted to stay with the other women.

'I don't like you talking to those other women. I think you must pray more and talk less,' he cautioned.

As the altitude of the plane decreased, Hester was amazed to see the row upon row of houses lining the streets below. Too few trees, she thought, and she could not work out how people could live with such deprivation. The roads and curling bridges covered with ant-like cars made her smile, thinking how like animals and insects people were. She was further astonished by the prodigal amount of water studded with small boats and larger ones.

John Jacob saw the roads as gigantic winding serpents. How well he knew that snakes were regarded as the devil's representatives; he felt they were an omen. He wished he had a sign to ward off the evil they embodied. Furtively, he tried putting his two index fingers together to form a cross. Sodom and Gomorrah. Abigail closed her eyes to avoid seeing where the Twin Towers once stood. It was like seeing a smile with two missing front teeth. New York looked unreal from the air. Hester was filled with amazement that people could construct such tall buildings, yet she thought it strange that they wanted to live so far away from the earth. Louise closed her eyes and prayed for their safety. God opened a pure white wing of light over the plane, how peace-giving was the protection of her Lord's love. Her fear left her. She was ashamed of John Jacob's squirming lack of trust and hoped no one noticed. She was embarrassed just by imagining how his flock would react if they witnessed his behaviour.

Curt sat sipping one soda after another. Roberto and Tom recognized his innate masculine power and were drawn to him. Megan had heard of his reputation as a forest ranger and firefighter; she told them of it, and when they congratulated him, he modestly thanked them and told them politely that Megan was exaggerating. He could barely concentrate on the plane ride and was preoccupied by his desperate longing for a drink. His only protection was his twelve-step mantra. He wished he could call Brady, his sponsor, flying was that bad!

Limousines with tinted windows awaited them and they were driven to Carnegie Hall. Hester spotted the homeless people and identified with them, aware of how much worse it must be in this frightening treeless place. Nowhere to hide or grow sustenance. Louise gaped at the way people were dressed and was afraid of the large crowds.

Francesca Burns had long since recognized her son in Gladdie. They never actually told her, but she knew. She knew. The child she had taught to play the piano and escorted to New York, was her granddaughter. Tom had once intimated it. Now that Gladdina, as Francesca privately called her, was spending more time with them, Francesca saw how much happier Tommy was. She was thankful that Megan was more at ease, at times even serene. She wondered if her granddaughter had inherited her genes, that is, if musical genes can be inherited. She took Gladdie shopping, bought her tiny bras and panties and the tight tops and denims her granddaughter chose. She bought her extravagantly feminine dresses, and an outrageously expensive silk outfit for her appearance at the concert. It was a dusky pink colour and was scattered with handmade roses of the same silk. It rustled. Gladdie didn't like it. Ugh. She didn't even know if she would play. She didn't want to and agreed to the fussy dress only to please her piano teacher. She felt pressured, angry that they wanted her to play; they were just about forcing her and she resented it. Why did it matter to them so much? She agreed to wear the dress if, she warned her teacher, if she played.

Francesca indulged herself even more than her granddaughter. This was sacred time for her, she took her for a manicure and Gladdie chose a pearlised pink nail polish. She took Gladdie, just to see, to the Julliard School of Music, to see some of the other pupils. She told Gladdie that she respected her decision not to play the piano any more, but what was the harm in visiting Juilliard? Grandparents should have more rights, she again told herself. Especially, she smiled grimly, illegitimate grandmothers with Italian blood.

The group arrived and the limos disgorged their fares. Hester was fascinated by everything she saw and felt, from the stair rail to the carpeting and lighting. The auditorium dimmed and a diminutive figure walked on to the stage. Gladdie was only doing this to humour them. She sat at the Steinway making herself comfortable, removed and then replaced her Alice band, and moved the piano stool back and forth, studying her nails. She draped her new skirt around her and peered out at the small group who sat huddled together. Hester stood up and stretched her arms out to Gladdie in a loving gesture that bespoke both vibrant strength and excitement. She didn't want to disappoint her mother; she played a scale, as though to loosen up. Strangely, she wasn't certain if Hester could differentiate between the mechanical playing of scales or music; then smiled at her foolishness remembering her mother's singing.

She raised her hands to play and everyone held their breath. Then she lost her impetus. She trailed off and sat, head bent and arms at her sides, limp and lifeless. Francesca stifled a sob and everyone sat paralyzed with anxiety. The auditorium, a vast womb of promise, void of all but memories of past performances glimmering like hymns against the walls, remained silent. The silence grew louder, threatening to engulf them all. They felt fear and the beginnings of panic. Gladdie picked at one of the roses on her skirt. Without any expression on her face but with methodical violence, she tore it off and threw it onto the floor, leaving a ragged hole in her dress, she jumped up, stomped on it as if it was noxious insects then started to work on another and then sat at the piano and appeared unaware of what she had done. Megan leapt up into a running crouch, Tom's head sunk into his fists. The moment stretched time, unraveling Gladdie's supporters. Francesca held her breath, her hand stopping over her mouth. Abigail's nails almost bit into Roberto's arm. He covered her hand with his own. His teeth clenched into a mirthless smile. The torn silk roses tore Louise's heart. Gladdie's audience didn't move: her frightening behaviour impaled them. She sat and waited, her arms dangling her defeat. The solid impasse was broken by the unlikely whirring of a raccoon quickly repeating itself, followed by the night call of a whip-poor-will, clear and pure as mountain air.

Gladdie was recalled to herself, she looked blindly in the direction of her mother. Her blood throbbingly registered that her mother had endured the same nightmare; it happened to both of them and her being took strength because they had both prevailed and survived. She, like her mother, would never be part of the crowd, never quite belong. Grasping this undeniable reality, tears filled her eyes. She was deeply, deeply disappointed and saddened, yet in almost the same moment, liberated from hope. Hope, that seductive deluder, slipped away from her. Understanding and accepting, she was free to be. Free and unafraid. Just like her mother.

She gathered herself together and corralled her strength. It would not be easy. But if her mother could do it, so could she.

She raised her hands and, with the first chord she played, took back her identity, revealed her uniqueness and gave herself to her future. Her body leaned into the music, her head tilted upwards, her straight back swayed. The wave of passion rose within her, she became the music. Her concentration was absolute. Beethoven's *Appassionata*, her most difficult piece, wove its power and while she played, it was all that mattered.

Unbeknown even to Roberto, Abigail had called her friend Mrs Newton Ball-Green. She knew that Newtie was a tremendous benefactor to the city's orchestra and she asked her for a big favour. That afternoon a conductor and the musical director had quietly taken their seats behind the family. They didn't have the time to be there, but neither could they refuse Mrs Newton Ball-Green.

During her playing, John Jacob didn't know what to do. He stealthily put his hands over his ears and wasn't sure if he wanted these sophisticated people to witness his behavior. Louise sat still, transported, delighted. He was galled by the expression on his wife's face and his body began to shudder in apoplectic fury. John Jacob clenched his teeth as he tried to work out how to take his revenge on Hester, his hands gripped and clawed at the arms of his chair. She was to blame and he would do his duty and make it his business to see to it that she paid for her crimes. He wasn't going to let the Devil beat him – she was a devil herself. A sly smile stole across his face, a fire warmed his brimstoned heart. Oh yes, she would pay, he was determined but enraged by ferocious doubts that his plan would work. His body stiffened in an awful way as a sharp pain shot into his head.

They had gambled, they had won, and when the wildly applauding group eventually stopped clapping the only sound they could hear was of a man sobbing. It was Curt. He empathized and understood too much of his daughter's journey. Hester clasped her arms around his quaking frame, and Gladdie flew up to hold her father and tell him how much she loved him.

Francesca stood aside, waiting for her moment. All her efforts and hopes were realized. Her granddaughter was greater than even she had dreamed possible – she was awestruck. There was no uncertainty about the role she would play in Gladdina's life. She would talk to Hester and get her permission for the child to receive the best tuition possible, would assure her that once she was with like-minded young people she would achieve the sense of belonging that she craved. Francesca was profoundly sad for her son, her Tommy, but it was plain that the child regarded Curt as her father and the child had been disturbed enough. Yes, she would persuade Gladdina's parents to allow their daughter the chance to fulfill herself. That, she fervently hoped, would be of comfort to her son.

Francesca would tell them that she, together with her husband, would escort the child and even live in the same town. Randall was semi-retired anyway, they would keep her safe. The school she thought would best suit her granddaughter was the Curtis. Hester had doubtless by now realized that she, Francesca, was the grandmother and only had the very best interests of the child at heart.

She intended telling her about the Curtis Institute of Music in Philadelphia. Here there was no need for charity as the students receive full scholarships based on merit alone.

She walked over to Hester, her steps purposeful. The two women looked at one another Francesca was about to speak when Hester smiled at her and said, 'Yes. Whatever Gladdie wants. That's what I want.'

No one noticed that John Jacob hadn't participated in their shared happiness until Louise looked around for him. She found him still in the same place only his body looked deconstructed. His eyes followed her but that was all that appeared to move excepting for a slow dribble from his half-open mouth. Louise recognized a stroke when she saw one, hadn't she helped nurse old Mrs Cayhill for over a year until she died. She saw what had happened to her husband and knew at once the Lord had sent her a hard task, but also knew that she would not fail Him.

First published in the United Kingdom by

Elliott & Thompson Limited
27 John Street
London WC1N 2BX

ISBN 1 904027 54 7
(10 digit)

ISBN 978 1 904027 54 6
(13 digit)

First Edition

Book design by Brad Thompson

Printed and bound in the UK by the Athenaeum Press